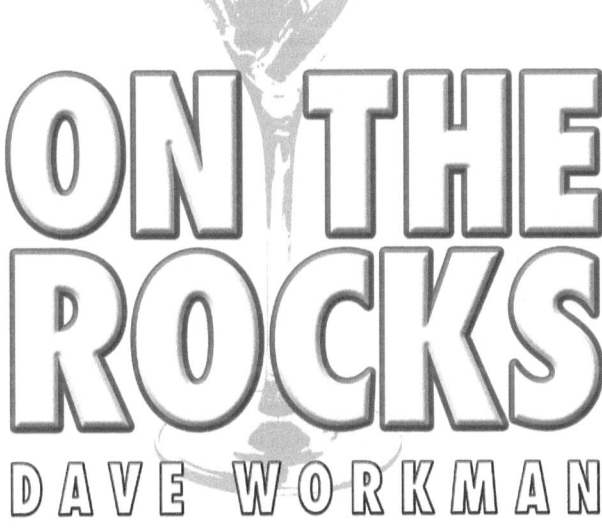

ON THE ROCKS

DAVE WORKMAN

Muse Harbor Publishing

ON THE ROCKS

A Muse Harbor Publishing Book

PUBLISHING HISTORY
Muse Harbor Publishing paperback edition published
SEPTEMBER 2012

Los Angeles, California
Santa Barbara, California

For more information, contact Muse Harbor Publishing.

Cover design by Timm Sinclair
Cover photography by Melissa Wolf
Interior design by Typeflow

ISBN 978-1-61264-132-4

Visit Muse Harbor Publishing at
www.museharbor.com

v 1.4

For Eileen,
my love,
my muse.

Books by Dave Workman:

The Hole

On The Rocks

On The Edge

Like a California Dream (coming in 2018)

On The Run (coming in 2019)

Acknowledgements

Very few writers function in a vacuum. I'm fortunate to have been part of Joan Oppenheimer's workshop (San Diego) for wayward wannabes and to have, for many years, participated in the insanely beneficial Santa Barbara Writers Conference. I'm grateful to Matthew Pallamary for his friendship and sage wisdom. Thank you Margaux (aka Margaret, Maggie) Hession for being brilliant. And for loving Komo.

Among the ears I've bent over the years, I thank the amazing Suzanne (Kat) DeCayette and also John McSweeney (my high school English teacher—yeah, like, *really*). Thank you, Karma Christine Salvato, fellow *autore*, for rejuvenating this novel and one day debuting your own magical gem.

I'm also grateful for the friendship and energy of a new crop of young and extremely talented artisans: Zeina Baltagi and Ciscandra Nostalghia—to whom I wish (and anticipate) the best of luck and success. A nod, as well, to Roy Gnan, for just being too cool.

Also—thank you Anita Gnan for being so utterly Angie.

Danke to Matthew Scott Russell, having survived Desert Storm, the Inland Empire, Eileen's front-porch philosophy and the quintessential Tahitian holiday, and whose own *eight bottles* are just a few million keystrokes (!) away.

Thanks to Jim and Lisa Rule for keeping me writing (as part of America's best newspaper) over these last several years. I became a bona fide L.A. film critic and loved every minute of it. I mean, what's *not* to love? And thank you Idie Emery for exceptional editorial assistance—and for a most charming friendship.

Much gratitude to Timm Sinclair (book design) and Melissa Wolf (photography) for making me look suitably *noiresque.* Thanks Keith Snyder of Typeflow (N.Y.) for your specialized knowledge and support. Last (but hardly least) thank you Ian Wood for being an integral part of the madness. Life without you would be way too ordinary.

In the non-literary arena, I'd like to thank Kristin, Nicky and Bryan for growing up so damn perfect. *Mais oui,* we encountered a few speed bumps—but weren't they fun? And the rest of the time was, of course, priceless. Jamez, you're pretty much okay too.

And thank you, my lovely Eileen, for learning to make sushi.

MICKY AND THE NAKED BLONDE

are giggling in the Jacuzzi.

Elvis waits in the shadows by a wall of climbing jasmine, wearing a jacket and tie, a 9mm Glock in a leather quick-action holster tucked beneath his right arm. Swirls of mist drift up from the sunken tub and every so often a drop of sweat rolls down his nose, plops on the Spanish tile between his polished Florsheims.

He wishes like hell Micky'd get it over with. He wants to get back inside the house, linger in front of the fridge and crack open a Tecaté.

Elvis stays close to Micky because that's his job, Micky Logan on the demanding side of paranoia but more often than not just wanting a nursemaid—someone to fetch his slippers, crank up the stereo or top off his Johnnie Walker Blue on ice. So Elvis lingers, trying not to pay attention, but occasionally wondering about the flesh beneath all those bubbles.

Micky and the naked blonde splash each other, having fun. Suddenly Micky grunts and stops laughing. The blonde's maybe taken one too many pulls on his unit and now Micky's pissed, the way he sometimes gets after too much whisky. Telling her to take it fuckin' easy—go on and wait for him in the bedroom. Elvis holds out a towel and watches her saunter up from the tub and toward the French doors, the towel draped indifferently over one shoulder.

"Angie's got hands like a frickin' crescent wrench," Micky says, slurring his words, speaking loud enough for the blonde to hear. He waits until she disappears into the house and his voice gets a mean kind of quiet. "Maybe you should go an' break her fuckin' fingers, huh? Let Angie know what fuckin' pain *feels* like."

Elvis listens to the ice cubes rattle angrily in Micky's glass. It's the sound Jesse Nevada's skull made after Micky cracked him a few in the face down in El Monte, back when Micky Logan kept a Luis Gonzalez autographed Rawlings in the trunk of his Lincoln Town Car.

"Nah, Angie's okay," Elvis says. "We don' wanna be messin' her up none."

"Yeah, an' you don't wanna be givin' me no fuckin' lip," Micky tells him with a look.

"Jus' sayin'." But Elvis knows better and lets the comment fade. He glances toward the night-shrouded house as Angie strolls past the open doorway, still naked, still wearing the towel over her shoulder.

Truth is, Elvis doesn't much care for the junkies and whores Micky sometimes brings around. Angie—she's different somehow. She smiles at him every so often, says *thank you* and makes small talk whenever he takes the Mercedes, picks her up on Santa Monica Boulevard or sometimes over on Westwood. Not many *nice* girls hanging around when you're selling crack to half the people in South Central. But Angie? She's as close to nice as Elvis has seen in a long while.

He remembers a few years back, when Consuela had been his steady girlfriend. Micky hadn't liked the idea. He didn't want Elvis getting lazy, maybe slacking off those evenings he needed someone around. And the last thing he wanted was Elvis running off to have some fucking kid.

That was Micky's problem—he didn't like the feel of loneliness. Crazy, because he owned this big house, tucked into the Santa Monica Mountains without a neighbor in sight, a nice view of the ocean a few miles away but nothing except the owls and coyotes—and his own raging insecurity—creeping around at two or three in the morning. Once, out with Consuela until after midnight, Elvis came home to find Micky clutching a Remington twelve-gauge, drenched in sweat, staring at shadows. That night, Micky simply said *no mas*.

And Elvis, he usually did what he was told.

So nine nights out of ten, they sit around and stream adult flicks on the flat-screen TV, or play with Micky's Wii. Elvis fetches drinks or potato chips or makes sandwiches at all hours, because when is Micky ever *not* hungry?

Every so often, Micky's fears hiding behind half a bottle

of Johnnie Walker, he'll drop a few bills and tells Elvis to
go take a night off, have some fun before his fuckin' pecker
shrivels up. So Elvis drives his *lady d'jour* to Zuma Beach
or catches a few clubs off Sunset. Sometimes they wander
upstairs, listen to Santana or Los Lobos and smoke Mexican weed. They fall asleep together, Elvis on that fuzzy side
of reality, and before morning she's up and gone again. A
quick kiss and a tossed smile but gone again because *hey,
amigo*, this is L.A. and a lady's got to make a living.

Although he'll never admit it to Micky, Elvis doesn't
appreciate his women bought and paid for. He has family down in Baja, a grandmother who walks a dirt road to
church every morning, and where sex with a price tag is
still considered a sin.

But women don't easily warm up to Elvis. He stands
a foot above the usual crowd and towers another several
inches over the squat, cookie-dough expanse of Micky
Logan. Elvis isn't bad looking, although he lets several days
pass between shaves—Elvis usually sporting an itchy black
goatee—and can't be bothered about combing his hair,
which sometimes falls below his eyebrows. A scar etches
one cheek, a thin slash that points to a mangled earlobe.
He seldom smiles, his stare resembling the countenance of
a grumpy bear.

Then again, people tend to give Micky an extra latitude of respect with Elvio Tejano Zapata hovering nearby.

Micky sucks at the remnants of his Scotch and spends
another moment with his eyes shut, his huge body blan-
keted under a torrent of bubbles. He says to Elvis, "Hey, you
take the Lexus in this afternoon?"

"Yeah. Be fixed up tomorrow."

"You tell 'em about the fuckin' brakes?"

"I tol' em."

Micky loves big cars. He's not obsessed with performance like some guys, though Micky's cars have to be comfortable. He keeps six of them in the air-conditioned garage that can hold two more. Micky's collection includes a powder blue '57 Cadillac Eldorado, a silver Bentley Mulsanne, and a '72 Lincoln Town Car that had once taken Brando to Vegas and back.

Micky can't drive worth a damn, so Elvis chauffeurs him wherever he needs to go. Every time Micky hears a noise or smells a vapor, he bitches at Elvis and then spends three or four hundred for a mechanic to tell him nothing's wrong.

"Hey, I almost forgot," Micky says. "You talk to Sal today?"

"Sal? Yeah. You owe him three large."

Micky opens his eyes, suddenly alert. That's what money does to Micky. Sobers him up. *"Three?"*

"Yeah."

"Fuckin' Dodgers."

"Sal says he'll wipe the vig if you talk to his nephew."

"Sal's got a nephew?"

"Uh huh."

"And this nephew of Sal's, he wants to talk to me why?"

"Says the kid wants into the business."

"Into *my* business?"

"That's what he tol' me. Knows you been lookin' to replace Santos. Says the kid's got the *cojones*."

"Sal got any idea what happened to Santos?"

"Dunno, Micky." Elvis absently rubs the ragged scar on his earlobe. "Tol' me his nephew wants more'n what he's got to give."

"Bookin' ain't good enough for him, huh?"

"Says the kid loves to fuck with guns and knives and shit."

"What, Sal afraid he's gonna make a bad impression? Cap some upstanding family man over a five-C late call." Micky hiccups loudly. "Blow away half of Sal's clientele, I imagine."

"Sal says he'll appreciate it."

"What's his name?"

"Sal's?" Elvis asks.

"No, the kid's," Micky says patiently.

"I think it's Dwight."

"No fuckin' way."

"Yeah—*Dwight*."

Micky holds out his empty glass toward Elvis. "And Dwight don't mind killin' people?"

"Nah. Sal says the kid'll get a kick out of it."

7:30 PM THURSDAY

Dwight D'Angelo Manetti walks into a room the size of a 7–Eleven, filled with leather furniture the color of chocolate ice cream and dark, funky shaped lamps. Paintings crowd the walls—the biggest one, over the fireplace, of violet-tinged, jagged-edged women. *Naked*, Dwight thinks, though he can't be sure.

Micky Logan sits on a La-Z-Boy, wrapped in a green silk bathrobe, wearing matching slippers. Dwight stares into rust-colored eyes and a wide face full of freckles. Micky's orange hair frizzes around his scalp like a dandelion. He wears a mustache the same color, like a stain across his upper lip. He's a short guy, going on three hundred pounds, maybe three twenty, his belly slopping over the armrests of the recliner. The other dude, tall and mostly muscle, looms over Logan like a dark shadow.

Dwight knows Elvio Zapata by reputation. Thing is, Micky calls him *Elvis* and how can you take a spic named Elvis seriously? His suit's out of date, steampunk, reminiscent of some late-show flick in black and white; a dark tweed jacket with long, narrow lapels and a button-down white shirt that could have come from K-Mart.

Dwight notices that Elvis doesn't move his hands much. He feels the pull of the little holstered Walther under his jacket and wonders if he can outdraw the big guy, thinking it could easily be *him* dogging Micky's moves, holed up here in a fancy house every night—man, having chicks and loud parties and shit, enjoying the life.

Micky clears his throat. He wipes his hands on the skirt of his silk robe and says; "You look like a fuckin' gangster."

"Yes, sir," Dwight replies without expression.

Micky likes the kid calling him *sir*, showing respect. Elvis has called Micky *Micky* since he can't even remember. Dwight isn't much older than twenty-three, twenty-four, wearing a black shirt, slate gray tie and a fitted, black

Armani suit, and why Micky thinks he looks like a gangster. He's not as tall as Elvis, not nearly as big, but he looks
sleek, like he could run circles around Elvis. The kid's voice
sounds gravelly, like he smokes too much, or maybe it's the
jitters. His hair is long and straight, shiny black, secured
with a gold pin the shape of a bullet. Micky doesn't appreciate ponytails on guys, but the kid looks okay in it. Give
him a flattop and he could be a ball player, maybe even a
movie star.

"So you wanna work for me, huh?"

"Yes, sir, Mr. Logan."

Micky glances at Elvis to see if he's picked up on the
deference. Except if Elvis ever calls Micky *mister*, it would
gag them both, having grown up together in the bad end
of Pacoima, and Micky a few years younger.

"Uncle Sal tell you what I need?"

"Said you needed talent, Mr. Logan."

"An' that's what you got?"

"Yes, sir, that's what I got."

Micky grins, amused by the kid's bravado. "You ever
hear of Santos Boja?"

"Boja? Squirrelly little guy, right? Used to run for you."

"Santos was my carrier. Right after Jesse Nevada quit.
Hey, another story. Boja helped Elvis with collections.
Helped keep my people in line. Kinda what you'd be doin',
you come work for me. I had Santos about—what, eighteen months? Ain't that right, Elvis?"

"Aroun' that."

"Never gave me no trouble, neither. 'Cept one day he
tells a coupla my boys down on La Cienega how I'm such

an asswipe 'cause I don't pay no fuckin' OT. You hear about this, kid?"

Dwight shakes his head.

"Word got back to me, from what you might call a reliable source. That same night, we sit down in the back yard an' have a couple Scotches. No, Santos liked one of them sweet mixers—wha'd he drink, Elvis? Whassit?"

"Seven an' Seven."

"That's right."

"With a twist," Elvis says.

"Yeah, whatever." Micky offers a dismissive wave. "So I wait 'til he's had a few, an' I casually say—yo, Santos, any chance you call me an asswipe this morning? Boja, he gives me a shit-eatin' grin, like it's no big deal. I had on this very same bathrobe, a couple towels on the chaise and underneath I had my Steyr nine. I pick it up and *bang*. No fuckin' muffler or nothin' because we're out here in the fuckin' boonies. You shoot off a bazooka and nobody knows shit.

"So that's what happened to Santos." Micky gestures, gun-like, with his thumb and forefinger. "'Cause I don't like my people giving me lip. Whaddaya say to that, kid?"

Dwight spends a quiet moment thinking. "Then I guess I don't ever call you no asswipe, Mr. Logan."

Micky cracks up. Laughs so hard his body spasms. "That's fuckin' rich," he says, tears welling in his eyes. Micky wipes his nose with the back of his hand, and all of a sudden his expression changes, Micky deadly serious. Tears still staining his cheeks, and his gaze becomes icy granite. "Elvis, tell Dwain, *whassit?*—Dwight here, tell the kid what he's gotta do first, if he ever wants to work for me."

"You wanna work for Micky, you prove your bones."

"Go ahead, ask me anything, Mr. Logan. You won't be disappointed."

"Like the ultimate," Micky tells him.

Elvis gives Dwight another hard stare. "Prove your loyalty, you gotta snuff someone. Let Micky know you're serious about business, that he can count on you, no matter what's asked."

The kid doesn't move, watching Micky like it's no big deal.

Trying to play the big shot, Micky thinks, but that's cool. Micky likes cool.

"You ever whack anyone?" he asks.

"Not people."

"Not people? What, you blow away, what, like mice and frogs and shit?"

The kid frowns slightly. "Did a couple dogs, mostly, testing my piece. Getting the distance, accuracy. I file down my front sight an—"

"People ain't cats an' dogs, y'know."

Dwight sucks in a deep breath and lets it out slowly. "Mr. Logan, you want me to off some dude, consider it done. You want me to pop two or three, hey, that's up to you." He gives Micky a squint.

Almost a dare, Micky thinks. That's cool, too.

"Whaddaya say, Elvis? We should give the kid here a try, huh?"

Elvis doesn't reply. Something about Sal's nephew bothers him. People usually have to warm up to the idea of wasting a complete stranger. Whacking people for fun is different than holding a grudge. But Dwight seems a little *too* eager. Elvis imagines Micky pointing to some guy off the street and Dwight pulling the trigger, no questions asked, the mark maybe a good husband or a priest or something.

Elvis remembers when Micky'd first thought up the pre-req. Elvis didn't like it, having known Micky so long, he didn't see why he had to waste somebody to prove his *machismo*. But he also knew better than to balk—Micky Logan with a short fuse and a temper sometimes out of nowhere. Besides, Micky was worth twenty-five, maybe thirty million, wholesaling crystal and coke and a bunch of synthetic shit, with a hundred guys willing to work for him at the drop of a hat.

Elvis didn't see what choice he had.

One night they sat down—this was three, almost four years ago—Micky with his Scotch and Elvis sucking on a Mazatlán Manhattan, a red chili pepper floating down there amid all that whisky and vermouth. Micky explained why he thought the pre-req was important and wondered about who maybe had it coming. There was Elvis' boozed-up father, an unemployed cement mixer who'd used a rubber hose on Elvis until, at thirteen and standing six-six, Elvis put an end to that shit with a single left hook that flattened the old man's nose. But the guy had liver cancer and wasn't expected to live much longer.

"So that wouldn't count," Micky told Elvis.

They decided on a guy named Rags Taglioni, a burned out street punk so coked up he couldn't use his grandmother's Sicilian heritage to get into the business. Taglioni favored a three-inch safety razor as his weapon of choice. He'd once sliced up a dealer who'd shorted him a couple of grams, Taglioni wearing the guy's left pinky on a gold chain around his neck until the thing began to putrefy.

They set him up one night, out on Mulholland near the park, dangling a bag of Mexican flake as bait, and Micky there to watch. Elvis walked up behind Taglioni and said, *Hey.* Taglioni turned, saw the over-under eight-gauge and, *boom, boom,* just like that it was over. Micky said it was kind of a social service, what they did. They found close to twenty-five hundred in Taglioni's pocket and Micky let Elvis keep the roll, letting him know that sometimes you get perks.

Over the years, Micky lost a few potential runners over the pre-req. Jesse Nevada didn't have a problem. Santos eventually gave in and popped a one-eyed Crip Deuce-Five with a bad disposition down in Compton. Funny how the promise of money could spin a moral compass. Could turn swans into swine, as Micky would sometimes say.

But this kid, Elvis thinks, he's too ready to play *caballero.* He wonders if maybe Dwight's all fuckin' talk.

"You got anyone in particular you don't like?" Micky asks.

Dwight thinks for a few seconds. "Nobody I can't handle on my own, Mr. Logan."

"Nobody you got the hots to whack, eh?"

"Can't think of no one. You want, I'll drive down Sunset

or to Chinatown, find some drunk nigger or somebody like that."

Micky leans forward and raises a stern finger. "One thing I gotta tell you, Kid—" Micky realizes he likes calling Dwight *Kid*, a little wet behind the ears but ready to listen up, "—my father was Irish. You know what ignorant fuckers call the Irish? They call 'em *micks*. My mother, she was half Italian, half Jewish. Some asshole comes up, calls me a wop or a kike or a mick an' there's a good chance they don't see the sun go down that night."

Micky points at a spot between his eyes, his fingers gun-like again, giving Dwight a clue. "Know what I'm sayin'? I don't disrespect people for no reason. If you wan' go down to Sunset, find some wino who happens to be African-American, that's up to you. But you give him a little respect. Don't slap him around or anything and don't be callin' him names. You waste him, you do it clean. Don't blow off a kneecap or his pecker, waitin' for the guy to die in agony. It's important I can trust you, but it's also important I know you work clean. I ain't hirin' no fuckin' freaks."

"Yes, sir, Mr. Logan."

"So then." Micky spreads his hands. "You got any particular African-American gentleman in mind?"

"No, sir."

Elvis watches without a word, although he *does* have a sudden thought. He wonders if Micky might get a kick out of watching the kid squirm—see if Dwight's anything more than mouth.

"I gotta idea."

Micky blinks once or twice. He appears genuinely surprised by the notion.

"What about that little *puta?*" Elvis says.

"Say what?"

"The hooker here a coupla nights ago."

"Angie? Bitch practically tore my cock off. What about her?"

"Said you had no further use for her."

"Hands like a fuckin' crescent wrench." Micky's confused as to how the hell Angie's name gets pulled out of nowhere, here in the middle of business. Then it dawns on him.

"You're sayin' we whack *Angie?*"

Elvis raises an eyebrow to let Micky know he's joking— although he's not sure Micky notices.

"Fuckin' hooker," Micky says. He stares vacantly across the room for a long moment. "Teach her a fuckin' lesson, huh? Yeah, I like that. You think you can do a woman, Kid? You got the balls?"

"Whoever you want, Mr. Logan."

Micky nods and—*whoa*, Elvis thinks. It's supposed to be a gag.

"Where you want me to do this, Mr. Logan?"

"You packin'?"

"Yes, sir."

Micky snaps his fingers. "Elvis, go pick up Angie. Tell her I'm a veritable horn toad tonight. Bring her around the side gate to the patio."

Elvis hesitates, not wanting to give Micky lip, but unsure of how to stop this terrible thing. He's aware of

Micky's eyes, glowing like embers in a hot breeze. Elvis gets midway to the door and hears Micky say, "Maybe I should get laid before you do her, huh, Kid?"

8:45 PM THURSDAY

Angelina Breusser calls herself Angie Love and hooks upscale in Westwood, near the park. She has a solid clientele and often hangs around Frebo's, a coffee and burger stand with a half-dozen outside stools. She drinks decaf and occasionally lights up a True Menthol, reads Cosmo and keeps Frebo company after most of his dinner crowd has split. He's sweet on her anyway, Frebo nearly eighty and Angie good company. Every now and then she'll slip him a twenty. Kind of like rent money, she figures.

Angie likes Westwood, her tricks mostly white collar and straight-laced. No winos or street pervs. She's willing to do kinky but has her limits. She's about five-five, maybe a little underweight but endowed with a healthy chest that she accentuates to the best of her ability. A natural blonde, she tells customers who want to know. She dresses the part, although in certain sections of Melrose she can pass for punk—tonight a fake fur miniskirt and black stretch halter, fishnet stockings and red stiletto pumps.

Angie's aware of Micky's royal blue 560SL midway up the block, already off her stool as the car pulls to the curbside. Tossing her hair back as a tinted window descends.

"Angie," Elvis says. "Hey, get in."

She peeks inside, giving him a wallop of Cherry Congo lipstick and bright white teeth. "What's up, honey?"

"Micky wants you. Says to tell you he's a vegetable toad."

"He is, huh? That's cute." She opens the door and sinks into the leather upholstery. She notices Elvis staring at her funny and gives him another smile. Micky Logan's a businessman who can afford the lay, up in the hills above Malibu in a house that feels like a hotel, how big it is. But Micky's a good tipper, so Elvis can stare all he wants. She thinks he's a bit goofy anyway. A little slow on the uptick.

"You mind some tunes?" she asks, reaching for the radio as Elvis pulls the Mercedes back into traffic.

Micky's not sure if doing Angie before letting the Kid do her is psycho or not. He spends several minutes pacing, trying not to feel sleazy about wanting one last screw. This is a business decision and sex might throw a whole different light on things. He considers maybe doing Angie *after* the Kid pops her, but he's not sure if that might send him straight to hell.

Better, he decides, to keep this strictly business.

He has time to pour a Scotch and then another one after that, feeling the buzz like an electric current through the back of his brain. Still wearing his bathrobe and slippers, Micky moves outside to the patio with a plastic rhododendron spritzer, making a half-assed pretense of killing some bugs. Truth is, he doesn't want Angie spilling all over the Berber carpet.

He tries making small talk, but Dwight's not exactly a socialite. So he gives up, puttering with some azaleas under the porch lights while Dwight watches from the shadows. Micky's still lost in thought when he hears the chime that signals the front gate sliding open. It will take Elvis a minute to crawl up the long driveway, pull the Mercedes around to the pebbled walkway that leads through the side gate. Micky wonders if he should feign indifference, or give her a big smile, happy to see her again. Yeah, he likes that. No sense being morbid about the whole thing.

Micky notices Dwight shifting his weight from one foot to the other and says, "Cool your jets, Kid. You'll get your chance." He spritzes a few more flowers, excitement sizzling inside his head like a firecracker, ready to explode.

"Micky," Angie says, coming around the wall of climbing pink flowers, heels click-clicking on the Mexican tile. She glances past Micky standing by the Malibu-lighted palms. Her gaze settles on the Jacuzzi.

"Want another bath, honey?"

"Angie, sweetheart, how you doin'?" Micky spreads his arms and she scurries over, kissing him on the cheek. He hugs her, barely able to get his arms around her because of his barrel-size gut. He grunts and she giggles, a soft, ticklish sound.

"Hey, a couple Scotches for me and Angie," Micky says, Elvis hovering in the darkness behind her, so Elvis goes to do what he's told. "None for the Kid though. He's gotta keep a steady hand. Maybe later, huh, Kid?"

Angie turns to look. She notices Dwight in the shadows for the first time.

"Oooh, a hunk."

"Angie, this is Dwight, my new business associate if things work out. Kid, this is Angie, a hooker."

"Glad to meet you," she tells him.

Dwight remains silent.

"This going to be round-robin, Micky?"

"Nah. The Kid here has some business to attend, in a little bit. I want him to hang around awhile. You don't mind, do you?"

She shakes her head and offers Dwight a smile. "He can watch if he wants."

Elvis brings two glasses to the patio and hands one to Angie. She grasps the glass with both hands, taking baby-sips, trying to get the whisky down without burning her mouth.

"By the way, you tell anyone you was comin' around tonight?" Micky asks. "Anybody see you get into the car or anything?"

"What, this a secret rendezvous or something?" Angie doesn't seem at all concerned with the direction the conversation's taking. She doesn't see Elvis, behind her, shaking his head *no*.

"Nah, just talking. A guy's gotta be careful, you know."

Micky watches her, taking in the swell of her breasts, the crook of her hip. Even though he's made up his mind, he wonders if he should unmake it, hop in the Jacuzzi for a quick one, step out and let the Kid do her in the tub. Let her bleed out, then pull the plug and drain the water.

Hell, why didn't he think of this before?

"Yo, Elvis," Micky says. "Go crank up the bubbles."

Elvis isn't happy about the turn of events, frowning and moving his lips, as if he's talking to himself and not liking what he's hearing.

"Me and Angie, we're gonna take a dip," Micky tells Dwight. Laying it out nice and simple, so there's no confusion later on. "Then I'm going to climb out, at which point I want you to do that thing we talked about."

The Kid looks at Angie, still baby-sipping her Scotch. He nods and watches Micky, midway to the Jacuzzi, shrug his way out of his bathrobe. In the shadows, the Kid shudders to himself at the sight of all that flesh, at Micky Logan's pale round butt.

Elvis waits by the Jacuzzi. "What are we doin'?"

"Angie," Micky says. He gestures impatiently at the blonde. In case she doesn't get the message, he snaps his fingers. Twice.

"Yeah, I know that."

"No. I mean *I'm* doin' Angie. Then the Kid's doin' Angie." He pokes Elvis with an elbow. "Guess what? You're the only one not doin' Angie tonight."

"You're gonna—" Elvis frowns. "Tha's loco."

"An' when I want the Mexican Pope's opinion, I'll ask for it, huh?"

Angie's lamé top is halfway over her head, her breasts bouncing, nipples dark patches in the moonlight. Micky kicks off his slippers and dabs a toe in the frothing water. He lumbers down the steps, balancing his bulk against the churning water. Micky enjoys sex in the Jacuzzi, the water's buoyancy allowing him to do things he can't accomplish in a bedroom. It's one of those deep, deluxe models, stooped and contoured. When he's not drinking too much, Micky can usually fit himself into some pretty funky positions.

"Is it hot, baby?" She hands Elvis her skirt, stockings and halter, naked now, her long legs disappearing one step at a time into the water. She's not badly put together, Elvis thinks—a blue and green gecko tattooed above one shoulder blade—admiring the flat of her back and slim hips, a last peek at the crack of her butt before she slips under the foam. Micky says something and she laughs, the words lost behind the whir of machinery.

Elvis backs away, staring at the Jacuzzi with a clinical fascination, not much to see, mostly shadows and an occasional flash of skin. He's still holding Angie's bunched up clothes, not quite sure what to do with them. The Kid steps beside him and clears his throat, one fist balled up in front of his mouth.

"I, uh, got a problem here."

Elvis wonders if he has to pee or something, but the Kid leans close and says, "I don't know if I can do this."

Elvis stares at him and thinks, *See? All fuckin' mouth.*

"Can't pop a woman. A naked woman in a Jacuzzi? Man, that's fucked up."

"Then you're right you got a problem."

"Mister Logan, what, he gonna be pissed?"

"Look, Kid—here's the thing." Elvis realizes he's calling Dwight *Kid* too, getting into it just like Micky. "He don't like to be embarrassed. Not even in front of dead people.

That means now *I* gotta pop Angie. Then prob'ly waste your sorry ass too."

Elvis watches Micky's broad backside rise above the froth like a whale breaching the ocean's surface, wondering how to change the direction of things already in motion.

Micky can't believe it. The thought of getting off on Angie and then having her blown away in his own goddamn Jacuzzi is too amazing to comprehend. Getting ready, feeling himself about to explode, Micky turns to sneak a glance at the Kid. Angie somehow slips away from his grasp. He pumps for her and misses—abruptly shooting his wad into a churning eddy of water.

"Shit," he says, like a whimper, the moment ruined, the fantasy skittering away. The last thing he wants is for Angie to start yanking on his pecker again. "Shit. Fuckin' shit. Shit a brick," he says, standing up.

"What's the matter, baby?"

"Shit," Micky says again. He climbs up the steps. "Wait here."

"You coming back?"

Micky stands dripping, watching the two guys who haven't moved out of the shadows yet. Like the Kid's going to pop her from way back there? The fuck's going on*!*

"Oh, man," Dwight moans. Elvis watches him reach into his Armani jacket, aware that the Kid's a left-hander like himself. Dwight pulls out a semi and hold it tight against his leg, the barrel as black as the Kid's suit.

Micky stares at them.

"You gonna *do* it?" Elvis whispers.

The Kid steps forward, exposing his back even after what Elvis said about maybe having to shoot his ass. *Neophyte*, Elvis thinks—one of Micky's twenty-dollar college words, but Elvis is pretty sure it fits the situation. He lets Angie's clothes drop to the tile, slipping a hand inside his jacket, fingers curling around his Glock's rubber-ribbed handle.

"Mr. Logan?"

Micky glances back and forth between Angie and the Kid. Dwight's shaking his head so much his ponytail's flipping from shoulder to shoulder.

"Micky?" Angie says, aware that something's wrong.

"You got a problem, Kid?"

"Mr. Logan, I don't think I can do this. Not a naked woman in a hot tub."

"I cannot fucking believe this."

"Mr. Logan—"

"Will you fuckin' *shoot* the bitch!"

"Micky?" Angie says again.

Micky lifts his foot and stomps hard, like a tantrum. He looks back and sees Angie scrambling up the steps, reaches out and gives her a shove. She squeals and tumbles back into the water.

"You fuckin' moron!" Micky screams.

The Kid raises his gun. Elvis sees Angie pop to the surface, drenched and coughing, sees the Kid's Walther waver, then jerk a tad to the right. Surprised to realize the Kid's not aiming at her any more.

The Walther makes a pebble-in-a-tin-can sound. With all that flesh to absorb the impact, Micky barely moves.

Elvis blinks, aware of the dark indentation above Micky's belly button, a tiny hole like a freckle.

Micky's mouth forms a small oval. He takes an uncertain step backward. Elvis remembers watching an old German blimp burning on The History Channel, crashing to the ground, and that's what he thinks as he stares at Micky teeter near the edge of the Jacuzzi.

The Kid pulls the trigger again and suddenly Micky's bleeding from the shoulder. Micky glares at Elvis as if to say, *you're just standing there?*—and Elvis too goddamn amazed to move, knowing it's far too late to ever make things *buena onda* with Micky again.

Elvis lifts his Glock, the bullets 129–grain hollow points, ninety-seven cents apiece. He fires and hits Micky below the throat. Micky's head snaps forward, his suddenly limp frame dropping backwards into the Jacuzzi, throwing up an enormous fountain of water.

Elvis watches in fascination and wonders if Micky might have killed Angie anyway.

10:15 PM THURSDAY

Angie Breusser, wearing Micky's silk bathrobe and gulping her Scotch—*screw* the baby sips—sits wet and shivering in the living room, dripping on Micky's Berber carpet. She's not cold, the alcohol burning a deep warmth inside her.

She shivers again at the recollection of Micky's insides

spewing out a sudden, fist-size hole in his back — Micky Logan plummeting like a broken rag doll on top of her. She barely had time to grab a breath, ducking under the foam, a crash dive to the bottom of the Jacuzzi. The last thing she remembered was a sharp *thump* and spinning lights, unable to breathe, unaware of Dwight's hand reaching down, pulling her out of the tub.

"I need a cigarette," Angie says.

"Micky don' want nobody smokin' in the house."

"Oh, yeah, I forgot." Dropping it and none of them thinking it through.

The Kid's on the couch beside her, his shoulders hunched. Elvis paces in the wide area behind them. Angie realizes that both men, in shirtsleeves, are wearing gun holsters. Realizes that something — and she can't quite put her finger on *why* — but something terrible was supposed to happen here tonight.

The Scotch makes her cocky. "So, what...like you schmucks were supposed to *kill* me?"

"Yeah, kinda like that," the Kid says, aware that Angie's lost the fluttery squeak. Her hair falls in damp tangles around her face, her mascara forming a raccoon circle under one eye. She's frowning, not at all the same sort of person he saw dolling up to Micky in the Jacuzzi.

"Why? What'd I *do?*"

"It was a test," the Kid tells her, glancing at Elvis for confirmation.

"A test?"

"Yeah, like a loyalty thing."

"You were going to *shoot* me? To prove your loyalty to

Micky?" Angie takes another sip and peers out the French doors toward the patio. She can see a few palm trees and part of the Jacuzzi and, jutting above the lip, floating on a current of pink bubbles, a mound of bloodless belly.

She's not sure why, the booze she supposes, but she says, "I guess you boys flunked *that* one, huh?"

A few minutes pass before anyone thinks to move. The Kid pulls the crystal decanter from a cabinet, pours himself a Scotch and, without asking, refills Angie's glass. He looks at Elvis. "So what now?"

Elvis stares at him, saying nothing.

"What we did—you think anyone's gonna notice Mr. Logan being dead? I mean, he's got friends. Am I right?"

Elvis remains silent a long moment, then says, "Micky didn't have friends. What Micky had was business partners. An' yeah, I think they might notice Micky bein' gone."

"You mind me asking?" Angie glances at the floor-to-ceiling sound system, flat-screen digital TV, all the expensive furniture and paintings. "What Micky did? I mean I know he wasn't a Boy Scout. He told me once he was an art dealer. But you guys don't, like, strike me as artists or anything."

Elvis isn't sure what to tell her. Micky'd always been too paranoid to talk about business. He never flaunted the fact that he was pulling down ten, sometimes twelve grand a day. He never kept coke in African teak bowls to share with his dealers or people like Angie. Micky hadn't been a user, either. Just twenty-year-old Johnny Walker, two hundred bucks a bottle.

Under the circumstances, he figures Angie maybe has a right to know. "Micky was a street doctor," he says.

"A what?"

"Cooked up crystal and stardust, feebs and pink rock. Had a bunch a guys selling for him out on the street."

"Crack? You're shitting me."

"That's what he did. Owned a bunch of labs and—"

The phone rings and they turn and stare at it. Angie waits for a machine to click in, but the ringing continues— six, seven, eight times. Elvis finally walks over, picks it up.

"Yeah?"

He listens with his mouth open, Elvis finally saying, "Micky?" Like he's never heard the name before.

Angie watches the big man's gaze flit back and forth along the floor, as if trying to find answers scattered about the white Berber carpet. Out of nowhere she gets a sudden scared rush and stands up. Elvis gives her a look. She mouths, *he's not here!*

"Micky ain't here."

Another pause. "Where?"

"*San Diego,*" she whispers.

"San Diego." A heartbeat. "Why?"

"Business."

"Business," Elvis says. "Yeah, later. Maybe tomorrow—" Angie shakes her head furiously. "—or, y'know, the day after that."

Angie crosses her fingers and waits, watching Elvis nod once or twice.

"—Yeah, try then.

"—Nah, why should Micky fuckin' tell you?

"—Don't sweat it none."

Elvis on his own now, getting the hang of it. She imagines something like a light bulb burning dimly inside his head.

"—Nah, you run it by me first. *I'll* tell Micky."

He hangs up and stares curiously at Angie. "Why would Micky go to San Diego?"

"I dunno. I have a sister, Jeannie. She lives near San Diego. Couldn't think of anywhere else."

"What'd they want?" the Kid asks.

"Wanted Micky," Elvis says. Like *sheesh*, is this kid stupid or what?

The silence creeps back. Something about the sudden lull makes Angie nervous. "Look, I better be going." Although she wonders if walking out the door will really be that easy.

"Can we do that?" Dwight asks. "Let her go?"

Elvis shakes his head. "I don't think—"

Angie scrunches her eyebrows together, trying to look fierce. "I didn't have *anything* to do with this."

"You saw us kill Mr. Logan," the Kid says. "You go to the cops an—"

"Cops? Why would I go to the cops! Micky wanted to *shoot* me, for heaven's sake. It was self-defense, what you guys did. You guys are like heroes."

The Kid looks at Elvis as if to ask, *okay, so why can't she go?*

Elvis tries to speak the words spinning around his brain—the thin-hipped hooker watching him with her big eyes, on the verge of tears. He's used to people passing him by in conversations, him with his mouth half-open and suddenly everybody talking about something else. He's not stupid; his brain comprehends most things even when people don't realize it.

Micky told him once there was like this brick wall between his thoughts and his lips. Said his brain formed ideas, but something happened before they got to his tongue. *Like a roadblock*, Micky explained. At the time, Elvis thinking, *yeah, that was it exactly.*

So Elvis is used to other people's impatience, people wondering if he's a stump when he's just trying to scramble over that roadblock. But now something's different. The Kid and Angie are waiting for him, hanging on like he's about to spit pearls.

"More'n a few people know you're Micky's hooker," he tells them finally. "A few days from now, they're gonna start askin' around. The kind of questions you don't walk away from."

"You're saying they'd hurt me?"

"They'd use pliers on your tongue, maybe one of them hair *aparato*—y'know, a curling iron—on your eyelids if they thought you had somethin' they wanted. And what they'll want is me and the Kid here."

"You can't *keep* me here." Her voice hikes up half an octave.

"We're sayin' you stay for your own good." The Kid looks at Elvis. "That's what we're tellin' her, am I right?"

"Maybe a coupla days," Elvis says with a shrug. Too much has happened too fast and Angie's not a priority at the moment. Elvis wants to go to bed but certain things need doing. He gazes past the French Doors and sees Micky's belly protruding from the hot tub like some kid's beach ball.

"You won't...*hurt* me or anything?"

"We wanted to hurt you," Elvis says, "we wouldn't be havin' this problem in the first place."

Angie admitting to herself that he had a pretty good point there.

1:30ᴀᴍ FRIDAY

Elvis wraps Micky in a king-size Ralph Lauren bed sheet. For reasons he doesn't explain, he brings out matching pillowcases and lays them across Micky's bloated mid-section. Green-and-brown stripes. Micky's favorite colors.

The Kid digs maybe four feet down, occasionally hitting rock, still wearing his black silk shirt, his Armani slacks. He pauses, breathing hard, wiping dirt and sweat from his forehead. He gets a whiff of fabric softener and it seems creepy, out here with the clean linen, digging a grave. There's not much light, only the dim Malibu lamps on the patio and an amber glow trickling through the French doors. Elvis' shadow throws a diagonal black swatch across the expanding hole.

Dwight glances up now and then, skittish, occasionally wondering whose grave he might be digging here.

Elvis listens to the crunch of the shovel and the Kid's breathing—but the sounds seem far away, like the volume of a TV turned low in another room. He can't take his eyes off the big-bellied lump of bedding at the edge of the patio. Gonna be different, he thinks. Life without Micky.

They'd gotten used to each over the years—like an old married couple, Micky would sometimes joke. Elvis wasn't sure *what* he'd call these last dozen years, but it wasn't no marriage. He can't deny that he'd grown accustomed to the lifestyle; a Cadillac in the garage and his own bedroom upstairs with satellite TV, money in his wallet and respect on the streets. But Elvis won't miss Micky's temper. Santos Boja and Jesse Nevada aren't the only guys Micky ever whacked out of sheer meanness—Elvis having driven up Decker Canyon more than a few times after midnight to unload guys suddenly dead because of Micky's 'tude.

And Micky always grousing at him for one thing or another, complaining about costs and expenditures, flying into a rage every time he thought a dealer maybe shorted him a C note or two, but not blinking twice about buying a new Mercedes every summer. Or investing in art. Micky'd been crazy about oils and acrylics, one time dropping three hundred grand on some dead guy's painting of a French garden. Fucking nuts, the way Micky spent money. But you had to tread lightly around Micky Logan, never knowing what might make him snap.

Like last summer, when Elvis' cousin Simone called. Simone owned a cantina in Baja, the place doing okay— and Simone out of the blue asking if Elvis wanted to come down and help her run the bar. Micky'd been there a few years back, marlin fishing with some of his big shot buddies. Elvis thought it would be nice to see his *gran'mama* again and maybe get out of L.A. in one piece, but Micky hadn't seemed thrilled about the idea, telling Elvis he'd have to think about it.

Elvis had brought up Simone's cantina a few times since, wondering if Micky'd got around to thinking about it. Only last month, Micky pulled a Steyr semi-automatic from under his shirt and jammed the gun under Elvis' chin.

"You leave when *I* leave. Can you hear me now?"

Essentially telling him, finally, no fuckin' way.

Elvis had been born near Todos Santos, a few miles south of where Simone owned *El Culo Perezoso*. When he was six, his father finagled a green card and moved the family to Pacoima. His mother had been a schoolteacher who taught her children passable English, but she died from blood poisoning when Elvis was nine. By the time their father drank himself to death, his children had long since gone their separate ways. Elvis' older sister, Francesca, cleaned house for a rich widow in Sausalito. His younger sister, Rosa, worked at a Holiday Inn near Sacramento. Elvis sometimes wondered if he'd be working for Micky the rest of his life—a notoriously short longevity, the kind of shit Micky did—but then Simone had called and Elvis suddenly imagined himself pouring margaritas and frying up tamales, maybe hiring a cute waitress or two.

And it sure beat the hell out of killing people.

El Culo Perezoso wasn't exactly a hot spot, although Simone pulled in a fair share of passing tourist busses and seasonal sports fishermen. It was a cozy bar, salmon pink walls with blue shutters and a terracotta floor, a couple of *palapa* umbrellas out front, shading tables and chairs. A mural on the wall depicted a big, sleepy eyed donkey. The cantina sat on a hillside overlooking a wide slice of the Pacific. Where Elvis *should* be, Simone told him, suspicious of his life here in Los Angeles.

A secret Elvis kept from Micky was the bartending book he often studied when Micky wasn't around. Elvis memorized drinks with names like Fuzzy Navel and Luscious Lady and — he liked this one — *Screaming Orgasm.* The trouble with Micky, he only drank Johnnie Walker Blue, telling him now and then to shut the fuck up about the Singapore Slings already.

So when Elvis pulls his Glock on Micky, what flickers through his mind is Simone's hillside cantina, for a single instant tickling the back of his brain before he squeezes the trigger.

"Wha'ya think?" the Kid asks finally, breathing hard, wiping his brow.

"Maybe another foot down. Micky had a gut."

"Yeah, tell me about it." The Kid glances again at the Ralph Lauren designer mound. "Maybe I could make it deeper, y'know, right here. Put him face down, stick his belly in the deep part?"

Elvis shrugs. He has no problem with that.

The Kid lifts another pile of dirt, then pauses, poised over the shovel. "Hey, I gotta ask you."

"Wha's that?"

"About Angie. The people Mr. Logan worked for, you really think they'll come looking for her?"

"They know he liked hookers. An' maybe someone happened to see me pick Angie up. They'll get around to askin' everyone Micky knew, sooner or later, wondering where he's at."

"They'd hurt her?"

Elvis stares at him.

"I'm just saying—shit. What about you and me? *Are* we gonna hurt her?"

"She knows we killed Micky."

"Doesn't mean she'd tell anybody."

"You wanna take that chance?"

The Kid thinks about it. "So, tomorrow an' she goes to leave—then what?" He peers up at Elvis, expecting an answer. He gets none and shrugs and, for the next several minutes, digs in silence.

When the Kid stops again he's panting, sweat trickling down his throat and soaking his shirt. He reaches up without a word, one eyebrow curiously arched. Elvis grabs his forearm and hoists him out of the hole. The Kid wipes a smudge of dirt from his cheek and says, "Y'know, me and you leavin' might not be the dumbest thing we ever did."

Elvis only grunts. The two men strain to move the body enough to tip it over the edge and finally drop Micky into the big-bellied grave. Elvis covers the body with the linen sheet, throwing in the pillow cases because what else is he going to do with them? They peer down at the shrouded form for a long moment before the Kid says, "My uncle's gonna be pissed. I mean Mr. Logan, he was one of Sal's best customers."

It's as close as Micky comes to a eulogy.

7:15 AM FRIDAY

Waking up in a king-size bed in a guest room with the door locked and a chair propped against the knob, Angie can't remember having a more restful sleep. Funny, considering the circumstances—Micky exploding in front of her, dropping on her like an anvil. The two guys with guns pulling her out of the Jacuzzi and the whole experience like something out of a late night movie. For a moment, when she opens her eyes, she wonders if it's all been a dream.

Angie's been hooking about eighteen months. The money beats the hell out of cocktail waitressing, and she never graduated from the Moody-Lebowitz School of Cosmetology—mostly because of Mr. Moody himself and, come to think of it, why she started hooking in the first place. She'd been an enthusiastic student at Moody's school, a few months shy of graduating, her hair always done pretty and her make-up and nails flawless every day in class.

One afternoon Mr. Moody suggested dinner at his place, which at the time she thought would be okay. She wanted to talk to him about some of her classes and he'd told her, *Sure, why not?* But midway through her second glass of wine—his fifth—Mr. Moody started groping at her breasts and thighs. She tried to wrestle away but he pushed her to the floor, hiked up her skirt and entered her there beneath the dining room table, Frank Sinatra crooning in the background about a farewell to love. Moody took his time, smelling like warm Merlot, his mouth uttering sweet assurances in her ear.

Somewhere on the spotted grey carpeting that night, something snapped shut inside Angie's head and she stopped struggling. It wasn't much different than her first time, Angie a sophomore at Green Valley High and Freddy Cochran shit-canned drunk. He was a senior and a half-back on the football team, the two of them necking in Jimmy O'Shaunissey's basement. Before she knew what was happening, he'd stuck a hand up into her business and ripped off her panties. Telling Angie he was hot for her sister — Jeanne also a senior — but that she would do in a pinch. Freddy popped her cherry in twenty seconds flat and when he finished, Angie sobbing in a corner, he tossed her a beer and told her she liked it.

She didn't have much to do with boys after that. She was shy, preoccupied in her own little world — but she always had Jeannie as a friend. But she never told her sister about that night in Jimmy O'Shaunissey's basement.

When Moody finished, he politely helped her to her feet and offered Angie another glass of wine. Not too different at all, really. She was still in shock, quivering, and when he excused himself for the bathroom she got the hell out of there, half-dressed and still putting on her blouse when she hit the door. She never returned to the Moody-Lebowitz School of Cosmetology. When Moody called her apartment the following weekend, sounding a little drunk, inviting himself over for another *date*, she'd packed her suitcase and left Pasadena flat out.

She started waitressing at Goodtime Charlie's after that, her squeaky laugh and big boobs like a neon *do me* sign for all the perverts — and now and then she'd find herself in a compromising situation. But Angie realized that having sex wasn't much different than taking out the garbage. It smelled a little and sometimes you get grunge on you, but you could always wash up afterward and pretend you were normal.

She started asking for a few dollars because—well, why the hell not? Then started asking for more. One day she typed *How do I become a prostitute?* on Google and discovered pages and pages of information. She found a smarmy wellspring of cynical and callus material (God hates sluts and queers), but she also uncovered heartfelt advice from women who'd asked those same questions over the years; women with the same sincerity, the same needs, hoping to make ends meet. She even discovered a Wikipedia page. Who knew?

She started hooking freelance—no pimp, no middleman, no Form 1040s—clearing three or four hundred dollars on good nights, and soon enough double that, her mind in some far away place those times a man asked for a hand job, or lay groaning and writhing on top of her. She was amazed at how little she remembered each encounter, but in a year and a half she'd accumulated nearly twelve grand in a savings account—sending another fifty-five hundred to her mother, whose only income was social security and who thought she was a fancy hairstylist up in Hollywood, because that's what Angie's told her.

She spends a long time thinking about her mother, standing under the hot spray in Micky Logan's shower before she towels dry, staring at the doorknob long enough to swear it's moving. She allows herself to relax finally and begins to peek around the room, smoking her first cigarette in way too long, wondering how much everything costs. Thinking this is only a *guest* room for heaven's sake; more lavish than any hotel suite she's ever seen. She slips a pewter ashtray into her purse as memorabilia, then dresses quickly and sticks her head out the door. She listens to the silent house around her.

Time to go.

Angie sneaks around a couple of corners and emerges from a hallway, carrying her stiletto pumps, her feet silent on the tiled foyer. She's a few steps through the living room, her eyes on the front door—surprised to see the Kid slumped in the La-Z-Boy and Elvis on the couch, doing nothing, like two storefront mannequins.

"Oh," Angie says, unintentionally aloud. The Kid raises his head. They're in shirtsleeves, Elvis mostly sweat, the Kid mostly dirt. She notices a couple of shovels leaning against a sliding glass door and, beyond the doorway, the empty Jacuzzi.

The Kid's lost his ponytail, long strands of ebony hair falling to his shoulders. He has a smudge of dirt on the tip of his nose and something soft kicks at Angie's stomach, like she's seeing an innocent side, Dwight with a boyish charm, bandy-eyed and tired.

She hesitates for a heartbeat, contemplating the awkward silence between them, not wanting them to know she's like, the fuck *outta* here. She sneaks her stiletto pumps behind her back.

"How about I rustle up some breakfast for us, okay?" She

gives the doorway a longing glance and wanders off to find the kitchen. She'll leave, she tells herself, after they eat. How can they say no? Bellies full and the three of them feeling like they've accomplished something together. *Compadres.*

Angie snoops around the big almond-colored kitchen. Copper pots hang here and there, above solid wood cabinets and polished stone counter tops. The room strikes her as overtly masculine, no fresh flowers or fruit in pretty bowls. No cheerful colors. If she owned a home like this, the kitchen would smell like a country meadow every day of the week.

She fries up mushroom and bell-pepper omelets with plenty of Swiss cheese and diced onion, the two men shuffling to the table, downing their food without conversation, cleaning their plates inside a couple of minutes. Angie sips on coffee and nibbles a wheat bagel.

The Kid swallows his last mouthful and glances toward Elvis. "You want me to tell her?"

"Tell me what?" she asks.

Elvis makes a noise, like he doesn't care one way or the other.

"What Elvis and I talked about, last night when we were planting Mr. Logan. We got two choices here. Either we get the fuck out of Dodge or—"

"Who, you two?"

"*All* of us. You can hang around if you want, but I don't recommend it. These guys we told you about last night? They're not gonna understand why we capped Mr. Logan—I mean why it made sense at the time. The fact

that you happened to be here, they're not going understand that either."

"Terrific," Angie says. Guys who don't understand the
meaning of *coincidence.* "So now I'm supposed to be out of
town the rest of my life? What's the other option?"

"We don't let nobody know that Mr. Logan's dead."

"And how do we do that?"

"There's the problem." The Kid shakes his head. "We're
not exactly sure."

"What I figure," Elvis says, pausing to drink his coffee,
using the time to push the thoughts toward his tongue, "is
we got maybe three, four days 'fore they start wonderin'
where Micky's at. Where their money's at."

"Money?" Angie says. "What money? Who said anything about money?"

"What Micky owes them each week. By the time they
figure out why Micky's no longer paying, on account of him
being dead, we better be somewhere else."

"Them," Angie says. "*Them.* The same guys who might
want to kill me because I was in Micky's Jacuzzi? Would
someone please explain to me who these guys are?"

"Micky's business partners."

"I don't suppose we're talking IBM, someone like that."

"Micky didn't sell no computers."

She waits for more, but neither man speaks. The realization comes to her in a flash — the guns, the drugs, Micky
living large in his king-size mansion. Angie's mouth drops
open, her eyes saucer wide. "You mean, like the *Mafia?*"

Aware of Elvis' sullen, steady gaze, she shakes her head
and says, "But Micky's *Irish.*"

"Micky wasn't one of 'em. Worked with 'em is all."

Angie thinks about her sister in San Diego again, but she doesn't believe San Diego is far enough. Her mother lives in Phoenix—but no way is she going to involve her mother, not to mention the fact that if she moves home, her mother will make her go to Mass every morning and nag her about marrying a nice Catholic man and in general bug the shit out of her.

Which means Angie doesn't know where to go. But she's not too sure about staying either.

"Can't we tell them somebody *else* killed Micky?"

"Like who?" Elvis asks.

"Christ, I don't know. Hoods? Gangs? Micky's a drug dealer, for heaven's sake. Didn't you guys ever see *Scarface*? Pushers killing each other all over the place."

"Nah, Micky had it good. Nobody's gonna touch Micky, not knowin' the guys he worked for."

"What if we pretend somebody kidnapped him?"

"Yeah, hey, I thought of that too," the Kid says, giving Angie a grin.

But Elvis is already shaking his head. "Mob guys don't snatch other mob guys. It's like a—" Elvis searches for the right word. "—like a *courtesy*. Somebody wants what we got, they pop Micky and me straight away, then take out Teddy Sparks and three or four of his guys before they get noticed. Maybe then they got room to negotiate."

Teddy Sparks? Angie wonders.

"We say Micky got swiped an' they'll look at us first. When nobody makes a move on Micky's territory, they'll start to worry about me an' the Kid here. "

She begrudgingly concedes the issue. "We could say Micky had a heart attack?"

"In *this* business?" Elvis crooks an eyebrow. "They're gonna take a peek."

"Then what about—?" Angie closes her mouth. *Forget it, Angelina.* From her chair, Angie can see past the living room and into the foyer. She thinks about getting up and running as fast as she can. See how far she gets past the front door.

But *then* what?

She takes a deep breath and leans forward with her elbows on the table. "These people, these Mafia guys, they don't have any particular sentimental feelings toward Micky, do they? I mean he wasn't even Italian, right? Since you work for Micky, why can't *you* give them their money?"

The comment makes Elvis blink. "Me?"

"Wait, you can do that?" the Kid asks.

"Nah, Micky kept a lotta shit to hisself. Numbers, schedules, names. The stuff he wrote down, I don't know nothing about that."

"But Mr. Logan, he told you things," the Kid says. "Am I right?"

"Sometimes he tol' me things, yeah. What to do and when."

"Isn't that enough?" Angie asks.

"Enough for what?"

"To keep Micky's business partners from caring one way or the other."

Elvis releases a heavy breath. He stares at the punk sitting here, the big-eyed hooker, neither of them with a clue.

Believing it might be so easy. He should have headed south the second they finished burying Micky. Let the fuckin' Italians take their best shot.

Angie watches Elvis grumble and scowl—and the idea pops out of nowhere. She jerks upright in her seat, one hand pressed against her chin. Her gaze flickers back and forth rapidly between the two men.

"What if we told them Micky wanted to, like, *retire*? Like Micky's stressed out—wants to move to Tahiti or go live down in Florida or something? Would they *buy* what he's got?"

"Buy it?"

"If they think Micky wants to *sell* them his part of the business?"

"I don't know nothin' about selling Micky's shit."

"Micky had accountants, didn't he?"

"Just Leo." Elvis runs his fingers through his black mop of unruly hair and shakes his head. "Leo, he's got a backbone like mashed potato."

"This house," Angie says. "It's gotta be worth *millions*. My sister in San Diego? You know what she is? She's a CPA. An accountant," she adds for Elvis' benefit.

"Jeanne keeps books for some schmo out in Jamul. You can practically spit into Mexico, where she lives. But she's an *accountant*, get it? Jeanne looks around, tells us what everything's worth, and we make Micky's partners a sweet deal."

"Won't they be suspicious, wondering why we're givin' 'em Micky's business without him sayin' boo?" the Kid asks.

"What do they care, if we offer them a good price? Like

these shoes." Angie stretches out a slim leg and wiggles a red pump. "I got these at Macy's. I have another pair almost exactly like them, but these were on sale—seventy percent off! I *had* to buy them. Don't you get it?"

She wiggles the shoe again. Elvis and the Kid glance at each other with lost expressions. Angie waves her hands in frustration. "What I'm saying is nobody can pass up a bargain if it's too good to resist. Jeanne tells us what Micky's worth and we go to these Mafia guys and tell them—hey, all this shit? It's yours for half price! Two-thirds off! Bottom dollar! What, they're gonna say *no?*"

Elvis sits there, rubbing his scarred earlobe. "Your sister, she can tell you this over the phone?"

"She'll have to drive up and take a look at, y'know, Micky's books. He's gotta have records, tax returns, a checkbook. Can we get all that stuff from Leo?"

"Micky keeps his shit here, in the safe."

"Even better. We show everything to Jeanne and she tells us what it's worth. Then we give Micky's partners the deal of the century. Pennies on the dollar."

"Yeah," Dwight says. "Why can't we do that?"

"This is Friday, right? What about I tell Jeanne to come tomorrow? We'd have to, like, pay her for her time," Angie says hopefully. "She might have to spend the weekend, okay?"

Elvis stares at Angie without a word. Nobody will come looking for Micky over the weekend. He can put Leo off a few days and, who knows, maybe the hooker has a point? Because the thing about running, sooner or later you have to stop. Sooner or later, somebody catches up. Everything's

happening too fast and Elvis wishes Micky was here to figure things out — but that's the problem, isn't it? Micky ain't
here. Angie's idea sounds better than nothing — and nothing's all his brain can muster at the moment.

"Yeah, alright," Elvis tells her, but when Angie slips her
cellphone out of her purse, he frowns. "Use the phone on
the table over there. Your li'l phone, it don't work none
in the house. But, yeah, go call your *hermana* in San
Diego."

So Angie phones Jeanne, gabs about Jeff and the weather,
and then her voice gets low. Elvis hears her say it's an emergency — but also an opportunity for Jeannie to pull down a
few bills if she doesn't mind working the weekend.

And since Jeff is still on disability...?

Yeah, she doesn't think so either. Angie looks up and
smiles. They talk another few minutes. She gives Jeanne
directions up the 405 and over to Route 10, merge north
with the Pacific Coast Highway toward Malibu. Remember
that time eating lobster at Gladstones? Yeah, go past that.
Up Las Flores Canyon until it gets really steep and spooky,
then turn right on Barranca Vista. When Angie hangs up
she seems happy.

"She's coming?" the Kid asks.

"This afternoon. Around two-thirty or three."

"*Today?*" Elvis asks, surprised. "You tol' me tomorrow?"

Angie shrugs. "I explained it was an emergency."

The Kid's nervous, packing his mental bags, ready to
get the hell out of town. "This CPA stuff, it won't take
long, right?"

"She and Jeff can hang around until Sunday evening if they need to."

Elvis nods, having no problem with Sunday, but concerned at the speed in which things are spinning into motion. Something else bothers him. It takes Elvis a few seconds to think it through.

"Jeff?" he asks finally.

"Oh, yeah, Jeannie's husband. He's a real nice guy. Did you know he's one-quarter Cuyapaipe Indian? She didn't want to drive all this way alone, so I figured it wouldn't matter, Jeff with nothing to do the next few weeks because of his leg."

"Wha's wrong with his leg?"

"Drunk driver hit him. He's been on disability since February."

"He's an accountant too?" Elvis asks.

Angie starts to reply, but her expression freezes. She reaches up and cups her mouth with her hands.

The Kid thinks it's cute—her reaction like that—except her eyes are round and wide and maybe it doesn't seem all that cute after all. He leans forward in his chair. "What's the matter?"

Angie doesn't move.

"C'mon, *what?*" the Kid says again.

"I forgot." Angie draws her fingers away from her face, leaving the tips of her polished nails resting on her lower lip. "All this going on, it sort of slipped my mind. I don't know if it's important or anything, but Jeff—he's a cop."

11:00 AM FRIDAY

Jefferson Russell shifts his weight in the Volvo's passenger seat, stretching the muscles in his left leg, scratching at the thick band of elastic girdling his thigh.

"Comfortable, babe?" Jeanne asks.

"Not too bad."

"You want to stop and rest a while?" Jeanne knows he's worried about Angie and smiles. "She sounded fine. Really."

"She called pretty early this morning."

"She said it was an opportunity for me. And this will be a good excuse to spend some time together. All of us." Jeanne watches her husband shift his weight again. "You're sure you don't want to stretch?"

"I'm fine." He puts a hand atop his wife's, their fingers entwining on the gearshift knob. A few moments pass before he starts scratching again.

Jeff doesn't particularly like riding shotgun. Jeanne's a good driver, but he finds it comforting being behind the wheel. Jeanne likes to sing, today a bunch of old Supremes songs as she watches the scenery go by. Jeff feels the need to stay alert, have control over this mass of speeding metal — a feeling far more prevalent since February 4th.

The old woman had been doing at least eighty, her headlights splashing the empty night, in a hurry home to catch The Tonight Show. Jeff had pulled his Jeep Cherokee to the side of the road, rack lights flashing, but the glow only served as a beacon — the woman having staggered from the casino two hundred dollars and six White Russians to the better. That last instant—her headlights playing over the Cherokee and Jeff, standing where he'd dragged the dead coyote—she spun the wheel. The big Buick fish-tailed before it rolled, the rear panel catching him in the thigh like a giant fly swatter, spitting him up and over the embankment almost as if he had wings.

He regained consciousness harnessed to an EMT's stretcher. A half dozen San Diego County sheriff's cruisers marked the area, flares throbbing like angry red welts against the night. Jeff saw the distant Buick in the glow of floodlights, pretty much flattened because it hadn't stop rolling for seventy or eighty yards, the woman having missed Jimmy Fallon for the last time in her life.

Jeff turned thirty a month after the accident. Two years older than her husband, Jeanne found herself occasionally bothered by their age difference in a way he never understood. Especially since she could pass for twenty-one and got carded everywhere they went. She'd been an aerobics instructor for six years, when she wasn't keeping people's books and, in Jeff's opinion, she had a body to die for. Jeanne kept her dark blonde hair short but full around her head and he liked the way she'd shake it loose after they showered or spent a day at the beach. She wasn't very tall, about Angie's height—and Jeff loved her with a totality that often bordered on a physical ache.

In their five years of marriage, if he could name one failing to Jeanne's character, it's her blind devotion to her younger sister. Jeff sees the difference between Angie and Jeanne like night and day. They share many of the same features—the same dazzling smiles, pert noses, innocent

green eyes, (something of an irony in Angie's case, he feels).
Yet their personalities are radically divergent—Jeanne
thoughtful and organized and demure, but Angie always
on the edge, half the time because she likes it there and
the other half because she can't stay away from trouble.
And yet the two of them close, in spite of their differences.

Back when Angie stopped cocktail waitressing, started
working the streets, Jeanne tried to keep it a secret. Not
that Angie began hooking all at once. She worked odd jobs
sporadically, but turning tricks became more frequent and
then routine. Jeanne drove to L.A. and begged Angie to
come live with them until she could find a job and get her
life together. But Angie wouldn't budge. Jeanne had cried
off and on for a few weeks, refusing to tell him what was
wrong, until Jeff eventually coaxed it out of her.

He was normally good at reading between the lines
when it came to people—people being his job, after all.
He liked the sheriff's department, liked working the streets.
He was smart enough for pre-law but enjoyed police work.
He knew a few guys in law enforcement who were in it for
the ego trip, guys who liked to bust heads, but those people
disgusted him. Jeff spoke fluent Spanish and visited schools,
and genuinely felt gratified by helping people.

But then there was Angie, one of the few lost souls he
felt powerless to reach. He'd known Angie almost seven
years, felt certain that she was a good person down deep,
but she confounded him. Like he was talking French and
she was speaking Italian. The two of them *trying* to com-
municate but most often failing. Jeanne would sometimes

tell him he was trying too hard—that Angie wasn't someone who needed rescuing, just a little latitude.

What Jeff wouldn't admit to anyone was the newfound leniency he proffered these days to the runaways and prostitutes he came across out in Jamul, by the casinos or cowpoke bars. He'd often take time to talk rehab or family counseling, and once gave a seventeen-year-old Navajo girl bus fare home. Angie's doing, he suspected.

Jeff's leg throbs and he starts to scratch again. "Damn."

"Poor baby."

The injury's almost four months old. Jeff's still part-time desk-jockeying, the doctor promising a full return to active duty—because he's damn lucky, the way his leg's knitting—maybe sometime in the fall. He's scheduled for two hours of physical therapy on Monday and this weekend, while Jeannie works, he hopes to fit in a strenuous regimen of exercise. He's thrown a couple of paperbacks, a few magazines, into his SDSD duffel bag, but Jeff assumes he'll be bored out of his skull most of the weekend.

The way he figures, what else is he going to do?

It takes Angie awhile to calm the big guy down. *No cops*, Elvis says, *no cops, no way, no cops*—over and over until Angie gets mad and tells him to chill *out* already. Jeff's a deputy sheriff out in Jamul, for heaven's sake, and this is L.A. And it's not any big deal anyway, because he's family.

"He won't even know what's going on," Angie explains. "We'll tell him that you and Dwight are a couple of businessmen. Looking to sell a company." She eyeballs the two men; Elvis a hulking presence like something out of that *Terminator* movie and the Kid with a ponytail, in a black shirt and black suit snap-snapping a wad of gum. Angie thinking to herself, *fat fucking chance Jeff's going to buy it,* but she sticks to the agenda because Elvis is finally beginning to loosen up—and what other choice does she have?

She takes a breath and says; "Come on, we have a lot to do before they get here."

"Do? Whadda we gotta do?"

"We're not going to tell them, y'know, that you shot a guy in the Jacuzzi last night and now we want to sell his place to a bunch of drug dealers. I mean, are we?"

Elvis draws a blank.

"Don't sweat it, I'll think of *something,*" she supposes morosely.

They finalize Angie's plan later that morning, by chance about twenty minutes before Micky's accountant, Leo Sussman, phones. Angie gets nervous but Elvis takes the call like it's no big deal. She listens to him explain Logan's whereabouts, Elvis making the appropriate noises about not being Micky's fuckin' keeper.

"Some place called Heavenly Acres," Elvis tells Leo, although Angie belatedly realizes it sounds more like a cemetery than a health resort. An exclusive spa in Escondido, thirty miles east of San Diego, or so she visualized in her head. The type of place for celebrities wanting tucks or lifts or lipo. And far enough away, she hopes, that people won't go snooping around—and realize Heavenly Acres doesn't even exist.

"No. He don't want to be disturbed," Elvis says.

"—Not even you, Leo.

"—You gotta question, you ask me. I ask Micky.

"—'Cause Micky said so, is why.

"—Yeah. That's what he tol' me.

"—You too. Bye."

Elvis puts down the phone and says, "Leo's pissed."

"Will he be trouble?" Angie wonders.

"Nah. Had some questions for Micky is all."

"He's going to call back?"

"Maybe tomorrow."

"You're doing good," Angie says with a smile. But she's not sure what they're going to tell Jeanne when *she* starts asking questions. You don't sell a guy's house because he's at a fat farm for a few months. And if Jeanne discovers Micky's a dealer—even a dead one—she'll freak. Not to mention Jeff will cop a 'tude and everything will fall to shit. Angie wonders why they can't pretend that *Dwight* is Micky Logan, but both the Kid and Elvis have trouble with that angle.

"Do I look fuckin' Irish to you?" Dwight asks miserably.

"So you're *half* Irish. What's it matter?"

Elvis pulls at his mangled earlobe. "If anybody comes around askin' for Micky, and the Kid here shows up, then what?"

She hasn't considered that.

And there are questions Jeanne will inevitably

ask — *When did you buy the house? How much did you pay? Where's the bathroom?* — and Dwight won't have any answers. So Angie concedes the notion. She decides that Micky Logan is Dwight's stepfather — his *estranged* stepfather and recently deceased, so Dwight can play dumb and Jeanne won't get suspicious.

"Micky's name is going to be all over the place," she tells Dwight. "Once Jeanne starts poking around, we're going to have to explain that. Why you're living here and why you care how much everything costs."

"So everyone's gonna call *me* Mr. Logan now?"

Angie frowns, realizing that Dwight will be tripping over his tongue the entire weekend. "No, hon, you stay who you are. We'll make an excuse to Jeanne when the time comes."

Later that morning she discovers that Micky really *did* sell art. He owns three high-priced retail galleries called Toadflax that Elvis calls dummies. Micky's the CEO of his own corporation that doesn't really exist. Angie's seen enough gangster flicks to know what *that's* all about.

"Micky was laundering," she confirms, pleased with herself.

According to Elvis, Leo pays a legitimate accounting firm to track gallery sales, in case the feds ever get suspicious. But how money is transferred between the galleries and Leo and between Micky and Micky's other partners, he doesn't know.

Micky has a floor safe the size of a small refrigerator in the study. Earlier that morning, Elvis spent a long time removing fat envelopes and wads of paperwork, placing the contents in neat little stacks on Micky's desk. He put Micky's two fat, leather-bound ledgers on top, knowing these were somehow important, Micky telling him once, *If the fucking house ever catches fire, grab these first, then come save my ass.*

Angie's surprised to hear about Micky's ledgers. She figures everyone in the world uses QuickBooks and Turbo-Tax. Ledgers? She not sure if Jeanne will know how to deal with those.

"Micky got *hacked* once, a few years back," Elvis says. It's one of the few computer terms he knows and only because, at the time, Micky had screamed the word every few minutes, like a mantra. That was the same day Micky discovered his phones were bugged.

"Since then, "Elvis says, "Micky didn't trust nothin' he had to plug in."

Elvis knows that Leo occasionally hands Micky thin stacks of paper in vinyl folders, pages filled with rows and columns of laser-printed numbers—several folders piled on Micky's desk too—but, otherwise, Elvis doesn't have a clue about the business end. Everything Micky pays his partners, and everything he keeps for himself, Elvis knows that Leo tracks by hand.

"He was pretty fuckin' paranoid," Elvis admits.

Angie still worries about Jeanne. This morning everything sounded so simple, the way it came out of her mouth. Now, three cups of Greenwell Farms Kona coffee later, she's not too sure.

She's also keenly aware of Elvis and Dwight talking, their voices low—the conversation stopping once when she brings them a lunch of leftovers. She can feed them for weeks, the way Micky's kitchen is stocked. Fancy labels and high price tags — like the boutique coffee and the Himalayan goat cheese and the tiny jars of fish eggs. Micky Logan dearly loved his food.

But seeing the suspicious look in their eyes, Angie begins to wonder if she's made a mistake calling Jeanne. She's not worried about herself anymore. She already thinks of them as kind of a team — and believes Elvis and Dwight feel the same way. The only problem is, Jeanne and Jeff aren't exactly in the game yet.

11:45 AM FRIDAY

Going on noon, Angie begins to fret. She tells Elvis she doesn't want to meet her sister looking like a hooker and wonders if she can borrow a car. Dwight says he'll tag along, make sure she doesn't forget the way back — and, hey, maybe stop over his apartment in Redondo to pick up some extra clothes. Elvis tells them to take the Mercedes — and to hurry it up. He's not as worried about losing Angie as he is about getting his story straight.

So Elvis doesn't do much except pace until they return, Dwight carrying a brown leather satchel and Angie wearing a short teal sundress with white flowers, with her overnight bag over one shoulder. Elvis is still anxious, so they sit down in the living room and go over the story again and — because Angie wants to be *absolutely* sure — they go over it one last time. Elvis mostly listens, not saying much. A hopeful sign, she thinks.

Now if *Dwight* would just fucking relax.

She watches him fidget in Micky's Logan's La-Z-Boy, absently squeezing his hands together, his mouth moving, as if rehearsing lines inside his head. He's dressed in baggy black gym pants and a yellow muscle shirt. Looking at him now she's aware of the definition of his shoulders, the hard curvature of his arms, not grotesque like he's self-absorbed, but nice, like he enjoys working out. She has an idea, so she runs to the kitchen and returns with an ice cold Dos Equis.

"Chill, baby," she says.

"Yeah, easy for you to say."

"You'll do fine." She doesn't have a fix on how his mind works yet—aware the *last* time he got perturbed, Micky Logan ended up six feet under. So Angie wants all of them nice and calm.

He takes the beer and quickly downs a mouthful. She crouches beside him, her hand on the big chair's armrest, her fingers brushing his elbow.

"Hey, tell me something."

"What's that?"

"Why you did it."

The Kid looks sheepish—not at all an expression she's been expecting. He's wearing a thin gold chain, a small crucifix hanging below his throat. She likes that too, a nice touch without being gaudy. Some guys drape themselves in it, two pounds of gold around their necks, *bling bling.* Sitting here, the Kid seems innocent. Like somebody's kid brother.

"What do you mean?" he asks.

She smiles at him.

"You mean me shooting Mr. Logan? I couldn't kill a woman for no reason." He shakes his head and blushes a little, then takes another sip of beer. "Maybe somebody who deserves it, yeah, a hard ass or a freak. I can maybe do that. But I went and popped my mouth off—" He shrugs, like the rest is obvious.

"You could have walked away."

The Kid thinks a moment. "Probably wasn't the brightest thing I ever did, huh? He pissed me off, yelling at me like that. What Elvis told me, if *I* didn't shoot you—Mr. Logan, he woulda popped me, too."

"I guess I should say thank you."

"Nah, don't mean nothin'."

"Not like we're going steady or anything," Angie jokes, but the Kid doesn't get it. He continues to watch her. Angie understands men's stares, but this is different. Not like she's meat.

"You feel bad?" he asks her.

"About what?"

"About Mr. Logan being dead?"

"You're serious?"

The Kid shrugs again, giving her that one. But there's something else on his mind. "I mean, did you like Mr. Logan very much?"

"Like him?" It's Angie's time to think. "He was a good tipper."

"It seemed, last night, like you were sweet on him."

"On *Micky*? Look, Dwight, here's how it goes—it's make believe. Gush over some guy and make him feel, you know, like he's a knockout lay, and it's the difference between four and five bills, know what I'm saying? He was my rent check, sweetie."

She's aware of a surprising gentleness in his eyes.

"You have a pimp or anything?"

"Don't need one. I pick my customers, don't let them pick me."

"But a guy's still payin' for it."

There. Angie finally understands where the conversation is heading. She feels a wall of static rising up inside her head. It blurs the Kid's cute expression and the buff tone of his shoulders. She forces herself to smile again and, when he opens his mouth, she beats him to it.

"So how come they call you the Kid?"

"Oh... I dunno. Micky started calling me that last night. I guess I'm getting used to it." But Dwight's not ready to let go. "You enjoy it? Being a hooker, I mean?"

Angie stands up and hovers next to the La-Z-Boy. *So much for idle chatter, kiddo.* "I don't mind it, no," she tells him, surprised by the harshness in her own voice. "I don't mind it because sex doesn't matter."

Dwight's mouth forms a tight slash but she's not aware. "I don't feel a thing, being with a man, because I spread my legs for five minutes and get two hundred bucks. That's why."

"It's important to you, huh? The money?"

"Let's put it this way. I find a million bucks in the street and I'll stop hookin'. You okay with that?"

She turns her back on him, not waiting for an answer, not really caring one way or the other.

They call Theodore Sparanzano *Teddy Sparks*, Sparanzano a *capo*, a captain in an organization that would easily make Forbes Global 2000 — had anyone been able to track its assets. Sparanzano's superior is underboss Duke Capriccio, a 76–year-old Sicilian who oversees much of the synthetic drug trade between Tijuana and Ventura. Despite the Chinese Triads, the Mexicans, the Vietnamese, the Russians and the Columbians, Sparanzano's organization is making profits hand over fist these last few years.

Once a week, Capriccio talks privately to Sparanzano while Sparanzano's accountants, wearing cordless headsets, talk to Micky Logan's accountant, tapping in complicated sets of figures on Dell laptops between idle chitchat about lasagna and the Lakers. Sparanzano's accountants are elated, Sparanzano's happy and Duke Capriccio isn't unhappy, the Duke every now and then calling Micky Logan "that okay Irish guy." Once, sipping on too many glasses of Chianti, the Duke admitted that Micky shoulda been born Sicilian.

The fact is they've stumbled on a smooth deal, and all of them smart enough to know it. Nobody gets paranoid on a couple or three down weeks in a market mostly so wide-fucking-open that the manufacturers can't keep up with the demand. Last month, Sparanzano financed two new synth labs in secluded desert stretches northeast of L.A. — eleven altogether — Micky's boys bringing most of the stuff to the coast hidden inside dairy and produce trucks. Even with the new labs, they can't keep up.

"Numbers like these," Sparanzano tells Capriccio, "and pretty soon we'll be out of booking and loan-sharking completely." Putting all their efforts into tiny crystallized, meth – and opium-based granules called Pink Pussies, Sunflower Seeds and Mind Grinders.

"Down in the jungle, they can't get enough of this shit," the Duke agrees with a sparkle in his eye.

Micky Logan's penchant for privacy meant Elvis pretty much doted on Micky's whims over the years, everything from carrying Micky's gadabout money—forty or fifty G's in crisp hundreds—to ordering his Saturday night pizzas. Because Micky didn't use a cellphone, people either called the house phone or called Elvis' cell.

So when Elvis calls Vinnie "Li'l Spark" Sparanzano that afternoon, nobody considers it any big deal. Vinnie is Teddy Sparks' nephew, barely twenty years old and drunk much of the time, not the deepest crater on the moon. Vinnie has a flawless '66 Corvette Stingray and a silver Porsche Carrera in his garage, because his uncle *is* Teddy Sparks. Vinnie's an easy reach to Sparanzano—a man who also appreciates his privacy. When Micky wants something from Teddy Sparks, Elvis talks to Vinnie who chats with his uncle and eventually gets back to Elvis.

"Like, so who needs fuckin' Facebook?" Micky used to say.

On the phone, Elvis tells Vinnie, "Micky wants Teddy to know he's outta town awhile. I'm runnin' the numbers this week, so nobody's gotta be bothering Micky none."

He hears a ball game in the background, Vinnie's mouth full of pretzels or nuts and Vinnie distracted, telling Elvis, *Yeah, okay, whatever.*

They chat for another moment, Angie standing at his shoulder, nodding and smiling—giving him a big thumbs-up when he finally tells Vinnie *adiós.* Elvis shrugs, thinking to himself, *this ain't so hard.*

He's barely hung up when the house phone rings again. It's Leo Sussman.

2:45 PM FRIDAY

"This is it? You're sure?"

Jeanne looks at the Post-It Note stuck to the dashboard. "Positive."

They stare past an arched, gated entry, up a long, palm-lined driveway. There isn't much grass, the landscaping mostly rocks and desert scrub. A few plump fruit trees in the distance. They can see part of the house, peach colored stucco, cathedral windows. Peach and orange tiled roof pitched at various angles.

"Christ, it's a mansion," Jeff says.

"Angie told me it was ritzy."

"What, some director or producer lives here?"

"She said he was a business man."

"One of her clients?"

She shoots him a look.

"I'm only saying the last time we saw her, she was in that studio off Ocean Boulevard."

"The one with the cockroaches." Jeanne makes a face.

"What exactly did she tell you again?"

"That she needs some business advice. Financial help."

"Guy who owns this place must have accountants up the wazoo."

"Should I pull up to that little box?"

"Yeah," Jeff tells her. "Push the button. Whoever answers, tell them you're here to ensure their financial security."

Jeanne barely stops the car before Angie's out the front entry and down the brick stairway, all bouncing arms and legs. Elvis waits beneath the portico roof in his dark suit, observing the Volvo with a frown, Dwight beside him in a tan sport jacket and brown tie, white shirt and dress slacks.

"Jesus, they look like hoods."

Jeanne says, "Shhhh," in a nervous whisper and pushes open the door to greet her sister.

They hug under an enormous Sega palm, both woman making happy squealing noises.

Jeff takes his time pulling Jeanne's overnight bags out of the trunk, stealing another glimpse at the two guys standing in the doorway. He can't shake the feeling that something peculiar's about to happen, the place worth a few million and Angie living off hooker's pay. Jeff keeps a Smith .38 service revolver in a padlocked canvas wrap under the driver's seat. He considers bringing it along with the luggage. But Jeanne would *not* be happy and he reconsiders, slamming the trunk and moving with a stiff-legged gait toward the house.

"Jeff!" Angie says, peeking past her sister's shoulder.

"Angie," he replies, cautious and reserved.

"Jefferson?" Giving him that big smile of hers, opening her arms.

"Angelina," he says, aware of his own begrudging attempt to smile. The woman has an innate ability to disarm his suspicions. Somewhere deep down, Jeff wants to believe that Angie's a great deal like Jeanne. If only he could reach down there, grab hold and drag it out of her. She wraps her arms around him and squeezes, then kisses him fully on the mouth. Biting his lower lip playfully.

"Jesus, Angie, oww — what's this all about?"

"Lots and lots of money," she breathes.

"I mean with you. Who lives here?"

"Oh, it's so bizarre. Don't freak, Jefferson. Please, don't freak. I know what I'm doing, all right? Don't make a fuss."

"And you're going to tell us what's going on?"

"I promise."

He nods uneasily.

"I promise," she says again, hoping for some semblance of a concession, squeezing his arm to let him know she's serious.

He glances at the doorway again. The two men haven't moved.

"This is going to be good for Jeannie," she whispers. "Trust me, okay?"

"Uh huh."

"When there's time, I'll explain everything."

"For this," he says, "I can't wait."

Angie cautiously makes the necessary introductions, standing in the polished marble entry, inside the twin oak, hand-tooled doors. They shake hands. Jeff's tense, wary of Zapata's ominous gaze and of the way Manetti's animated jitters swell up, overpowering his pretense of polite charm. Jeanne is affable and warm, making up for Jeff's silence. They step inside and Jeanne *ooohs* appropriately. From what Jeff gathers—first impressions—Manetti owns the place, Zapata an associate or a bodyguard, the way he keeps two steps back, observing. The way Zapata stands, Jeff can discern a discreet bulge beneath his right arm. The guy's packing.

Not a good sign.

Jeanne's oblivious, of course, holding Angie's hand. Angie leads them through the foyer as if she owns the place. Jeff wonders if she and Dwight are intimate. Maybe he's misconstrued everything and Angie's scored big time, Dwight a producer or mogul—one of the young and rich Hollywood elite.

Jeanne's still ogling, saying things like, "Isn't that pretty, isn't that gorgeous!" and, "Oh my God, is that a Pissarro?" Motioning toward an oil painting on the wall. Manetti looks around—*What? What?*—without a clue. Finally looking at Zapata, who doesn't have any idea either. Jeff's foreboding returns.

Angie precedes them into a sunken living room with high ceilings, intricate molding and detailing—three steps up to a large dining area farther the back, near a wide wall of glass and shuttered French doors overlooking a flower

– and vine-shrouded patio. Through a wide doorway, they can see a kitchen the size of Rhode Island. Copper pots climb one wall. A center island with *two* sinks. Turn your head the other direction to there's a walk-in fireplace, done in pink and gray marble, and more tall windows that present the distant Pacific against a cloudless sky. Jeff notices an inlaid chessboard on a coffee table, oversized pieces in dark and light woods, standing at rapt attention.

Angie suggests drinks—sure, everyone's amenable—Manetti and Jeff asking for beer, Angie and Jeanne opting for white wine. Mr. Zapata declines refreshment, the big Mexican hovering, keeping his distance. Jeanne's good at casual conversation and Jeff's relieved, having nothing to say. He's still studying the chessboard, the pieces intricately carved medieval lords and ladies, knights and lancers, jesters and wizards—the board itself inlaid maple or maybe zebrawood against a dark, rich walnut. Jeff figures there's a month's salary sitting on the table. Jeanne and Manetti talk about the warm weather and the typically lousy traffic driving up from San Diego and finally everybody's holding drinks, sitting comfortably in plush chairs, Jeanne and Jeff together on the leather couch. The conversation ceases. In unison, everyone looks at Angie.

Showtime, she realizes, nodding discreetly to Dwight, her fingers crossed. If they can pull this off with Jeff and Jeanne, she's sure they can pull it off with Micky's partners. Convincing her sister will be the trial run.

Dwight clears his throat. "I understand you're a law enforcement officer, Mr. Russell, so I'm telling you this up front." He folds his hands in his lap, like some miscast kid in a B-movie, playing a family patriarch. "I want to be absolutely sure of your discretion in this, um, situation."

Jeff nods without comment.

"The reason Angie's invited you here—obviously this isn't an ordinary circumstance. But here's the thing—" He swallows hard, the quintessence of nervous politeness—"this house, the wealth, needless to say, it's not mine."

"Needless," Jeff replies.

Jeanne gives him a look.

"My stepfather, Michael, is recently deceased. He was an art dealer, but I'm afraid he wasn't the most scrupulous of people. I suspect that some of this shi—pardon me, the paintings that he bought and sold, we believe may be stolen. I wasn't aware of my father's dealings until a few days ago. Which is why you're here. I want to rid myself of my father's, uh—"

"Assets?" Jeanne suggests.

"Yeah." The Kid smiles at her. "All this stuff."

"You realize," Jeff says, "if you're dealing in stolen property, sell it or not, it's still a felony."

"Dwight wants to *return* any stolen property," Angie says quickly.

"Why we need to sort out what belongs to Mick—to my stepfather, and what might not be his to sell," Dwight explains.

"Oh?" Jeanne says. She exchanges a glance with Jeff, who's still frowning. "Didn't your stepfather have financial advisors? I mean, *legitimate* advisors?"

Dwight looks at Angie before he nods. "My stepfather

died in a plane crash a few weeks ago. He was traveling with a group of his, um, people—"

"His entourage," Angie says.

"Yeah. His accountant people were all with him. Which is why this is a sort of, sort of—" He looks blankly at Angie.

"A dilemma," she says.

"Right. When Angie told me her sister was an accountant, naturally, it came as a great relief."

"Naturally," Jeff echoes. He catches Elvis' sideways glance, turns and stares back.

"Like I say, I want you both fully aware of the circumstances before we proceed. I want that there's no misunderstanding."

"You realize," Jeanne says politely, "I can't offer you specific advice. Under the circumstances, there are people with far more expertise than me. Art appraisers. Attorneys."

"For the time being, we need to keep this hush-hush. Y'know, confidential."

"Until we have more information," Angie adds.

"Well, I can take a look at your stepfather's records, his tax returns, but what you have, frankly, Mr. Manetti, it's beyond my capabilities."

Dwight looks surprised.

"Perhaps I can offer a general idea of his worth…?"

"That's cool. See, what we're looking for here, Mrs. Russell, is ballpark."

"Ballpark?"

"Peace of mind," Angie says.

He seems to like the word and nods agreeably. "Yeah, peace of mind."

Jeff has gone along for the first half-minute or so, but now his mind's reeling. Whatever they're selling—it's bullshit. He stares at Angie, but she's watching Manetti with a rapt intensity. Maybe intentionally avoiding his gaze.

"You have a bathroom?" Jeff asks.

"Down the hall, first door on the left," Angie tells him, pointing.

He glances at Jeanne and catches the look in her eye. She's not buying it either, but she's not scared. He feels okay to leave her and pulls himself stiff-legged from the chair. Jeanne's asking questions again, Angie doing most of the answering.

Jeff finds the bathroom and glances back, sees only empty hallway and walks past. The home is magnificent, doorways all over the place and little niches where tropical plants grow, skylights throwing random patterns of sunshine. Heavily framed oil paintings hang on the walls and Jeff notices brushstrokes, aware that these aren't store-bought prints. He glances for signatures, confident that Jeanne will recognize the names. He wonders if they're all stolen.

He confronts a second room—some sort of den with a big desk, a couple overstuffed chairs, a fireplace and bookshelves climbing the walls. He's aware of several distant doorways but doesn't want to chance venturing too far. He turns back.

Elvis is watching him from the end of the hall. The big man's presence is startling, but Jeff moves without expression, limping a bit, pausing a moment to return Zapata's stare before slipping into the bathroom. Despite his attempt at self-control, Jeff feels a wave of dizziness, suddenly wobbly and sponge-kneed. He leans against the door, his eyes closed, waiting for the feeling to pass. He takes a few steps, reached down and flushes the toilet. Takes his time running some water, splashing his hands and face.

When he returns to the hallway, Zapata's gone.

Jeanne regards Jeff with a big, tenuous smile, her gaze wide and filled with awe. She stands, rubbing her palms against her skirt, smoothing non-existent wrinkles. "Do you mind if I talk this over with my husband?"

"No, no," Dwight tells her, motioning agreeably.

Before he has a chance to speak, Jeanne grabs his hand and maneuvers him back into the hallway. Her eyes seek the closest doorway — the bathroom again — she pulls him in and shuts the door.

"You're *not* going to believe this."

"I don't like—"

"Jeff, listen. Mr. Manetti's going to pay me five thousand dollars. For the weekend. For looking over the books."

"It's dirty money, babe."

"Five *grand*, Jefferson! They're not asking me to wash it, for goshsakes. They want my advice."

"That's not the point."

"They're not asking me to lie or cheat or—"

Jeff shakes his head.

"—*Damn* it. Five thousand dollars."

"It's dirty," he says again.

"Why? Because Angie's involved?"

"Because…" He doesn't have a reason. Intuition. He looks away, a vein pulsing at his temple.

Suddenly Jeanne's mad too, about to pursue it, but a tiny sound tap-tap-taps against the door. Angie's trademark knock, nine or ten timid raps. Jeff lets out a deep breath and Jeanne runs her fingers through her hair, calming herself. Their eyes touch, barely a second, before Jeanne opens the door.

"Can I come in?"

"Sure, Sweetie."

"Did you tell Jeff?"

"I tried."

"Jeff?" Angie says hopefully. "Isn't this too cool?"

"It's horse shit, Angie."

"I don't understand." Her big hazel green eyes brim with hopeful innocence.

"About the only thing Manetti's not lying about is that this place isn't his. I'm surprised he can find his way to the front door."

Angie seems more disappointed than chastised. "You're not buying it? Any of it? Even about Dwight's stepfather?"

"Seriously?"

Jeanne reaches out, touches her sister on the shoulder. "Angie? Are you in some kind of trouble?"

"Not the kind you're thinking."

"What I'm thinking is we're out of here," Jeff says. "Right this minute. Save your games for—"

"It's not a game!" She whips her head back and forth, her blonde hair washing over her face. She jabs a finger against her lips, pantomiming silence. "You promised me

you'd listen. Well *listen*, damn it. This is a chance for me —
for *all* of us."

"Manetti's talking about stolen property. If he tries to
unload it, that's a felony. You're an accessory."

"Let Jeanne look at the books. Please."

Jeanne glances at her husband, then back at Angie.
"Who are these people? Where did you meet them?"

"They saved my life. Don't ask me to explain more than
that because it's complicated." She reaches out, takes
Jeanne's hands in hers and squeezes. "I wouldn't do anything—*anything*—to hurt you or Jeff. You know that. I
swear to you I know what I'm doing."

When Jeff doesn't respond, Jeanne touches his shoulder. "Hon?"

He stares at the floor. A few seconds float by, long
enough for him to realize the tiles are real marble, a for-
tune under their feet.

"Jeff?"

They're watching him with expectant, eerily similar expressions. "*Shit*," he says finally, the word a hot rush
under his breath. "Yeah, go help Angie." Blurting it before
he can pull it back or go with the instincts eating him up
inside. He raises a finger, one last-ditch effort. "I think for
one second that Jeanne's not safe here, if *you're* not safe,
we're out of here. All of us. No arguments."

"Thank you," she says. "Nothing bad will happen. I
promise, Jefferson. I *promise*." Her words are a fierce
whisper.

3:45pm FRIDAY

Every couple of days for the last five years, Elvis would climb into his copper-colored Fleetwood and head south on the Pacific Coast Highway. He usually took the Santa Monica Freeway east, across town, sometimes in rush-hour traffic that ate up a couple of hours just to go the twenty-three miles. Elvis would pull into the weed-choked parking lot of *The Alhambra Children's Library*, a single-story cinder-block building that had seen better days—hard to tell the color of the building lately, the walls mostly obliterated by taggers in layer upon layer of dancing graffiti.

Elvis would grab an empty satchel from the back seat and pop the trunk, then walk to a steel door with no handle and a triple Mallory lock. He'd knock and sooner or later a black guy named LeRoy Beers would appear. They'd chat a minute or two in the doorway, a few of Beers' guys hanging around, smoking Marlboros. When Beers felt like it, he'd poke at his iPhone and a short while later a black BMW or sometimes a fluorescent violet Mercedes 320SE would park next to Elvis' Caddy.

The switch never took longer than five or six minutes. Elvis would be back in his Fleetwood with a bag or two filled with cash, listening to *Café Tacuba* or *Maldita Vecindad*—or more recently thinking about his cousin Simone and how to make a Sahara Scorcher or a Mai Tai.

Today's no different. Elvis finds himself stuck in traffic an hour and a half before he reaches the library. The crazy thing is that Micky Logan owns the building. Crazier still is the plaque inside from the mayor, commending Logan's

contribution to the community. Every year, Logan takes in
an eighty grand write-off on the property. Beers' guys sometimes hang around out back, selling kids cherry-flavored
crack-laced poppers in dollar bags.

Elvis feels peculiar this afternoon, jumpy, with Logan
dead and people he doesn't know in his house. He arrives
early and unlocks the back door, waiting in the shade for
several minutes before Beers shows up—him and three
other young men in the Mercedes. Beers is a skinny
guy with a bobbing Adam's apple and a gold tooth like
Tyson. Beers' steps out of the back seat, his silk Versace
shirt unbuttoned to the waist. He wears a half dozen 24–
carat rope chains around his neck and another few pounds
of bracelets and rings that offset the contrast of his baby
smooth skin.

Micky calls LeRoy Beers his foreman—Beers a man
with *juice*, a dozen foot soldiers in his own army, guys
who'll keep the peace or keep him alive out here in the
zone. Beers directs a network of street dealers, owns himself a fluid twenty-five or thirty intersections around the
city. Beers could have been a Double-Deuce Crip, could
have been Wilshire Baller—hell, could have been a U.S.
Congressman—wise and cagey beyond his twenty-eight
years. But he cleared three hundred grand last year, tax-
free, working off Micky Logan. Not many Crips raking in
that kind of bread.

Beers nods at Elvis, then tosses a by-the-way frown in
his direction. "Hey, how come Micky didn't call t'other
day?"

Elvis stares without a word.

"Tol' me he's gonna give me a head's up. Said we be gettin' some new v-mail scramble code. Somethin' the feds can't sneak no listen to. You know Micky, thinks the whole world can hear him takin' a piss. So how come, hombre?"

"Micky got busy is how come."

"Too busy to take care o' business?" Beers arches an eyebrow, like what's Chico trying to pull here?

"Micky's away."

"Ain't nobody *that* far away." Beers and Elvis watch a kid in sagging denims and a skin-tight T-shirt transfer a stuffed duffel bag into the Caddy's open trunk.

"A couple weeks," Elvis tells him. "I'm runnin' *pago* while Micky's gone."

"You? Why you?"

"Micky said so is why."

Beers squints at him. "You harshin' my buzz, Chico. Micky didn't say nothin' to me."

"Micky comes back, you bitch at him, huh?" Elvis walks to his Cadillac and looks inside the trunk. The black duffel holds ten or twelve grand in small, crumpled bills — singles and fives and nothing over a twenty because the people who buy on corners, they usually don't see more than crumpled twenties in a lifetime.

Elvis shuts the trunk and climbs back into his Cadillac. Pulling away from the library, he glances in the rearview and sees Beers staring after him. Elvis wonders if the man's going to be trouble.

4:30 PM FRIDAY

"He's *where?*" Sparanzano asks.

"Fat farm," Joey Segal tells him, gazing up from a computer screen. Cigarette smoke infuses the small room. "Out in the desert somewhere."

"You're serious?"

Segal's eyebrows dance with curious cynicism. Joey Segal is Sparanzano's chief accountant. An hour before, Leo Sussman called, saying, *Hey, hey, Zapata's changin' up the game plan.* Leo Sussman is a loose-skinned Jewish guy going on seventy who makes no bones about being scared shitless of Sparanzano's organization. To Sussman, any divergence from the ordinary foreshadows a few guys coming over in the middle of the night, taking him away in his pajamas and the neighbors never seeing him again. Sussman had opened the conversation with a rush of breath. "Look, this ain't my fault, but..."

"Funny thing," Segal says, "because Zapata's never got in the middle of runnin' numbers before."

"Pretty much wipes Micky's nose when he wants."

"Yeah, but keepin' score?" Segal shakes his head. "Why not give 'em to Leo? Zapata's a gorilla. What's he know about the tally?"

"He talked to Vincent this morning."

"Zapata did?"

"Yeah."

"Wha'd he say?"

"That Micky was making some changes. Nothing about a fat farm. He asked Vinnie to pass me the message."

Segal tries to imagine a phone call between Elvis Zapata and Vinnie Sparanzano. An entire conversation in monosyllabic grunts, the way he hears it in his head.

"You worry too much," Sparanzano says.

"Meh."

"What exactly *did* Sussman tell you?"

"That Logan would be out of touch, on account of some doctor told him he had to lose a hundred pounds or his ticker was gonna explode."

"Yeah?"

"Like an egg in a microwave, what Leo said the doctor told Micky."

Although Sparanzano is in pretty good shape for a man recently turned fifty, he puts a hand to his chest, feels his own heart give a sympathetic quiver. "Leo tell you how long Micky'll be gone?"

"Four weeks, give or take."

"Which is why Zapata's running the numbers. Makes sense."

Segal nods.

"Micky make provisions?"

"Leo said June's fourth quarter might be a half-week shy is all."

"Any problem there?"

"No. Nearly thirty grand *up* as a matter of fact."

"Oh yeah? The new labs," Sparanzano offers with a satisfied nod. He's quiet for a moment, then says, "Micky been having any trouble with Sussman lately?"

"You kiddin'? Leo was with Micky's uncle from the old days. Been a bean-counter since Hector was a pup."

"Fat farm, huh?"

"Yeah. Elvis told Leo that Micky didn't want it getting around. Y'know, guys on the street having a laugh at his expense."

Sparanzano spreads his arms, like, *there you go.* "You blame him?"

"Nah, shit. Whadda I know? Just strange, out of the blue and all."

Sparanzano feels Segal's brooding contemplation washing over him in distracting pulses. Segal's a Capricorn and that pretty much explains it—especially where Micky Logan is Aries, and the two never meshing well in matters of finance. Not many people know that Sparanzano consults astrological charts when weighing the consequence of business matters—and he's careful about the few people he lets in.

Sparanzano lifts a finger. "Will you feel better if I have Danny check it out?"

"Probably no big deal."

"You lose sleep, you make mistakes and pretty soon numbers don't add up. Then it's a big deal. I'll have Danny take a look."

"Yeah. A little strange is all."

Sparanzano puts a hand on the back of Segal's neck and gently squeezes. "Hey, you know what? You worry too much. Maybe you should try yoga. I'll tell Danny not to bother the poor guy, simply make sure everything's kosher, okay?"

Segal nods.

"Joey, you worry too much," Sparanzano tells him again.

Micky Logan had been born fat, told all his friends he'd die fat, and on that account he hadn't been wrong. Sometimes, sipping his twenty-year-old Scotch, he'd tell Elvis, "Chicks don't mind fucking the fat, man. Some even dig it. The ones that mind, hell, they fuck the money." Micky had his clothes and suits custom made on East 9th. Sometimes, dropping two or three grand on a new suit, Micky would feel like a million dollars.

He bought a room full of exercise equipment several years back — once rode an exercise bike for seven minutes, a plastic tumbler of Johnnie Walker in one hand, before he decided it was a fucking bore. Still, Micky liked the idea of Elvis working out, building muscle.

"In case you gotta throw yourself in front of a bullet or somethin'," Micky told him once. "Hit something solid, not come through your blubber and get to *my* blubber." Micky with a wink at the time, but Elvis not quite sure, touching the scar on his ear, knowing Micky was serious about certain things.

Elvio Zapata first met Micky Logan when they were kids, Elvis usually hiding from his old man, who spent most of his time drunk and full of rage. In those days, Elvis kicked around the streets because street life was safer than going home. He did odd jobs for an assortment of loose knit Mexican street gangs, pop-capping cars and ripping off vending machines, occasionally getting high on 'ludes and home-grown weed.

Micky Logan came down from Bakersfield, his parents recently deceased. His uncle Paddy was a small-time hustler, well on his way into the big leagues and usually on the move — somebody or other after him for various reasons. The house fire that killed Micky's parents was "of suspicious and unknown origin," inspiring Paddy to disappear for eight days afterward, taking young Micky with him and telling his protégé to stay close. "Family's the only folk you can trust," Paddy would often tell Micky. "Family's all we ever got." Paddy considered everyone else in the world to be either marks or enemies.

By age eleven, Micky was already rotund and clumsy, fair-skinned and glaringly out of place amid the converging ghettos of dark-skinned Latinos. But Micky had his uncle's instincts. He hustled because he had no other options.

Micky sold weed and an assortment of pilfered pills in schoolyards and playgrounds, usually carrying wads of singles stuffed into the pockets of his baggy Levi's. His biggest problem seemed to be keeping his money. Those first couple of months in Pacoima Micky got stomped and mugged a few times too many. One afternoon he spotted the thirteen-year-old Zapata — already six-foot-four and built like a bear — standing with a group of bored *vándalos* near a corner liquor store. Micky walked up, waving a couple C-notes in his face, ready to take a chance. "Just keep me safe, dude. That's all I'm askin'."

Elvio was skeptical, but two bills was more money than he'd ever seen in one hand. He shrugged and told this pudgy blanco he'd give it a shot.

So Micky started calling him *Elvis* — Uncle Paddy had

been a fan of The King—and more than a few times over
that first year Elvis pulled Micky's ass out of harm's way.
There was also the time Elvis turned his back—Micky
fourteen by then and Elvis standing in line at a corner
deli, waiting for a salami, sweet pickle and cream cheese
sub because Micky was hungry. Three black kids came out
of nowhere, kicking and punching and taking almost six
hundred dollars off Micky, who sat sniffling and bruised on
the curbside, waiting for Elvis with a palmed blade. When
Elvis bent down to say, *Wha' happened?* Micky lashed out,
carved a hunk of skin out of Elvis' cheek and ear, almost
taking off the lobe.

"For slouchin' off," Micky told him between sobs, the
two of them bloodied and getting stares, sitting on the curb
until Elvis finally passed out, bleeding so much. The last
thing he remembered was Micky saying, "Here's the way
it is. You do good by me, you get good by me. You do bad,
you get bad back."

Uncle Paddy kept Micky in school—education and a
twelve-gauge, that's all you ever needed in life, Paddy told
him—and Micky went off to UCLA a few years later. Elvis
won an all-expense-paid trip to the Correctional Training
Facility in Soledad, three days after his nineteenth birth-
day. The cops had stopped him behind the wheel of a stolen
Corvette, an unlicensed pistol and a half-kilo of cocaine
under the seat. Who knew? Elvis pulled six to eight, got
out in three with a measly hundred in gate money, hanging around street corners when Micky came looking for
him. Micky had a B.S. in finance by then, and was eager
to get back into the biz. Uncle Paddy's standing had risen

dramatically, thanks to an infusion of capital from his new Italian partners—and Micky wanted a front-row seat.

"You're the fuckin' Man now?" Elvis asked.

"Me? Hey, just tryin' to make ends meet. These guys, they won't be no trouble. Me and the *goombahs* are both after the same brass ring," Micky told him. He handed Elvis five grand and told him to keep his nose clean, to do what he was told. Elvis has no problem with five grand and, a few years later, when Paddy's heart wheezed out after the third Barrera-Morales bout in Vegas, Micky inherited several million dollars, as well as Duke Capriccio's grumbling admiration.

And there was Elvis, along for the ride.

7:45 PM FRIDAY

Jeff asks Manetti—the Kid telling him, "Hey, call me *Dwight, okay?*"—if he could walk the grounds awhile, stretch his bum leg and get some fresh air.

"We got a gym down the hall."

"Doctor told me to do some distance work."

"Suit yourself," Dwight says. "Watch the fence though. It's juiced. You could fry an egg."

Jeanne's been in the library with Micky's books the last few hours, the door shut. Angie's with her, probably reading a magazine, keeping her sister company. Jeff's been watching an Angels game with Manetti, the big Mexican nowhere in sight, but after three innings of small talk,

Manetti drinking more than a couple of beers and getting skittish, Jeff figures it's time for a change.

He steps outside, into the dry summer evening. The sun hangs round and red above the sliver of ocean visible to the west. Jeff jockeys himself gingerly down the front staircase, ornate cement owls capping the bottom posts, and limps past the giant Sega palm toward the Volvo. He keeps an aluminum cane in the back seat, but rarely uses it. He doesn't like the feeling of needing a crutch. Doesn't like the implications. He casually looks back a couple of times like he's admiring the place. He half expects to see Zapata peering from an upstairs window, like an ominous shadow out of some Hitchcock movie.

Jeff opens the driver's side door and slides behind the wheel. He opens the glove compartment and removes a bottle of pain pills. He wants to have them, should anybody ask what he's doing in the car. He slips his cellphone from a pocket, his back to the house, and speed dials a number.

No signal.

The mountains, he thinks.

The driveway snakes down a hill toward the distant ocean. This close to the house the lawn is well manicured, but a dozen paces away clusters of pampas grass and outcroppings of gray porous rock reclaim the slope. A scattering of citrus trees dot the landscape midway to the front gate. Jeff figures it's maybe a hundred yards to the street, past a trio of spindly palms that sway in a gentle breeze and the electrified fence that drifts out of sight beyond the rocky slope.

Probably better reception closer to the road, he thinks.

Jeff moves slowly along the asphalt, testing his leg, scan-
ning the horizon but far more aware of the surrounding terrain, deep ravines to the north and south and nothing but
sage-scattered hilltops behind the house. These guys like
their privacy.

He spends a few minutes working out the kinks, feeling the bruised muscles begin to flex. He pauses near one
of the orange trees and speed dials again; for a half-second
a number appears, then blinks away.

Jeff stops again near the gate, one of the big palms cam-
ouflaging his intent. He's sweating, and feels a prickly damp-
ness he knows isn't from the heat. For the first time in a
long while, he recognizes the stinging sensation of fear. He's
not often afraid—but whatever's happening here, it feels
elusive, subversive, beyond his control. He taps his phone
again. The number blinks, disappears, then reappears.

A phone rings and he hears a familiar voice.

"Stacy? Hi. It's Jeff. I need a favor, an address check, res-
idential, up in Malibu. The number one, on Barranca Vista
Drive. Who's shown as owner on record?

"—Well, it's crazy. I'll explain later. Thing is, Stace, I
need it like yesterday."

He pauses. "Thanks, you're a pal."

Jeff glances back toward the house. Okay, so say Zapata
has binoculars, watching him from one of a dozen oversized
windows. Jeff can say he's checking messages, so what's the
big deal? *Get a grip,* he tells himself. *You're a peace officer,
for Chri*—

"Yeah, I'm here.

"—Logan, Michael Patrick," he repeats.

"—Anybody named Manetti?" He spells it.

"—What about a D.O.D. on Logan?

"—Nothing? Alive and kicking, huh?"

"—Okay, no, don't bother." He feels the seconds ticking by, unseen eyes drilling into the back of his head. "Thanks, Stace. I'll touch back later."

Jeff ends the call and gazes absently toward the ocean. So Michael Logan *is* Manetti's stepfather? If Angie's been telling the truth, he's going to feel like a complete ass. But as far as anyone knows, Michael Logan's very much alive. Why would Manetti lie about his stepfather's death?

Midway back to the house he wonders if he should pull the canvas satchel from under the Volvo's seat. He'd feel safer with his revolver within reach. Then again, maybe Jeanne's right. Maybe it's time he gives Angie a little slack.

She pulls a bagel out of the fridge and cuts slices of Jarlsberg to melt with a smear of honey mustard. Angie notices several empty Corona bottles near the sink and has an idea. She finds several more bottles chilling in the fridge, snatches one and pops the cap with a gold opener, the handle shaped like a dolphin.

"Thought you might like another brew."

The Kid's still watching the ball game, the volume turned low. She notices that he's changed back into his yellow muscle shirt, his black warm ups and unlaced Nike high tops. "Yeah, thanks, I'm runnin' on empty."

"I can read your mind," she tells him.

"Now *that's* dangerous." He takes the bottle and gave her a grin, all those white, even teeth.

"It's getting late. Mrs. Russell's still working?"

"She's almost done for the night."

"She got a clue yet, about what it's all worth?"

"It's probably still too early."

"Tomorrow, right?"

"Yeah, honey, I think so. She glances around the room with a sudden realization. "Where'd Jeff go?"

"Out for a walk."

"Is he okay?"

"Stretching his leg."

Angie's not sure if she believes that or not, but Dwight's watching her and she doesn't want to spook him. "Hey, you did good today."

"It felt *real*, y'know? Make-believing Micky was my step-daddy, and I'm washing my hands of all his shit. You think your sister bought it?"

"I hope so."

"Maybe we weren't so stupid after all, huh? Maybe we got the—"

The phone chirps and Dwight closes his mouth. Angie waits, expecting a machine somewhere to pick up, take a message, but the sound continued for almost a minute.

"Where's Elvis?" she asks.

"Must be out, too."

"Micky couldn't afford an answering machine?"

"Elvis tol' me last night Micky didn't want one in the house. Didn't want people leaving all sorts of weird messages that would maybe fuck him up some day with the cops. These don't work in here either," Dwight tells her, slipping his cell phone out of a pocket, juggling it in his hand.

"Micky's got some sort of jamming system built into the house. Elvis called it—ah, shit, I can't remember. Interferes with phone signals. Kills the reception. Micky doesn't own a cell phone either. Elvis said he thought it would give him brain cancer."

"He was one spooked out little guy, Micky was."

The kid nods. "Yeah, can say that again."

"Too bad he hadn't been more afraid of guns, huh?"

Angie leaves the kid thinking about that one, remembering her bagel in the microwave, telling him to hang on a minute.

Dwight takes a gulp of beer and watches Angie prance to the kitchen. She's still wearing her teal summer dress with white flowers, cut several inches above her knees, a slit up one side, showing a little thigh. He likes how she looks, her legs tan and well shaped. Something about a barefoot woman in a short dress that turns him on. Something about Angie that—

Across the room, a shadow moves. Dwight shifts his gaze and sees Elvis standing there. Hell, maybe the entire time, listening to them talk.

"Hey—what's up, dude?"

Elvis regards Dwight with a brooding slash of eyebrow. The Kid's starting to get used to the long silences, not taking it personally. He wiggles his Corona. "Have Angie chase you down a beer, why don'cha?"

"She done yet?"

"Mrs. Russell? Angie says maybe tomorrow."

She must have heard them talking—Angie returns from the kitchen carrying two bottles.

"Shit, we could get used to this," the Kid tells her.

"Ex-cocktail waitress." She offers a beer to Elvis. He seems uncomfortable, but reaches out and takes the bottle.

"On the house," she says with a wink, then turns around and retraces her steps. Elvis watches the kid's gaze follow her out of the room.

"Don't forget what I tol' you."

"What? About Angie? Man, you still think that way? Angie's a pal."

"Don' change nothing 'cause she's fetchin' you a bottle of Micky's beer."

"Hey, if it wasn't for Angie, man, you an' me, we'd be halfway to Bumfuck by now, running scared."

"Wasn't for Angie, Micky'd still be alive," Elvis reminds him.

"Yeah, and we'd be doin' what? Sucking shit off Micky's shoes every time he wanted? If we got a chance here, it's because of Angie."

Elvis isn't sure he likes the Kid's tone — Dwight wouldn't last two seconds giving him that kind of lip — except that the Kid's looking at him with big puppy dog eyes and suddenly it dawns on him. "You're tellin' me, wha'? You wanna *do* her?"

The Kid's cheeks turn red. "No, not *do* her. Like, maybe, you know, ask her out or something."

"*Jesucristo*," Elvis mutters, shaking his head. He wonders if maybe the whole world's gone crazy since Micky died.

10:00 PM FRIDAY

Jeanne, in her panties and a frayed Chargers T-shirt, slips into bed beside her husband. Jeff lets the Los Angeles magazine drop to the floor. She entwines her legs around him, pressing her belly against his thigh, a hand on his chest. "You won't believe this, babe."

"What's that?"

She rubs her cold feet against his calf. "What Manetti told me about his stepfather? All this time I've been getting numbers from these various art galleries—you know, Toadflax? I Googled the name, by the way, because it sounded funny. Toadflax. It's a *flower* that grows in Ireland. Anyway—the place caters to private investors, strictly big ticket sales, and I'm talking about the kind of art you'd see bought and sold at auctions. Artists you learned about in school."

"Uh huh."

"Most of the transactions, the money disappears—like, everywhere. At first I thought funds were being transferred to other galleries, but I don't think so. Michael Logan was the sole shareholder of MPL Enterprises, the umbrella corporation for everything he owned. MPL's like a sieve."

"Is it dirty? Is he laundering?"

"My God, Jeff, the man's pulling in close to three million dollars a quarter. Four-fifths of that is going in directions I can't begin to fathom. Doesn't mean it's not legit—but it is pretty strange."

"What about taxes?"

"Next to nada."

"Then it's dirty."

"Or creative." She shrugged. "I don't know yet."

"Can you find out?"

"Eventually, if I dig deep enough."

"How deep can you go by tomorrow? Because we're out of here, Jeanne. As soon as possible."

She pushes herself up on one elbow. "Not without Angie."

"Then talk to her. Or I will."

"I don't think I could untangle these books in a month. But I promised Angie I'd do my best. That's why we're here, right?"

"This isn't only about Angie any more."

"If you're asking me to look for illegal activities, there's no way I can scratch this mess in one day. Not and get Mr. Manetti the figures he needs. I'm not even sure I know how to *look* for this kind of dirty money."

Jeff's silent, staring into the shadows on the ceiling. Jeanne puts her head against his chest, listening to his heartbeat, a sound she finds comforting. She reads his silence as acceptance and closes her eyes, feeling peaceful again, her thoughts quieted.

Too soon. Jeff tenses again. "It's got to be drug money, Jeannie. Maybe it's—"

"Shhhh."

Jeff closes his mouth and she nuzzles her face into his neck, stretches up and brushes her lips against his ear. Kisses him lightly and says, "Not tonight, alright? No more business. I'm off the clock."

When he says nothing, she says, "Make love with me?"

One promise they've faithfully upheld during their

marriage — the world's problems would not come between them in bed. Not even Angie's problems. Jeanne's already surrendered her monsters this evening and he knows it's impossible to do battle alone. She allows him sufficient time to peel away any leftover vestige of anger.

He understands her need for intimacy tonight and kisses her.

Their playful hugs gave away to slower kisses — Jeff's mouth getting serious, brushing his tongue against her lips in a way that shoots tingles down her spine — a sudden yearning quiver in the pit of her belly.

Jeff turns out the bed lamp. Something about a strange bedroom that makes them both uneasy, more comfortable in absolute darkness.

"Where were we?" he whispers.

"Mmm, getting me all hot and bothered is where."

They make love with quiet gentleness, briefly suspicious of the subtle bed-squeaks beneath them, until they lose themselves against each other. Jeanne has a playful streak — sometimes coaxing Jeff to get his handcuffs off the bureau, or whispering obscenities in his ear, passionately arousing him in ways he's not quite sure he understands. Tonight she's content with gentleness, the feel of his weight atop her.

For a long while Jeanne loses her thoughts in the sheer pleasure of his touch, her body responding to his, her mind at peace. Her thoughts drift and float and touch upon a myriad of delightful visions, vague and pleasing snatches of memories, here and gone again. The first tingles of electricity spark between her thigh.

"Come with me," she says, her words a hot rush.

"Not yet," he whispers.

And Jeanne, holding back—trying to. Playing with the urge a few moments longer, her eyes tightly closed, before a surge of longing overcomes her. Jeanne moans and bites his earlobe. "Now?"

"No," he says and kisses her neck, their bodies moving in a passionate rhythm, the first traces of sweat trickling from his temples. She knows they're letting their bodies find the rhythm, letting themselves connect to every conscious fiber, feeling the other's tension and melding it with their own. Not even aware, she scissors her legs around his waist and squeezes; and when his body spasms—Jeff speaking her name in that hushed way she loves, she instinctively reacts—she bites his shoulder to keep from crying out. Electricity races from her groin and into her head, a wave of pleasure dizzying her senses. For a moment the sensation overloads her circuitry, the feeling like an explosive current ripping through the top of her head. Jeanne clenches her fists and grimaces, for a moment teetering between pleasure and pain. Then she feels a spreading warmth of satiation and total happiness, and kisses him fiercely.

"Jesus," he says.

"Jesus," she whispers back.

Neither of them moves again for a long, silent time and the darkness returns to invade their thoughts. They find comfort in each other's embrace.

"You know?" he says, several minutes later. "If Manetti thinks we're—"

But she silences him with a sound. "In the morning," she reminds him.

"Alright."

So they hold each other and Jeanne hears his breathing begin to relax. She strokes his hair and inhales his scent, content in ways she can't even begin to describe. She closes her eyes, on the verge of letting the night take her. Vaguely she hears a phone ring, so far away in this grand maze of a house. She half wonders if it's real or an imagined sound deep inside her head. But Jeanne is asleep before she can worry about who might be calling so late at night.

10:30 PM FRIDAY

Elvis answers on the fourth ring. He's still wearing a jacket and tie, his shoes off and feet crossed on Micky Logan's desktop, watching an old movie on *Telemundo*. He knows the call will be for Micky—Elvis getting the hang of it, comfortable with his part in the charade.

But he's unprepared for the voice on the other end of the line.

"Mr. Zapata, I presume?"

Elvis feels an icy sense of dread—tries to find his own voice and fails.

"This is Teddy Sparks, Mr. Zapata."

"How you doin' Mr. Sparanzano," Elvis says finally.

"I hear you're taking care of business while Micky's away."

"Tha's right."

"Good to know our venture is in such capable hands. I'd like for us to chat tomorrow, Mr. Zapata. Let's say nine o'clock. Bright and early, huh? You know the big parking lot over on Wilshire? Corner of Lateen?"

"Uh...," Elvis says.

"Since Micky's left you in charge, I know he'll be happy you and I had this little meet. Nine o'clock, Mr. Zapata."

Sparanzano hangs up and Elvis — for the longest time, Elvis stares at the dead phone.

11:45 PM FRIDAY

Angie lies in the dark thinking about her sister, unable to sleep. Wondering if she was wrong to involve Jeanne in her scheme. Her entire life, Jeanne's been coming to her rescue. Only this time, it feels like a genuine rescue.

She starts to drift off and hears the noise, a small click floating through the black veil. Immediately awake, she's aware of bare feet against the carpet. She hasn't locked the door, not tonight, feeling complacent and, with Jeanne and Jeff down the hall, safe.

The sound of breathing in the darkness startles her.

"Jeannie?"

"It's me," the Kid says.

"Oh." Relaxing and tensing at the same time, Angie knowing why he's in her room and desperately not wanting him here.

"I thought we, uh, could talk."

"It's late," she says calmly.

Before she can protest, she feels the weight of him beside her on the bed. She smells his cologne. Something musky, mingling with the remnants of stale beer.

"It's late," she says again, this time her voice sounds timid. She can vaguely see the color of his yellow muscle shirt through the darkness.

"Angie," he says. "Hey, I thought you liked me."

"I do." Meaning it, but feeling a sadness in the words, like scolding an uncomprehending child.

"The way you liked Micky?"

She doesn't know how to answer, about to try when she feels him lean close, the musk and beer a hot rush in front of her face. She feels his hair tickle her cheeks and knows he's not wearing the ponytail. She smells his hair, too, a soapy, woody scent.

He kisses her, lightly, his lips a wisp of sensation against hers. He isn't touching her and she doesn't know where his hands might be, own hands clutching a knot of blanket at her belly. She's afraid to move or try to push him away.

"We're partners now," the Kid tells her softly.

Angie lays silently.

The Kid hovers. She realizes he's giving her time to accept his presence, maybe even time to say no, but his closeness is too startling and she feels herself go numb, Angie's brain suddenly spiraling into a realm that leaves her body behind.

"*Baby*," she coos — Angie's voice, but not her voice. She reaches for him and feels the hard curve of muscle in his shoulders. "Ooh, baby," she whispers and raises her head, her lips mashing against his mouth. Her hands slid around the back of his neck and she presses him closer.

"Oh, yeah, make me scream, honey. Make me burn," Angie says, except that Angie's no longer in the room. Her thoughts hover on a distant plateau of blue and silver stones where a warm breeze blows and strange alabaster birds call out through distant mists.

MIDNIGHT SATURDAY

Like an unshackled ghost, Elvis floats silently through the darkened house. For a big man he moves with agility, avoiding the dim silhouettes of furniture, guided by a sliver of moonlight. He double-checks the perimeter alarms, then the back-up generator. He's unsnapped his holstered Glock, the safety off. His eyes prowl the darkness beyond the windows. It's a ritual he performs nightly, his sense of discipline unaltered even by Micky Logan's recent demise.

He knows that anyone attempting to make a move, they'll come around to the rocky peaks behind the house. They'll lay low in the inky shadows that loom not long before sunset, then maybe crawl in behind the stone wall, or slip past the patio, concealed by the cascading rhododendron. A series of French doors offer a half-dozen points of access. Pop a lock when everyone's asleep and walk right in. Or settle down amid the big rocks and take their time, set up a Bushmaster or some big-ass bore gun with a tripod and a scope, wait for someone to turn on a lamp inside the

house. Anyone with half a brain, half a reason, and that's
how life will end.

Elvis finishes his rounds, sets the alarm system for infrared and walks upstairs to his bedroom in total darkness.
Something inside him always feels safer, cocooned in the
grip of the night.

Teddy Sparks calls his wife and tells her he loves her. He
often phones while he's away, frequently with a suspicion
that each conversation may be his last. Never fully *believing*
it—but hardly oblivious to that possibility. To that even-
tual certainty.

Sparanzano has had many lovers in his day, although
he's been faithful to his wife for the twenty-six years of
their marriage. Delaney's a good wife, a great mother and,
for as long as he's known her, she's been a Wiccan priest-
ess. A witch. Delaney's belief isn't a black cat, pointy hat
sort of existence; she's a soccer mom and hospice volun-
teer, a soft-spoken, auburn-haired lady, still with a knockout figure and a wide, pleasant face.

Teddy Sparks first met Delaney thirty years ago, Sparanzano a street hustler and Delaney a casual ganja dealer,
a senior at UCSF. They'd often bumped into each other
socially—campus parties being both prevalent and lucrative, and one night she invited him back to her dorm room.
He'd been intrigued by the numerous white candles and

the scent of nag champa, her walls adorned with old English prints and mystical, moody landscapes—without a bare-chested celeb or glam band poster in sight. Among the textbooks cramming her bookcase he noted Faust, John Locke and Joseph Campbell—Sartre and Nietzsche, of course—a who's who of philosophical rhetoric and provocative ambiguity. The woman instantly capturing his fascination. Sparanzano had spent the night.

Few of Delaney's recent friends are aware of her spiritual journey. Although she dutifully accompanies her husband to Mass most Sundays at St. Lawrence, she's not thought of herself as Christian in a long while. She has nothing *against* Catholicism, but Delaney's staunch belief has led her down a far more ancient path. She blends herbal salves and casts spells—though without a single attempt at retribution or debauchery, the so-called *black magicks*. Over these last three decades, her efforts have been protective in nature and exclusively focused on her husband—keeping him safe, keeping him alive. Not long after their marriage, Teddy Sparks' longevity became Delaney's full-time spiritual preoccupation.

On the surface, Theodore and Delaney seem like a perfect couple. Few of their acquaintances ever hear a harsh word, a raised voice. When Sparanzano isn't flitting from hotel to hotel, they host backyard barbecues and attend the local theater. They have a son practicing corporate law in Manhattan, a daughter at Columbia and, when people ask, Teddy Sparks explains that he's a semi-retired aerospace executive.

Delaney Sparanzano is one of a very few Mafia wives

who know of her husband's intimate business dealings, mostly because Delaney Sparanzano is one of the few people whom Teddy Sparks trusts—and his trust isn't easily earned. Sparanzano doesn't even completely trust the Duke. The old man has his respect, his unflinching loyalty, but rarely does Sparanzano consult the Duke about day-to-day business. Sparanzano likes Joey Segal, but their conversations seldom drift beyond money matters.

Besides Delaney, Sparanzano's closest advisor is a seventy-four-year-old Milanese grandmother who calls herself Aunt Loretta. The old lady's sessions with Teddy Sparks involve a deck of century-old Tarot cards—Aunt Loretta convinced she can peek into Sparanzano's future. Not unlike Delaney, Sparanzano is a firm believer in the predetermination of existence, that every element of life, bad or good, has been calculated for eons by some grand scheme. Sparanzano believes that bad shit happening is the natural order of things, that success is obtained only by those clever enough to somehow crook the roll of the cosmic dice. He sees himself as an integral puzzle-piece, as needful to life as the rain clouds occasionally blocking the sun. He firmly believes in God and the devil and understands that he'll spend eternity with the latter, although he trusts in a standing of some importance.

"Without us," Teddy Sparks once told the Duke, both of them well into the Chianti, "there would be no peace in the world. No order. Peace and order cannot occur in existential reality without their polarities of adversity and chaos."

The old man grunting, thinking *what the hell?* but giving

Teddy the benefit of whatever doubt because, hocus-pocus or not, Sparanzano got the job done.

It was Aunt Loretta's recent dream of Sparanzano sprouting roots that entwined his body, dirt-crusted fingers crawling upward, reaching into his mouth, suffocating him — that prompted Teddy Sparks to conduct business from hotel suites that he randomly chose, sometimes for a day or two, but more often staying a week. Those nights at the Omni or the Bonaventure or the Pasadena Ritz, he would call Delaney and chat for hours.

Sparanzano's name has rarely been linked to organized crime in the media. He doesn't hang out in Little Italy with mob people or have girlfriends with loose lips. Even along federal pipelines not many people are sure of Sparanzano's status within the family. The ones who *do* know, they know because Sparanzano told them himself.

And Teddy Sparks has his reasons.

Sparanzano was born in Daly City, coming of age in the early-'90s, his mother a dry cleaner and addict who chronically ignored her seven children. He grew up distrustful and cynical, a generation behind the Haight-Ashbury craze. The drugs, the pimps and the street gangs had removed any vestige of peace and solace surrounding free love or communal happiness. Sparanzano belonged to a scattered group of street punks with no connection to organized crime, and who used their Italian heritage to hoodwink potential victims into believing they were *Mafioso*.

At age nineteen, his mustache drooping to his chin, his dark, shoulder-length hair parted in the middle and a red bandanna circling his head, Sparanzano, Norm Bombacci and Wiley Gordopf called themselves *Lobo Loco*, making a decent wage in low-level intimidation and by growing illegal weed. They'd hired farmers to tend vast, untamed acres up near Wilbur Springs, long before federal agents began identifying cannabis groves from airplane spotters or by chromatic scans from orbiting satellites.

The *famiglia* had come west generations before in search of expansion—first to Las Vegas, and later to the coast. By the time Capriccio had made capo in the late–70's, the family was already struggling in the Bay Area. Too many fingers already in the stew. When Capriccio turned his attention from pimping and loan-sharking to drugs, Lobo Loco was lucrative and cohesive enough to rate the Duke's irritation. Capriccio gave the boys a few warnings to step aside, which they duly ignored, and when he asked for a meeting to, as he put it, "clarify my intentions on the matter of my disappointment," Sparanzano was young and impudent enough to blow him off. The next day a hit-and-run Dodge Charger creamed Norm Bombacci in broad daylight on Balboa, and Capriccio asked again. Wiley beat it up to Oregon, but Sparanzano was belligerent enough to take the meeting, if only to look Capriccio in the eye.

Capriccio blinked first. "Cut your hair," the Duke told him, enjoying this street punk's brash confidence—what Capriccio called his *spark*—and that's how Teddy Sparks joined the family, under Capriccio's wing.

Several years later Capriccio would ask him, "How'd you like to meet some movie stars, get a tan?" Meaning L.A., of course, and Sparanzano jumped at the chance. Not so much for the tan, but because San Francisco has begun to burn out. Los Angeles would be a new beginning. A clean slate.

Delaney's influence and Tarot readings only go so far. Sparanzano augments Aunt Loretta's psychic abilities with a more modern magic — paying six-figure salaries to a USC computer science dropout and an ex-CIA mole who spend their days with a few million dollars worth of pilfered, state-of-the-art surveillance equipment in an upstairs warehouse off Sutter. Sparanzano knows the feds didn't have a monopoly on phone taps. He keeps most of his own people bugged, and many of their people as well, not excluding wives and lovers.

Only a scattering of Sparanzano's associates have managed to elude his curiosity, Micky Logan first and foremost among them — although never in a million years would Sparanzano have considered the mick a risk. But Logan's recent silence nags at Teddy Sparks. The cards have not foreseen this particular hiccup. He is concerned.

7:30 AM SATURDAY

The Kid's been acting strange most of the morning, his eyes flitting away from Angie whenever she speaks. The house is quiet, just the two of them up this early, Jeff and Jeanne still asleep in the guest room down the hallway.

"What?" she says finally, cornering him in the kitchen, him with a Diet Coke in his hand, standing in front of the open refrigerator door. "Wha'd I do?"

"Nothin'," the Kid says, closing the door with a soft *wump*.

"Is this about last night?" she asks; close enough to smell his musk.

The Kid hesitates, looking for a way out, not wanting to respond, his eyes finally locking on hers.

"Okay, about last night. What happened?"

"Happened?"

"You changed."

"What do you mean?"

A flush creeps from his throat. "You were like — a *whore*," he says quietly.

"I *am* a whore."

"With me? That's what you thought? What I wanted?"

"With any man," Angie supposes.

"That's what I am to you, huh? A fuckin' trick?"

She doesn't know how to respond. Doesn't want to hurt his feelings but she finds herself with nothing else to say. He steps around her and she knows what's about to happen, waiting until he says, "Hey, Angie?"

Turning then to look.

He places two one hundred dollar bills on the counter. "For last night."

She watches him walk away without a word, then reaches down and takes the money.

8:45ᴀᴍ SATURDAY

Elvis pulls the Cadillac into a lot off Wilshire. He takes a ticket and crawls the aisles until he sees two guys in mismatched sports jackets standing next to a black SUV and an adjacent open slot. He parks and they pat him down without a word, Elvis waiting patiently, smart enough to have stashed his Glock under the seat. He climbs into the back seat of the SUV, wedged between the same two guys, feeling naked without the familiar lump under his arm.

They take him up Melrose, midway to Beverly. Winos and hookers share the sidewalks with Japanese tourists and teenaged girls is ratty jeans. The Escalade stops amid a row of graffiti-marred, tired brick buildings. Elvis steps out in front of a doorway ensconced behind thick iron bars. Red neon in a window proclaims "Aunt Loretta's." Beneath the neon, a hand painted sign reads: Palmistry, Tarot, Crystal Healing. Further down, a scrawled piece of cardboard adds: *Psychic Massage.*

You can *do* that? Elvis wonders.

He finds Sparanzano lying naked on a fur-lined table, in a dark room that smells of incense and flickers with the light from maybe a hundred candles.

The two guys leave, closing the door with a tight click and Elvis stands for a long silent moment, staring into the dancing shadows. A pretty black woman in beaded dreadlocks rubs oil on Sparanzano's glistening shoulders. Another woman, older, with a nose like a retired prizefighter's, sits at a small table next to Sparanzano's head. She's wearing flowing purple robes and a matching head wrap, oblivious to Elvis' presence. She shuffles a deck of over-sized cards.

Sparanzano glances up and offers Elvis a polite smile. "Mr. Zapata, a pleasure to see you."

"Mr. Sparanzano."

"Excuse me for not shaking hands. I don't wish to disrupt my chakra alignment."

Elvis isn't sure what to say.

"Tell me, do you believe in magic, Mr. Zapata? There's some powerful shit at work at play here. Trust me on that."

Elvis nods, trying to keep his eyes off Sparanzano's backside. He isn't used to seeing a guy naked if it isn't Micky — and Micky with a butt like two overstuffed pillows sprinkled with red pepper. Sparanzano is in good shape, like maybe he often works out. He doesn't look Mafia either, his graying hair trimmed close and neat, like an executive you'd pass on Wilshire. One of the few mob guys who doesn't talk like he's walked in off the street.

The old woman continues to ignore Elvis, laying out a series of cards on the table like she's playing solitaire. Big and colorful picture cards, people with swords and spears, dancing, and one's riding a painted horse.

"My regards to Micky," Sparanzano says.

Which returns Elvis' attention.

"It's not like your boss to run off without telling us, Mr. Zapata. Might you know what Micky's up to?"

Elvis has the story in the back of his head and pulls it forward, Angie's voice an echo inside his brain, telling him to stay cool. He says, "Micky's been actin' strange lately."

"I have to be honest with you, Mr. Zapata. He has a few people worried about him."

"Been acting real funny," Elvis presses, his mind racing, aware that the next instant could go one of two ways. Tell Teddy Sparks the truth—*the fucking Kid put Micky down, Mr. Sparanzano*—knowing the Kid and Angie wouldn't live through the weekend. Maybe not him either. Or—

He glances at the young black woman, sucking in a jasmine-tinged breath and tells himself, *fuck it*, Elvis jumping into that bottomless hole with both feet. "Micky's been talking about, y'know, cashin' in."

"Oh?"

"On account of his heart. Doesn't wanna talk with no one these last couple days. Tellin' everyone he's got too much stress."

"Stress? I can appreciate that. Stress can do odd things to a man."

"He's been talkin' about gettin' out of the business, selling his share and maybe goin' to some island somewhere."

"An island," Sparanzano muses, quiet for a moment, the masseuse kneading muscles at the base of his neck. "Selling his share of what, might I ask? And to whom?"

"Well, I figure to you, Mr. Sparanzano."

"What makes Micky think he has anything to sell?"

"Micky said somethin' about equity," Elvis says. Angie's word. She's made him memorize it, and here it is, out in the open. Sparanzano's silent again, like he's thinking about it.

"Tell Micky to call me," Sparanzano says finally, "and we'll talk. We'll talk about his equity."

Sparanzano closes his eyes. Elvis gets the impression the meeting's over. He nods and turns for the door.

"One moment, Mr. Zapata. A card for my friend here, Loretta," Sparanzano says to the robed woman. "Can you tell us what's in his future?"

She acknowledges Elvis finally with a hard, level gaze. Her fingers cut the deck and pluck the top card, holding it for Sparanzano and Elvis to see.

"The Magician," Sparanzano remarks.

Elvis gazes at a bony figure dressed in red and gold, the guy wearing a floppy hat that covers his eyes, juggling five colorful balls while doing a jig. "That a good one?"

"Depends on your intentions, Mr. Zapata. It can be quite good. Or else, you know, very, very bad."

10:00 AM SATURDAY

"Where they take him?" LeRoy Beers asks.

"Pisshole. Place called Aunt Lo'etta's. Psychic voodoo shit." Tin Man doing the talking and Peanut B standing beside him, five foot even, wearing an oversized A&F hoodie and woolen skullcap.

"Suits?"

"Greasers in suits, man. Bunch o' big ol' fat guys."

Beers thinks it over. He's sitting in a dark booth in a dark bar, a shot of Courvoisier in his coffee, Beers the only patron at the moment—the six other black guys in the room watching the door or watching the bartender. Tin

Man and Peanut B stand close to Beers, feeling the electricity emanating from his every gesture, every twitch.

"Elvis, man, he's sellin' hisself out to the Mafioso," Beers tells them.

"Nobody we can't fuck up," says Peanut B.

"Yo, li'l bro, why you wanna tussle 'stead of makin' dough?" Beers winks at the kid. He says to Tin Man; "Micky never let Elvis do none o' his speakin' befo'. Now Elvis be talkin' to *suits*? Man, don't you get it?"

Tin Man and Peanut B don't get it.

"Elvis is sendin' Micky down the proverbial river."

Tin Man and Peanut B *still* don't get it. Beers stares into his coffee mug, letting them wait, his thoughts racing.

"Whassup?" Tin Man says, spooked by the lingering silence, the sudden sparkle in Beers' eyes.

"Our streets, man," he says finally. "They about to make a play on *our* streets. Maybe it's time we make a play fo' our *own* fuckin' streets."

"No more wipin' white ass," Peanut B says, giggling in an eerily childlike way.

Beers nods. "Tell Cool O an' Dr. Rod to saddle up, cuz it be comin' down to-*day*." All of Beers' soldiers with rap names, street names, half of them hoping to go down like Tupac or B.I.G. or Suge, many of them with shiny pink ovals scarring their young bodies—because unless you took some lead, you didn't have the respect. All of Beers' other soldiers jealous, ready to impress the ladies and Peanut B dying to earn a bullet, already fourteen, already a daddy twice over, but not yet with a shiny mark of his own.

10:15 AM SATURDAY

Jeanne's spent the last few hours in Michael Logan's study, pouring over XLS spreadsheets and glancing through the two oversized ledgers that Elvis gives her. Angie hangs out on a couch, looking bored, sipping coffee and reading *Vanity Fair*.

Silent all morning, Jeanne finally looks up and says, "What's going on, Angie?"

Her sister seems surprised. "What do you mean?"

"You're deep in the middle of something."

"Shhh, don't worry about me. Dwight wants out, remember? We all want out. A few days from now it's going to be someone else's problem."

"I'm scared, Angie. Why can't you tell me?"

"*Trust* me on this. I don't want you to worry or anything, but, well, what you're doing for me—the reason you're here?" She shakes her head, her eyes welling. Angie can't remember the last time she's cried. Alone with her sister, for the first time in a long while, she feels safe. She feels the tears tumble down her cheeks.

"What you're doing, Jeannie, is saving my life."

"Then why won't you—"

Jeff taps lightly on the door, pokes his head through. "Hey, Angie?"

Embarrassed, she dabs at the wet streaks and puts on a smile. "What's up, honey?"

"I need a small favor...."

Angie follows Jeff into the kitchen. "Guys?" she says.Elvis is standing at the coffeepot, the Kid eating breakfast at the table with the Sports section in his face.

"Jeannie's laptop died. I'm such a moron about those things. You mind if Jeff runs out, gets a special kind of battery. She's sort of stuck for the moment."

The Kid looks at Elvis, sees him shrug and reaches for his wallet. "Hey, you mind picking up some brew while you're out? Nothing's left in the fridge but this piss poor American shit."

"No problem, I got it," Jeff says.

He gives Angie's shoulder a squeeze. She tries to smile, hiding her concern because Jeff hasn't told her squat. She knows Jeff won't do anything stupid with Jeanne here. She watches him leave from a window in the foyer, nibbling at her lip. *Not with Jeannie here,* she thinks again.

10:45 AM SATURDAY

Jeff parks in a ten-dollar lot on Aiso Street and hoofs it the two blocks to the Federal Building on East Temple. It's a tall, rust brown building; a busy place, swarming with various guardians of democracy. He goes through the front doors, passes a metal detector and finds a directory. The Drug Enforcement Administration occupies the 20th floor and he takes an elevator up.

At an oval reception desk, a gaunt, silver-haired woman

wearing gray wool and a communications headset gives him a neutral appraisal.

He shows his badge and identifies himself as a San Diego County deputy sheriff. "Is there an agent in charge of criminal investigations?"

"How may we help you, deputy?"

"Can I talk to somebody?"

"Is this in regards to an official investigation?"

Jeff's aware that he's here on a whim, that there's a chance he'll be turned away without seeing a soul. But he wants to get higher up the food chain. He keeps it simple. "I'm looking for information."

She smiles politely, not impressed. "Information concerning...?"

"Concerning a local. Michael Patrick Logan."

The woman's expression doesn't change, but he's aware of a sudden, terse formality in her movements. She swivels in her chair, pressing buttons behind the partition, speaking softly into her headset.

"Just a moment," she tells him.

A tall black man wearing a tan blazer and chinos emerges from a hallway a moment later, walking briskly. He's about Jeff's age but bigger at the hips, at the shoulders, like maybe he's played ball or pumps iron. He wears small oval glasses, like the kind John Lennon once wore.

"Deputy Russell?" The agent holds out his hand. "I'm Terrence Cutter."

"How do you do."

Cutter smiles in a way that makes Jeff think the guy's

maybe PR or some sort of glorified paper shuffler. Well-groomed and polite, wearing cologne — the kind of guy they drag from some tiny cubical to deal with assorted oddities and two-cent bothers.

"I understand you're inquiring about a Mr. Logan?"

"Yeah, owns or owned a residence up in Malibu."

"You're a bit out of your jurisdiction aren't you, deputy?"

"Which is my problem. I'm not entirely sure what I'm doing here. Maybe I'm wasting your time."

"Would you come with me please?" Agent Cutter directs Jeff up the hallway. They walk a dozen steps in silence before Cutter points toward an office doorway and says, "In here, deputy." A plaque on the door identified Cutter as a Deputy Assistant, Criminal Investigations Unit.

Low head on the totem pole, Jeff figures.

Cutter closes the door. "Have a seat, Jeff."

He takes the single chair in front of Cutter's metal desk, glances at a framed print on the wall, an aerial view of a red-tailed P–51 Mustang trailing a smoking Messerschmitt.

"Coffee?" Cutter moves around the desk and sits.

"No, thanks."

"Would it bother you if this conversation is recorded, Jeff?"

He's not sure he appreciates the condescending tone of Cutter's voice, but at least he's got an ear. "No, I don't care."

Cutter leans slightly forward, his hands clasped atop the desk. "So why don't you tell me what's on your mind?"

"I don't suppose I could ask a few questions first?"

Cutter grins at him so Jeff parries with a dubious little smile of his own. "Well, it started with a call from my sister-in-law..."

11:30ᴀᴍ SATURDAY

The Kid finds Micky's exercise room in the hallway beyond the kitchen; an entire wing of the house he might never have discovered had he not gone snooping—three or four rooms like an afterthought between the kitchen and the garage. Dwight decides the exercise room must have been meant as a maid's quarters, a private bathroom and private entrance around back—but, *guess what?*—no maid. There's also a laundry room and a walk-in pantry—an entire room filled with food. Pretty cool, he thinks.

Angie finds him in the exercise room a short time later, sweaty in his black warm up pants and yellow T, lying on his back working on his pecs, going on fifty lifts when he notices her in the doorway. She's wearing tight jeans and a halter top. He hustles through a dozen more, showing off, then grunts and sits up.

"Angie, hey."

"Can we talk?"

"Sure, I was just finishing up." He swipes his face with a towel. Angie's aware of the artery pulsating in his neck, beating fast. Even hot and sweaty, there's something gentle about him. The way a few strands of ebony hair have loosened from his ponytail, falling across his cheeks.

Angie puts the two hundred-dollar bills on the work-out bench by his knees and a blush creeps from his throat.

"Man, I'm such a dick sometimes, huh?" He glance flitters around the room. "I was—I dunno. *Stupid*."

"Angry?"

"Pissed," he says. "Not at you. Shit, at myself. What happened last night, man, I thought maybe you and me'd hit it off."

"We have hit it off."

"I mean in bed."

"Is that important?"

"Well—" About to tell her, *fuckin' A sure it's important*, but he stops himself. Looks at her and rolls his eyes. "Is this where you tell me I got a nice personality? I remind you of your kid cousin?"

"This is where I tell you it's okay for us to be friends. You've got a lovely—sorry, a magnificent body. A wonderful spirit. You're a living doll, kiddo. Don't think for a moment that I don't find you sizzling."

"But?"

"But right now in my life, I don't want a bed partner."

The Kid's not sure how to respond. "You mad?"

"Of course not."

"I mean, God's honest truth, Angie. I never did a girl who didn't wanna be—well, you know. I never made no one like that. I never made you, last night. You *know* that, right?"

"You were a perfect gentleman."

"You mind me askin' you somethin'?"

"Shoot."

"Was I...?"

"...*Good?*"

He gives her that goofy smile of his.

"The truth? Don't take this wrong, Dwight, but I don't know. I wasn't there."

He doesn't understand.

"I wasn't... in my own head," she tells him.

"Because you're a hooker?"

"Yeah. Because I'm a hooker."

"And because I'm nothing special?"

She moves from the doorway. She's pretty in her white jeans. A flat, bare midriff. She has a big freckle below her belly button. She comes toward him and for a second he thinks she might slap him. But Angie takes his face in her hands, not seeming to mind the sweat. She tilts his head forward and kisses him on the forehead, then gently again on the lips.

Telling him what he needs to know and yet—and yet filling his mind with even more uncertainty. The Kid watches her leave, more confused than ever.

12:30 PM SATURDAY

Danny Fortuna's in a bad mood. He sits in the passenger seat of a silver Lincoln Navigator, the air-conditioner breezing on him as he watches the desert roll past at 80 mph. Shep Boco drives, Richie Moya moody and silent in the back seat, staring outside, thinking about the Dodger game last night. They'd blown a three-run lead over the Padres in the ninth. Moya had dropped five hundred on that one fucking slammer.

Boco had two bills on the Pads, and he's been giving Moya shit until Fortuna tells them to knock it the fuck off. That had been thirty miles ago. Neither man has spoken since.

While Boco has a passable IQ and a bad attitude, Richie Moya has a little sociopathic problem. Psychologically speaking, Moya's not a well man upstairs. He likes to inflict pain. Liked it since he was old enough to get away with it—starting with small animals and then later his baby sister, until a social worker found trauma bruises on her arms, legs and throat. Moya spent the next six years at St. Luke's Institution for Boys.

Even now, the need to inflict pain comes in overpowering waves. But Moya's smart enough to know that St. Luke's is no longer an option. Lompoc had come four years later on, at the age of nineteen. Followed by a stint in Atascadero. Moya doesn't like small metal boxes. The single certainty in his life is that he'll be stone cold dead before anyone ever puts him back in a small metal box.

Most people seeing Moya and Boco together, coming toward them with those dead BB eyes of theirs most people don't give them reason to get pissed. Yet here they are, Moya and Boco together, neither man daring to backtalk Danny Fortuna.

Fortuna's twenty-five, ten years younger than Moya, who's ten younger than Boco. Fortuna's the only son of a wise guy who handed him his first silenced Beretta when he was seven, had him point the gun and let loose a couple rounds right there in the house, to get the feel of the action.

Fortuna first killed at the age of sixteen, the same year he dropped out of ninth grade. He'd made and blown over a hundred grand by the time his former classmates were taking their final exams. Fortuna isn't much over five-six, a short guy who doesn't like being short. Acquaintances know enough not to chide him, rumor being that Danny once shot a man in the throat for calling him a weenie. Danny hadn't killed the guy, although his father's Beretta induced a chronic whisper. Moral of the story is, nobody jokes about Danny Fortuna's stature.

He's nice enough looking; dark hair that he likes to keep long, to his eyebrows and over his collar in back. He has a sharp, Mediterranean face, full lips and crystal blue eyes usually hidden behind black Ray Bans. He often tucks a whore on one arm or the other and sometimes both. Most guys his size go for tall blondes, five ten or more, stunning and decidedly upscale, showing off. But Danny likes them small, Asian or preferably Latina, five-two or – three, dark-haired and feisty. He has a reputation as a stud, although he has a tendency to overdo his Wild Turkey and sometimes gets rough. Danny put a girl in UCLA Medical with a ruptured spleen a few years back. Teddy Sparks gave him a talk and took care of the hooker's tab, moved her to a nice little place out of state. Sparanzano doesn't like rumors getting started about family matters, about his crew's extracurricular activities. What the whore might say fifty miles east of Albuquerque doesn't much matter to him.

Danny Fortuna is in a piss poor mood today, out here

in the middle of nowhere. Boca's been driving the last four hours, looking for some fucking fat farm where Micky Logan's supposedly holed up, but the place doesn't exist. Fortuna pretty much knows that before making the trip, finding zip in the Yellow Pages and making a couple calls, people telling him hell, no, they've never heard of Heavenly Acres either. Even fucking *Bing* doesn't help, and what's up with that? But there *is* a place called Hidden Meadows Spa and Clinic — and no, they don't divulge their client's names over the phone — so on the slight chance Micky Logan's there, they drive out to take a look.

But no Micky Logan.

"Want some tunes, Danny?" Boco asks.

Fortuna doesn't move his eyes from the passing desert.

"You mind if I turn on the radio, Danny?"

Nothing out of Fortuna. Not a sound.

Boco doesn't press it, drives the rest of the way home in silence. That's the way Fortuna is. You don't find any reason to give him grief. Mostly, to play it safe, you don't find a reason to make him notice you're even alive.

12:45ᴘᴍ SATURDAY

Something's different and it takes Elvis a moment to think it through. Maybe the way Beers doesn't even bother to ask about Micky. Calls Elvis up, saying, "Yo," talking one-on-one and telling him they'd had a ball-buster of a Friday night. Come an' get it because he doesn't like babysitting all this loose bread, maybe twenty grand lying around in garbage bags and Beers hoping none of it wanders off over the weekend.

Elvis wants to tell Beers it can wait, but he knows Micky would be screaming at him to make a Saturday collection. Elvis pictures Micky griping and swearing, telling him to get a fuckin' move on.

So Elvis says yeah, he'll be over.

Beers saying, "Coo."

Elvis stares down at the phone on Micky's desk for nearly a minute, then walks to the gun rack inside Micky's bedroom closet. He chooses the Mossberg pump, a modified 12-gauge, the barrel barely sixteen inches and short-stocked, an extra wide choke—what Micky called his *splatter* gun. Elvis takes two extra clips for his Glock. Micky once told a bunch of his dealers that Elvis wasn't the smartest guy when it came to college words or doing multiplication in his head, but put him on the street and, man, Elvis Zapata was fuckin' Einstein.

He takes Micky's Mercedes with the tinted windows— maybe fool some people into thinking Micky's in back, along for the ride. He tucks the Mossberg into the money satchel, an old towel loose on top, the satchel's zipper open enough to reach in, snag the trigger in a hurry.

Elvis considers taking the Kid as backup. Then thinks about it again. The Kid's a distraction or maybe worse, getting squirmy and maybe Elvis ending up like Micky, his last few seconds full of surprises, full of holes. Besides, if nothing happens, he'll feel like his *abuelita*—an old lady— bringing some young snot along for a simple collection.

This time of day, traffic on the 10 is light and Elvis makes the Alhambra Children's Library in forty-five minutes. He cruises around the empty parking lot a few times and then leaves the key in the ignition, gets out and walks to the back door. Elvis stands for a few seconds, listening to the silence before he unlocks the door and steps inside.

Instantly feels a hard muzzle press into the back of his neck.

"Check it out," LeRoy Beers says, stepping out of Micky's private john. Beers smiles at Elvis, a couple of guys spilling out of the bathroom behind him. Everybody grinning.

"What we got here is a' Elvis burger," Beers says. "Whassup, Chico?"

Elvis watches the two punks moving around Beers, all skin and bone, pearly white smiles. Young guys wearing high-top Nikes and holding black pistols. Cheap looking guns, mostly plastic. One of Beers' guys isn't much past puberty; a red woolen cap pulled down over his ears, down to his eyebrows, the kid waving a pistol around like it's a toy. Coming up to Elvis, reaching under his jacket, right side, snaking out the Glock. The boy with two guns now.

"Jus' wanna ax you a question or two, Chico. Sit down, make yourself t'home." Beers motions with one hand and Elvis feels a push from behind. The money satchel's slung over his shoulder, like always, nobody giving it any mind. He glances at the tall, stringy guy they call Tin Man pointing a plastic-looking pistol like the kid's. Elvis figures the only reason he's still alive, Beers has questions.

Beers waits until Elvis sits behind the desk. It's an ugly tan metal desk. An ugly tan metal chair on squeaky rollers.

Ugly tan metal file cabinet in one corner. The room's only furnishings. The guy behind Elvis steps away, toward the door—guy's name is Jell-O or some shit like that. Elvis puts the satchel on his lap.

"Word on the street says you be fuckin' Micky over," Beers tells him.

"Where you hear a thin' like that?"

"Word on the street."

"Word's wrong, man."

"Street ain't never *that* wrong," Beers says. "So, question is, why you be jammin' on your ol' frien' Micky? Sellin' out to the mob-a-roni, huh?"

Elvis wonders, *what the fuck?* Amazed that Beers already knows. Elvis makes a slight, casual move toward the satchel's open zipper.

"What I'm wonderin' now is *why*, Chico?"

"None of your business is why."

"We *makin'* it our business. Micky's lunch money. Me and my buff'lo soljas here, we like to eat lunch."

"Like to eat pussy too," Tin Man says.

Elvis takes his eyes off Beers. Tin Man and the boy are standing closest to Beers, Cool O peeking out the door into the lot, his pistol jammed in the waistband of his baggy shorts, his arms folded across his bare torso, showing off his tattooed pecs. Cool O keeps glancing over at him, quick edgy looks—maybe him and Tin Man coked up. Everybody wired and ready for a blowout.

"Dangerous to know too much," Elvis says.

"Dang'rous to be holdin' up my time, motherfucker." Suddenly Beers isn't smiling, his patience gone like a popped balloon. The boy in the wool cap shifts his weight from one foot to another. He's holding Elvis' Glock at his side, sticking his own pistol in Elvis' face, ready to pull the trigger as soon as Beers gives the word. Elvis knows the look dancing in the kid's eyes; that giddy anticipation of doing the deed.

"Chill it out, amigo," Elvis tells the boy. He knows he has few options at the moment, his entire life teetering. Elvis looks back at Beers. "Micky's dead."

A few seconds of silence pass before Beers utters a laugh that sounds like a fart, snorting a lungful of air through his nose. "You shittin' me, Chico? Micky Logan too bad ass *mean* to fuckin' die."

The others start to laugh because Beers has done so. The boy in front of him sounds eerily baby-like. Except for Beers, none of them are over eighteen. Elvis slips his fingers further inside the open zipper.

"Micky's dead," he says again.

"So the I-talians gonna take it away from us. That what you think?"

Elvis shrugs.

"*Our* streets, man. Fuck the I-talians. Let 'em take over fuckin' I-tally-land."

Beers smiles. His anger dissipates as abruptly as it has come. Elvis wonders if he's bought himself an extra few seconds.

"Micky dead, now *you* dead, so ain't nothing fo' the motherfuckers to take over." Beers nods toward the kid with the gun in Elvis' face. The boy grins as he pulls the trigger.

Click.

Elvis' hand finds the Mossberg. He pulls the satchel up from his lap, pushing away from the desk, the chair rolling back with a series of squeaks and everyone thinks it's funny, like maybe Elvis intends to throw the bag at them.

Click. The boy shakes his gun like a broken water pistol, his expression frustrated, turning to surprise as the Mossberg slides free. Elvis waits a heartbeat, giving the kid time to get the picture. The boy snarls, raising the Glock and Elvis squeezes the trigger. The Mossberg goes boom and takes the boy off his feet, sends him up and over, a whirlwind mixture of surprise and anger on the boy's face. Tin Man fires and Elvis feels a sudden, searing pain between his neck and shoulder blade. He racks the pump and fires and Tin Man's head explodes, spewing the air with crimson mist and pieces of bone and teeth. The other guy's already out the door, Beers nearly as fast on his feet, halfway there. Elvis pumps and fires, a little low, shattering the jamb and maybe catching Beers in the leg as he dives through the open doorway. He pumps and aims the Mossberg at the swatch of blue sky and asphalt— hearing screams somewhere off in the building. Elvis feels a trickle of warmth crawl down his back and the first throb of pain, like a knotted muscle spasming. Another scream. Time to vamoose.

He walks around the desk with the Mossberg still pointing toward the doorway. He bends over the dead boy in the wool cap, the oversized A&F hoodie, and plucks his Glock from the limp hand. The kid's eyes regard him with a distant, placid disdain. He stares at the boy's gun—streaked with dirt and oil—this *poco niño muerto* too young to have learned the rules of the game. Elvis knows if the boy had raised the Glock first, it would be *him* bleeding out on the floor.

A few inches, a few seconds. A single bad decision. Life on the streets.

1:00 PM SATURDAY

Jeff walks into Logan's study and finds Jeanne working through a new stack of manila folders and computer printouts, her laptop humming on the wide desk in front of her. Angie's curled up on the couch reading Glamour.

Jeanne hears the door close and glances up with a smile. "Hi, hon—" But she sees the look on his face and her smile fades. Angie looks up too, sees the same look.

"Jesus *Christ*, Angie—" Jeff's voice is a fierce whisper. "—Micky Logan isn't some goddamn art dealer. He's a major league narcotics trafficker. He's organized crime, Angie. He's with the fucking Mafia."

He pushes a finger toward her face. "I can't believe you'd pull this kind of shit. Endangering Jeannie. Putting her in the middle of—"

"You're not in the *middle* of anything. Listen, I can explain—"

"You're done explaining. I'm done listening. Nothing you can tell me is going to make—"

"Micky was going to *kill* me, Jefferson."

Angie looks at Jeanne and offers the room a resigned sigh. "I didn't know he was a drug dealer until yesterday. I swear to God, I didn't. And for your information, Micky isn't a drug dealer any more because he's dead. Dwight and Elvis killed him. Nobody's supposed to know."

Jeanne tilts her head, giving Angie a funny look.

"If it wasn't for them, I'd be the one buried in the back-yard, not Micky Logan. It happened right in front of me. What you might call up close and personal." Angie tries to smile, but her lips tremble. "That's how all of this started. We need to make believe Micky is still alive, or else we *will* be dead. We need Micky's partners to think he wants to sell his business and split. That's why I called Jeanne. Elvis didn't trust Micky's accountant and we didn't know how much Micky was worth. We needed to know how much to charge these Mafia guys."

"You not serious," Jeff says.

She looks at him with wide, innocent eyes. "Well, *yeah.*"

"Jesus, Angie," he says again.

She flips her magazine aside and slips off the couch. She stands chest high to Jeff, her eyes blazing. "So what's wrong with that? We're not scamming anybody. His partners are getting a real deal, and I'm getting out alive. Nobody else will be hurt. Don't you see? It's the only thing we can do."

Jeanne's been watching her husband for a long moment. "Jeff?"

"I talked to the DEA, Jeannie. Logan's part of—"

"*You what?*" It's the first time any of them have spoken above a whisper. Angie stares at him in disbelief.

"I went to the DEA. I needed to—"

She hits him, hard, an open-hand slap across the cheek. "Damn you!"

"Angie?" Jeanne says, startled.

She surprises him—shocks the hell out of him is what she does, the sting radiating deep into his psyche. He's aware of the astonished oval of Jeanne's mouth. Angie has never touched him in animosity before. Has never raised her voice to him. Her sudden rage displaces his anger, leaves it in scattered fragments.

"Angie, all of this—" His words sound almost childlike. "We're in trouble here. We're in serious shit." He realizes he's lost his edge, sounding almost whiny in front of them.

"For your information, Jefferson, I'm not leaving this house. If you turn us in, then turn me in, too. Send me to prison because I gave them my word, goddamn it." Angie's gaze narrows. "The people you talked to. They don't *know* Micky's dead, do they?"

"I'm sure they'd be tickled silly to find out."

"You can't tell them *anything* else. Do you understand?"

Jeanne moves from the desk and touches his sleeve. "Are we in danger, Jeff? Staying here?"

"He's a fucking drug dealer, Jeannie."

She blinks, not accustomed to obscenities from her husband. He takes a deep breath and offers her an apologetic glance. "If Logan's really dead and all the wrong people find out?"

"But *no*body knows," Angie tells them.

"And how long until they do?"

"Babe? I think I'm onto something here," Jeanne says quietly, nodding toward her computer. "What we talked about last night? I need more time. I need to track some more numbers. But I think maybe Angie's right. Sounds like what they did, Mr. Manetti and Mr. Zapata, they saved her life. And that counts for something."

They grow silent again. Angie fidgets, giving them time to think it through. Trusting her sister to point them in the right direction.

"The DEA," Jeanne says. "What did they tell you?"

"Not a hell of a lot. Mostly asked questions."

"But they wouldn't let us stay, right? Jeff, if they thought we were in danger?"

"I got the impression they had their own agenda."

"You told them we were leaving?"

"I said it would be your call. Give me the word, Jeannie, and we're out the door this minute. Else I told them we'd hang on through Sunday night, if we thought it was safe. They want to talk to me again, tomorrow morning."

Jeanne's silent for several seconds, then gives Angie a determined nod. "All right, here's what we're going to do. We stay through 'til Sunday. But only on one condition. We'll stay if you promise, Angelina, you *promise* to come home with us. You'll get off the streets once and for all, come back with us until you have your life in order. If you promise me that, then we'll stay until Sunday and give Mr. Manetti his numbers. Whatever happens after that, it's up to them."

Angie bites her lower lip, wanting desperately to tell Jeanne there's nothing in the world she'd rather do. Too damn afraid to drag them any deeper, her life suddenly a spinning top. She shakes her head. "Jeannie, I can't—"

"*Promise* me, Angie."

Tears tumble down her cheeks. "I'm so sorry, Jeannie. I'm so sorry."

"Promise me," Jeanne whispers, her words a sob.

Angie knows a hundred different reasons why she can't agree, but none of them find the way to her lips. She nods finally, almost unaware, her gesture loosening the tears. "I promise," she whispers. She reaches out and they hug, the two of them crying for a long moment, unwilling or unable to move again until their tears run dry.

1:45 PM SATURDAY

Terrance Cutter works down a swallow of stale, tepid coffee. "So why would Elvio Zapata be interested in the net worth of the Logan estate?"

The three federal agents wait in a paneled conference room, around a stained oval table covered with folders and printouts and half-empty Styrofoam cups. Cutter opens a Dell touch-screen laptop and begins to poke at files. They call themselves the *Barranca Vista Task Force*—the FBI with maybe a dozen agents on Duke Capriccio's heels and the three of them mostly mired in paperwork, largely overlooked, the DEA's contribution to the cause.

Agent Marx sits to Cutter's left, silently pondering the question. He's a blond, prematurely balding man with a pleasant face and the build of a long-distance runner. His name is Henry, but they call him Harpo. They call Cutter *Trip.*

Renee Torres stands behind Marx, her posture rigid, her gaze flitting to the wall clock every half-minute or so. She's thirty-five, a handsome woman with ebony hair combed behind her ears, cut straight an inch above her shoulders. She shuns nicknames and they respect that. Torres has said nothing for several minutes, uncomfortably listening to her two colleagues banter.

"Maybe Logan pissed off the Duke," Marx offers with a shrug. "Bought himself a one way ticket out of town. Else Micky's ankle deep in concrete, feeding fish at the deep end of Harbor Drive."

"With Zapata still breathing? That's unlikely."

Marx agrees with a sullen nod. "You think, what, that the Duke's buying him out? But why bring in—"

The door opens and Marx closes his mouth. Despite the overtones of mute reverence, Marx and Cutter do little to quell their excitement. They have good reason to be stoked, both Duke Capriccio and Micky Logan operating under the radar for a very long time now.

Special Agent Benjamin Roman gravitates to the nearest empty chair and sits. His tie is loose, shirtsleeves rolled to his elbows. Roman is forty-seven, thin, the type of guy who spends his off-duty hours staying in shape. Roman's strictly Type-A—his idea of relaxation either jumping out of airplanes or white-water kayaking the Colorado. His face is long and chiseled; hair slicked back and barely gray, Roman's gaze typically unwavering, penetrating. He seldom smiles.

The Barranca Vista Task Force hasn't seen much of Ben Roman over the last six months. The Chinese meth epidemic, a recent influx of bad Tapachula coke, has kept his attention diverted. The Mexicans and the Vietnamese, a few biker gangs East of Palmdale, share the majority of the city's streets. But users looking for a cheap thrill or a quick dose of cope aren't discerning. Most Angelinos are unaware that the Mafia even exists in Southern California. The three agents in the room are aware that their efforts have been largely considered an afterthought.

Roman glances at his agents, gives a curt nod that suffices as both introduction and a prompt for information.

"A new angle on Micky Logan," Cutter tells him.

"Our intel?"

"One deputy sheriff Jefferson Russell."

"You check him out?"

Cutter nods. "Peace officer in Jamul for the past eight—"

"Where?"

"Jamul."

"The hell's Jamul?"

"East San Diego County. Mostly desert and tract homes, strip malls and cowboy bars."

"What's he doing up here, Trip?"

"Came for the weekend with his wife, visiting his sister-in-law, who happens to be holed up at Logan's place. Angelina Breusser, no sheet, age thirty-one. She and another unknown, Manetti, Dwight D. White male, twenty-four."

"Russell came to us why?"

"Out of the blue," Cutter admits. "He smelled dirty money and assumed narcotics. He's worried about Ms. Breusser being under the influence of some pretty bad people.

Didn't need coaxing. Gave us info we wouldn't have cleared for weeks, maybe longer."

"How is the sister-in-law involved?"

"Ms. Breusser is—how do I put this? An occasional acquaintance of Micky's. A working girl."

Roman's expression sours. "*That's* gotta sting."

"Yeah," Cutter says. "Deputy Russell's none too pleased about it."

"How come we don't have her on a short list?"

"Breusser? Nobody we've heard of before."

"Why's that, Trip?"

The energy in the room stumbles over an icy silence. Torres has been studying the floor the last several moments. She lifts her gaze to meet Roman's. "She's a new face, Ben. No priors or warnings. LAVD doesn't have anything."

He nods. "Okay, fair enough. So what about this Manetti character? Did we dig up any connections to Capriccio?"

"Nothing so far," Cutter admits. "NCIC's got nada. The bizarre thing is that Russell says the guy's pretending to own Logan's estate—posing as Micky's next of kin. No sign of Micky, but if Zapata's playing along, Logan can't be too far away. Can't fathom why he'd set Manetti up as principal resident. Maybe to bluff out the Russells, but if that's the case, why invite them for a sleepover in the first place?"

"What's Logan's angle? MIA or laying low?"

"The fact that Zapata's out there in plain sight means that Micky's nearby," Cutter says. "Zapata's still making phone calls, still bouncing traces, so we're assuming it's business as usual. If Micky's hiding, we're not sure why."

"Question is, hiding from who?"

Nobody answers that one.

Roman sits back, fingers steepled behind his head, contemplating the ceiling's fluorescent tubing. "Any bad blood between Capriccio's people and Logan lately?"

Cutter shakes his head and begins to tap a series of keys on his laptop. "We've got several ears on The Duke at the moment. As far as we know, everything's kosher. No chatter about putting the big guy down, no barroom bravado, nobody bragging to *la moza amiga*. Only thing gonna take out Micky Logan is an extra cheese double crust."

"By the way, we checked," Marx chimes. "No FDIGs in the local morgues."

"FDIGs?" Roman asks.

"Um — fat dead Irish guys," Marx says sheepishly.

"Which still doesn't explain Manetti's place in the game." Roman sits up straight, bringing the name back into play again. "What's his connection to Capriccio? I need to know who he is, Trip."

Torres has been brooding the last few moments, still looming over the table, shifting her weight between one foot and the other. The room falls silent and she takes a deep breath. "What if Manetti isn't one of Capriccio's," she says. "Maybe he belongs to Teddy Sparks?"

The silence lingers.

Theodore Sparanzano's name isn't often broached in this room, the man a shadowy presence in the grand scheme. Various federal agencies have suspected his complicity in Duke Capriccio's organization, but without sufficient evidence to directly link them. The FBI believes Sparks to be a mob accountant, although Torres' street spooks insist

he'd made *caporegime*—a rumor she's been unable to vali-
date. She feels that Teddy Sparks has long been a missing
thread, and one that might directly tie Micky Logan to the
family. In her mind, Sparanzano's always been the elephant
in the room, frustratingly overlooked or dismissed for one
reason or another.

She's aware of Roman's probing curiosity. "You have a
hunch, Renee? Let's hear it."

She absently rubs her shoulders. "Manetti's a mystery.
So is Sparanzano. Maybe that in itself signifies a connection."

Roman blinks first. "Trip? What do we have on Manetti?
First impressions? Anything?"

Cutter's fingers continue to play over the keyboard. He
scans the data he's so far only hastily reviewed. "Nothing's
older than 24 hours, meaning fragmented intel and zero
corroboration. But, first impression? Manetti doesn't seem
to be mob material. He's a nickel-and-dimer; no drugs, a
couple of Class C's but no prison time. If he's got a juvie rap,
cajv's zeroed it out. Parents deceased—been living with
his maternal grandmother most of his life. And, *shit*, here's
something I missed. His uncle's Salvador Paglia."

"Who?"

"Shit," Cutter mutters again. He glances up from his
laptop and offers Torres a sympathetic frown. "Sal Paglia.
Micky Logan's bookie for the last three years."

"Well, there you go," Roman says with an accepting
nod. "So Logan's handing out favors. Paying off a debt?"
He glances at Torres, whose gaze returns glumly to the floor.

"Trip, does Russell strike you as confident?"

"You mean dependable? Yeah, I think so."

"How much does he know?"

"Enough."

Roman raises an eyebrow and Cutter throws up his hands. "*I* didn't tell him squat. He had Logan pegged before our meet. Probably ran an ID check with his own people. He put the pieces together from the few questions I asked."

"Are they safe staying at the Logan estate?"

"He asked me that himself. I think he's afraid for his wife. I told him not to sweat it. I'm pretty sure I convinced him to stay put through the weekend. But to tell you the truth, the situation's a little hinky. At least until we figure Logan's angle. Where he's disappeared to and why Manetti's playing landlord."

"I want to talk to Russell," Roman says.

"Yeah, I thought you might."

"You set something up?"

"Tomorrow morning, ten forty-five. The Café Latte over on PCH, the Colony Plaza. We'll put a team in the parking lot, make sure nobody's dogging him. I told Russell to drink some java and read the sports. If we don't show up after fifteen minutes, he walks out and we'll reschedule."

"All the covert crap didn't spook him?"

"Didn't seem to."

"Tomorrow," Roman repeats, standing, still thinking. He pauses at the doorway. The three agents remain silent.

"Renee, I want you riding shotgun tomorrow. You too, Trip. Let Russell see a familiar face. Yvonne have any trouble giving you up on a Sunday morning?"

"No, sir."

"Want me to pass this along to the Bureau?" Marx asks.

"Let's talk to Russell first."

"Right." Marx slides the manila folder to the back of his briefcase.

"Trip, set it up with Ops." Roman pauses for a final glance at Torres. "You have a hunch, Agent Torres, you spill it out. Give us a chance to kick it around in here." He gives her a wink. "You keep us sharp, understand?"

She nods.

"But for the moment, I want to keep our focus on Capriccio. If nothing pans out in another month or so, we'll think about taking a closer look at Sparanzano. But I still believe The Duke's our best bet. Meanwhile, let's find out where the hell Micky Logan's holed up. He's one—what is it, Henry?—one FDIG we don't want getting away from us."

2:15 PM SATURDAY

Elvis uses the garage entrance. He's dizzy by the time he gets home, his right side sticky with blood. He's driven wobbly the last several miles in the Mercedes, cars honking as they pass. He takes off his ruined jacket, the collar torn and ragged, then removes his stained shirt. He takes four Tylenol and spends a few minutes with a washcloth, dabbing at the wound in front of the bathroom mirror. The bullet's carved a two-inch trough of flesh between the base of his neck and slope of his shoulder. Half an inch lower and his collarbone would have shattered. Half an inch to the left and Elvis would have bled out in the library. He holds the cloth tightly against the red-rimmed gouge. Some iodine and gauze and he figures he'll get by. At least until the next time somebody sticks a gun in his face.

He stares at his reflection and realizes that despite his best efforts, it's all turning to shit. First Teddy Sparks trying to read his future, now LeRoy Beers trying to take it away. A desperate part of his soul wants to climb back into the Mercedes and head south, not slow down until he hits the border at San Ysidro. But he can't do that, and it's not LeRoy Beers stopping him. It not Angie or the Kid or their half-assed scheme.

What Elvis knows—why he can't ever go home to help Simone run the cantina or see his gran'mama again—is what happened a couple of summers back. Micky had invited some of Sparanzano's people down to Baja, Teddy Sparks and a group of drunk Angelenos trying their luck at deep sea marlin fishing. Micky'd got lucky that trip, hooked an eighty-eight pound yellow fin. When they hauled it aboard the boat, some shitfaced little Italian shot it five times in the head with a handgun. But it was Elvis' cousin Simone who put them up for three days, serving them lobster enchiladas, ahi tacos and fresh oyster shooters every night, along with plenty of tequila and Negro Modelo until one or sometimes two in the morning. Simone giving them the upstairs rooms she kept for special guests and Micky playing the big-shot host, dropping money left and right.

Elvis remembers Sparanzano kissing Simone's hand before they left, telling her it was a pleasure. How he'd never forget her hospitality.

If he leaves town, Elvis figures Simone's cantina will be the first place they'll come looking for him. The last place they'll look as well—a bunch of freelance gunslingers hanging around, waiting for Elvis to show up, a price on his head he'll never outrun. And maybe a couple of Teddy's guys getting impatient, using Simone as bait. So here he is, stuck between Teddy Sparks and LeRoy Beers and whoever else wants a piece of him. Man, get in fuckin' line.

Things *way* too loco since Micky Logan died.

Jeff stays close to Jeanne most of the afternoon, reading a paperback in Micky's study. The small mountain of paperwork gradually dwindles in front of her. Angie's come and gone a few times, the last hour browsing through a *Rolling Stone*, content to relax on the sofa. Jeff doesn't tell Jeanne that he's taken his Smith .38 from under the seat in the Volvo, the gun stuffed loosely in a pocket of his duffel bag.

He's starting to feel safe again—although he's not ready to let his guard down. By Monday he'll be back with his own people, ask to have his union rep present and tell them whatever he can about his weekend in LA. Maybe Manetti and Zapata saved Angie's life, maybe not. But Angie will be safe at home and Jeanne will have dug up *something*. Enough perhaps to impress Ben Roman.

Tonight, they'll eat dinner and he'll smile at Manetti, even have a friendly beer or two. Keep everybody relaxed.

At least if they run into trouble, they'll have somebody to count on. Jeff remembering the promise Cutter gave him. At least they'll have the DEA.

4:45 PM SATURDAY

Benjamin Roman drives his BMW740i to the Westin Bonaventure downtown. Outside, a quartet of silver oval towers appear out of place — futuristic, maybe — against the taller, cornered angles of the surrounding downtown skyline. Inside, the hotel is both muted and gauche, a cacophony of tans and once-rich browns, of porous cement columns and glass walls. The Bonaventure's like a labyrinth, a myriad of curves and bends and walkways that weave through the expansive lobby. Roman thinks the building a suitable metaphor for L.A. itself — a combination of flamboyant and expensive, of gaudy and elegant. Or maybe, he realizes, it's merely how you choose to look at it, how you feel at any given moment.

Like *life*, he muses.

Roman moves quickly toward the center courtyard bar, past a multitude of gurgling fountains. He orders a gin and tonic he doesn't really want and spends several minutes watching the business-suited world bustle around him. He sees nobody he knows, nobody who might know him, and eventually assures himself that nobody here recognizes him.

The Bonaventure's guest elevators are exposed glass tubes — exciting for the tourists perhaps, but Roman walks toward a private, executive elevator bank far from the lobby. He ascends to the thirty-first floor in thoughtful silence.

Two men greet him with slight nods. He knows them by sight, not by name and they walk through a gilded hallway without a sound, chandeliers winking diamond pinpricks of light from above. They stop at a door midway down the hall. One of the men taps twice before turning to leave. Roman steps inside alone.

The suite's palatial. Roman takes in the amenities, the expanse of elegant carpeting, enormous bar — a spiral staircase near one corner, bedrooms on the next floor up. He's been here several times before, in similar suites, his stay usually no more than five or ten minutes. Today might take longer.

He's alone in the room and begins to move toward a million-dollar view of the city beyond a haze of white chiffon curtains.

"Ben? Is that you?" A man's voice, from another room.

Roman clears his throat. "We have a problem."

Theodore Sparanzano pokes his head from an adjacent doorway. "Ah, there you are." He enters with a confident stride, his suit tailored, Teddy Sparks looking tan and trim. He offers Roman a relaxed smile. "There are no problems, Ben. Only solutions looking for a *cause célèbre*. Would you like some Chianti?"

6:00ᴘᴍ SATURDAY

"It's an approximation," Jeanne says, feeling foolish because it's a vague estimate, but the best she can do considering the restrictions. "I won't have a viable figure until I reference certain incidental expenditures and debits, but if it's ballpark you want? Yes, I can give you ballpark."

They're seating in Logan's living room. Elvis looks pale — sitting for once, not standing over them like some brooding gargoyle. Dwight Manetti's on the couch next to Angie, with Jeff and Jeanne on the chocolate colored sofa, their knees touching. Micky Logan's ledgers clutter the coffee table.

"Based on the financials I examined, the market value of this house, his considerable art collection, his real estate holdings, various statements and listed securities, managed money assets and your stepfather's bond portfolio, it appears we're looking at a net value of thirty-six to maybe forty million."

"Forty?" Dwight's eyes do a happy dance. "Forty million *dollars*? No shit?"

"That's based on what's presented here. It's not a complete inventory of either buried assets or hidden liabilities, and I'm only estimating certain properties and possessions. For example, the selling price of this estate could easily vary by half a million dollars."

"You mean it might be *more*?" Dwight asks.

"Considerably," she says. "Forty may be a conservative estimate, Mr. Manetti. I'm not including your, um, stepfather's art galleries. He's listed as sole owner and CEO, but

I don't have any corporate information regarding Toadflax or its management. As far as his personal collection is concerned—he lists an original Monet. A Pissarro. Thomas Couture. I'm no expert, but I wouldn't be surprised if the collection has appreciated considerably since their purchase."

The Kid's chomping at a mental bit. "Maybe we should—"

"No, it's forty," Angie says firmly. "I like that. That's a good number."

Jeanne glances at Jeff, giving him a *what-now* look.

"Jeannie?" Angie says, her tone apologetic. "Would you and Jeff mind giving us a few minutes alone?"

"No, no problem." She's surprised to find Angie taking charge, but realizes Dwight's still fumbling over the enormity of the number. Elvis raises an eyebrow but otherwise his expression remains vacant, as if he hasn't registered a thing she's been telling them.

"We'll take a walk," Jeanne announces.

They move toward the foyer, aware of the electric silence behind them, Jeff imagining the big Hispanic or the skinny hood going to the door after they've left, making sure they're not eavesdropping. Jeanne takes his hand and whispers, "Isn't this just so bizarre?"

"Forty million," Dwight says, his voice barely above a whisper. "You *knew* Mr. Logan was worth that much?" He looks at Elvis but gets nowhere and gazes back at Angie with big chestnut eyes—chagrined to find her expression strangely calm as well. He has a sudden urge for a cold beer. Maybe several.

"Here's what we do," Angie says. She glanced nervously around the living room, making sure they're alone. "We don't haggle. The people Logan worked for must have a rough idea of Micky's worth. Forty million's probably a lot of money, even for *these* guys. So I say we give them the bargain of a lifetime. We tell them it's all theirs for four million."

"What?" the Kid says. "You're fuckin' serious? Your sister said—"

"We're not getting greedy. Don't you get it? We want *them* to get greedy. So greedy they forget we ever existed. We want them to think it's a steal."

"And let us walk?"

"Why not? Bargain basement, remember? They're happy and we're alive. What's the problem? They'll leave us alone and we don't even have to leave L.A."

Elvis sits, letting the sounds filter through his head. His shoulder throbs, the pain muddying his thoughts. He's popped several pills already today and his thoughts are spinning. He understands Angie's logic but he still feels anxious, knowing it's not going to be this simple. LeRoy Beers is still very much on his mind—all those loose threads the hooker and the Kid don't understand. Threads all over the fucking place, tangling up the inside of his brain.

"What about Micky's accountant?" Angie asks. "What do we do about him?"

"Leo," Elvis says. *Another* loose thread. Elvis wonders about Leo. He thinks about Micky's floor safe in the den, only him and Micky with the combination. A bunch of Micky's stuff in there, passports, a few handguns and shit—maybe close to a million dollars that Micky's stashed over the years. *Mad money*, what Micky calls it, because if he ever had to blow town in a hurry he knew he wouldn't have time to stop at no fucking bank. Micky's stashed another few million here or there, enough for a comfortable retirement, but even Elvis doesn't know where or how much. Some things Micky kept to himself.

Elvis has been thinking about Micky's mad money these last few days. Maybe with the numbers Angie's talking about, it's not important any more. But he considers dangling some of that floor money in front of Leo, because no way in hell is Leo going to believe a word of this. A couple hundred large might persuade Leo to be on the next plane for Tel Aviv, one of those places he talks about going before he dies.

Elvis thinks about the money again, four million dollars being an impressive sum and enough to—

"Wait," he says suddenly. It's him, Angie and the Kid sitting here. Three million he can grasp, but the remnants are snagging him up.

"Four million," he says.

Angie blinks, drawing the word out like a long breath. "Yeeeah?"

"There's only three of us," Elvis tells her. "You're saying what? A million dollars each?" Wondering for the first time if maybe Angie knows how to count.

Angie isn't thinking that way. Not in her wildest dreams has she considered the money in personal terms. Four million's the first number inside her head. Yeah, okay, so maybe there's a little something in it for her. This is mostly her idea, after all. But the big guy's staring at her and—

"Each what?" she says carefully, feeling dizzy.

"You an' me an' the Kid here," Elvis tells her. "That's three. Three million dollars."

Angie leans forward, her tongue playing against her upper lip. "You're saying...we *split* it?"

"No way you gettin' it all," he tells her.

"No, no, no—you don't understand. It's *your* money. Like you being Micky's next of kin. I mean, sure, maybe giving me and Dwight here enough to—"

"Whoa, I get it! We're partners, the three of us. Even Steven." The Kid's quick on his feet, aware that he's on the verge of a cool million. "Am I right?"

Elvis is silent again, thinking about Simone's cantina. The way he figures, what's he going to do with four million bucks down in Baja? He gives it another moment, letting the silence simmer. The Kid and the hooker, they're all eyes.

"Yeah, tha's what I'm sayin'."

"Fuck a moose!" The Kid claps his hands together.

Angie, her mouth half open, isn't sure how to respond.

"Thing is, there's only three of us," Elvis adds with a frown. Still screwed up on fractions.

Angie's too numb to think straight. Before she knows it, she says, "Jeannie and Jeff helped, too." She holds her breath, watching the big guy mull over this new speed bump.

Elvis' mind is still traipsing through Mexico. He feels the sun on his face, making strawberry margaritas for a

gaggle of pretty ladies in short skirts. "Yeah, sure, why not."
He shrugs, relieved that the numbers add up. Realizing,
too—if the shit hits the fan—Jeannie and Jeff are going
to be as dead as everyone else sitting here.

6:45 PM SATURDAY

Elvis wants to tell Sparanzano over the phone, but the man
seems to have his own agenda. Elvis doesn't get more than
a few words in.
"You know the Bonaventure, Mr. Zapata? Downtown?"
"Yeah."
"One hour."
Elvis starts to speak, but—
"And bring Micky along if he's available, hmm?"
"Uh. It's about Micky, but he ain't here."
"One hour," Sparanzano says again, and hangs up.
What the fuck, Elvis thinks to himself.

"So," Teddy Sparks says with a weary sigh, "Micky didn't
want to talk to me directly?"
"No, sir. He's still keepin' pretty much to hisself."
Elvis sits on a burgundy couch, holding a glass of Chianti he doesn't really want, sweating inside his black tweed.
Teddy Sparks sits with his ankles crossed, in a gilded chair
with a high back, like he's the Pope or something. Beyond
the gauge drapes, a yellow glow has begun to spread against
the horizon. Between them, a wide glass table holds vases

filled with fresh flowers. They smell nice. Danny Fortuna
stands next to Sparanzano's chair, his eyes like hot coals
in a cool breeze. Why is it Fortuna always looks ready to
pop someone? Like the guy can't ever chill the fuck out?

Someone else in the room too, fidgety, clinking glasses
behind the wet bar. Elvis recognizes Vinnie Sparanzano,
Teddy Sparks' nephew—the punk kid with pocked, red-
dened cheeks and a scraggly goatee, with a grease ball
hairdo right out of the '50s. He's been staring at Elvis with a
crazy grin the last minute or so, clutching a Stoli and tonic.
Micky used to call Vinnie a flat-liner, without enough sense
to blink both eyes at the same time. "But, hey, it's who you
know, right?" Micky'd once used the word *nepotism*—one
of his twenty-five-dollar college words, and ever since Elvis
has equated the word's meaning as sorry-ass stupid.

"So, Mr. Zapata. What's this about?"

Sparanzano waits patiently, Elvis' mind finally getting
down to business.

"Micky wan's to sell you his part of the business. He says
he don' wanna do this no more. Drugs an' shit."

"Micky's ready to give up such a good thing?"

"Wha' he says, yeah."

"And he's definite about this?"

"Micky's pretty sure."

"What does your boss think we'd be willing to pay for
his—his *part* of the operation?"

"He wan's to offer you a cut rate, Mr. Sparanzano. Four
million dollars."

"Really?" Sparanzano raises an eyebrow. "Might I ask
how Micky came up with four million?"

"He didn't say."

"One would think his business might be worth five, maybe ten times that amount."

"Micky didn't wanna make no fuss."

"He's worth *shit* without us, Teddy." Vinnie sucks at his drink and makes a nasally, chuckling sound.

Sparanzano holds up a hand. Vinnie shrugs and tops off his Stoli tonic with more Stoli.

"I assume this offer is directly from Micky's lips?"

"Yes, sir."

"And Micky told you, did he, how he expects me to come up with four million dollars?"

Elvis hasn't considered that—assumes they're the fucking Mafia after all, money all over the place.

"I'm curious. Why is Micky so afraid to talk to me?"

"Well, Micky's still outta town."

"A fat farm."

"Yeah. A fat farm."

"No phones out there, where Micky is?"

When Elvis doesn't answer, Sparanzano continues. "He's putting a good deal of faith in you, my friend. An awesome responsibility, negotiating a man's worth on blind trust."

"Ain't no thing."

Sparanzano places two fingers to his lips, lost in a moment of thought. "Let me run your offer past my people, hmm? Four million dollars isn't a drop in the bucket. I'll let you know inside a few days. But I'm certain we can work out some equitable arrangement."

Elvis nods and that's that, Sparanzano having spoken

his peace. Danny Fortuna shows Elvis to the door and comes back, Sparanzano brooding in silence. Vinnie's making giggling sounds again, already drunk behind the bar.

Sparanzano looks up. "Get my cards, Danny. From the bedroom drawer."

"Sure," Fortuna says. "But if you ask me, the guy's full of shit."

"Most likely, Danny. Most likely. Question is: What's he up to? What is our Mr. Zapata hoping to achieve?"

A few years ago, when everyone suspected Micky Logan to be a lone wolf, Ben Roman's people pulled off a sting, busting one of Logan's desert labs. They found chemicals and propane and a decent amount of illegal substance. They also found a chemist, hiding in a closet. His name was Wallace Turpin, a Berkeley burnout with oversized glasses and a shock of unkempt hair like Einstein. Turpin was the type of guy who wouldn't last two weeks in a federal bucket, so Roman talked to an assistant D.A., who offered Turpin a sweet deal; minimum county time in exchange for the dirt on Micky Logan. Everyone expected Turpin to jump at the chance, but the chemist kept his mouth shut and was sentenced a few months later to a hard fifteen at Atascadero.

"You're so afraid of one fat mick?" Roman asked, the day of the sentencing.

"Ain't about Logan, man." Turpin's gaze danced behind

his bottle-bottomed lenses. "It's the guys he's married too. You piss off the Duke an' one morning they feed you your balls for breakfast, man."

That comment brought in the Bureau with a RICO gleam in their eye. Ben Roman had often worked with the FBI, has actually gotten along with a few of their guys and knew how to ride the roller-coaster of colliding egos. But the inter-agency paperwork mired him, suddenly piece-meal scraps of information coming and going everywhere at once, endless e-mails, forms and requests fed through a contortionist's labyrinth of rubber stampers and paper pushers—and all Roman wanted was to get back into the field and bring down Micky Logan.

The call had come early one Sunday morning to Roman's unlisted line in the den. When the phone rang the first time, Roman wasn't home. His wife dutifully ignored the call. Later that afternoon, and Roman still damp from a six-mile jog, the phone rang again. He answered.

"Mr. Roman, how do you do? My name is Theodore Sparanzano." Teddy Sparks paused long enough to gauge the reaction, pleased to find none.

"Go on," Roman said.

"Tomorrow morning, Pier 18. Long Beach. We're talk-ing before the birds get up. A freighter of Panamanian reg-istry, name of *Muevo*. The ship is carrying Peruvian cargo, touristy stuff. Straw hats and baskets and, oh, yes, about six point five million in street coke."

When he hung up, Roman sat uneasily, ready to dismiss the call as a hoax. Eventually he picked up the phone again, thinking *what the hell*. The next morning, before the birds were up, twenty-five DEA and U.S. Customs agents, in conjunction with the LAPD Special Services Narcotics Division backed by a dozen uniforms, waved the appropriate papers to a sleepy-eyed sea captain and boarded the *Muevo*. The coke was aboard, precisely as Sparanzano had indicated. Roman's bust made the front page of the *L.A. Times*.

A few nights later, Sparanzano called again. "I see you've been in the funny papers."

"What's the catch, Teddy?"

"There can be other victories, such as this one."

Ben Roman counted off the seconds until he heard the other shoe drop.

"What I'm asking in return is that you to ease off certain people. For instance, your agents have been squeezing Michael Patrick Logan. I think they'd be more valuable looking into the dealings of one Juan Buenitas. You might find an interesting pipeline that begins in Bogota and ends in certain Boeing 767 wheel wells at LAX. I can be more specific if you're interested."

"Sorry," Roman told him, "but I don't play that way."

"Then I believe you may have misconstrued the game. I'm taking a chance by talking to you. You're taking a chance listening. You see, Ben—may I call you Ben?— we're already bound by the whim of circumstance. By a collision of fates. However, I'm not asking for favors. I'm not even asking for leniency. If Micky Logan jaywalks, give him a ticket. If you discover him selling crack to school children, by all means take him away. But you've not found anything in a long while. Perhaps I'm nothing more than a concerned citizen, wanting my tax money put to better use, hmm?"

When Roman said nothing, Sparanzano added, "Five or six years from now, perhaps Logan will slip. I myself may inadvertently provide information about certain indiscretions. Until then, I have knowledge that will keep your people busy. You won't end crime in this city, Ben, but you will make a dent. Perhaps *this* is a game you'd like to play?"

Roman remained silent for a long moment, repulsed and intrigued—feeling truly scared for one of the few times in his life. A crooked dealer had slipped him pocket aces, a hand he'd win four times out of five—but the dealer was telling him to fold to some joker named Micky Logan. Sure, he could walk away and devote the rest of his life to drawing out against unknown hands, occasionally winning a big pot here and there on his own terms. But like most cops, the odds were good that he'd go broke trying to score.

He knew fifty agents who would have already hung up the phone, determined to play the game clean, but Ben Roman was not a patient man. "Tell me more," he'd said to Teddy Sparks, all those years ago.

8:15 pm SATURDAY

"A million bucks." The Kid smiles at Angie. "That kind of money can change a lot of things, huh?"

"Yeah, I guess." She hasn't thought about the money

much, too preoccupied with staying alive these last couple of days. The money seems merely a part of the charade.

"Like what you told this morning," the Kid says.

Angie tries to remember. "What'd I tell you, hon?"

"If a million bucks fell in your lap?"

She feels a sudden surge of anger. "What, this is about me being a hooker?"

"No. About you being an ex-hooker."

"I told you before, what I do—"

The Kid holds out his hands, a placating gesture. "All I'm saying, a million bucks can change who you are. Who you wanna be. Hey, we add up your share and mine, it's plenty to live on, huh?"

Angie opens her mouth. The Kid reaches out, puts a finger to her lips. "I'm not asking you to make plans. But, y'know, think about it. About you and me maybe hanging out after this is over. Maybe goin' to dinner someplace real, like down in Hollywood where they don't look at you funny because of who you are. Or drive over to the coast, pick up some corn fritters at the Santa Monica pier, where nobody don't give a fuck who you are either.

"Look, I'm sorry what happened last night," he tells her. "I came on too fast, okay? I thought you liked me. The way I liked you. That's all. I'm asking for that chance is all."

She reaches for his hand, warm against her lips. "I do like you." Their fingers intertwine. "But the kind of relationship you want from me—I don't think I'm capable of that."

Angie sees the hurt on his face. "It's not you, babe. Any woman in her right mind—well, she'd be all over you like grease on sausage."

"You're saying then—what?" Gently coaxing her. "You ain't in your right mind?"

Angie nods. "Yeah, I guess that's what I'm saying."

"Whoa, hey—I'm kiddin' here."

"I know." She squeezes his hand. "Don't worry about it. About me."

Dwight smiles. "I think I *like* worrying about you."

"A million bucks or not, you don't wanna get close to who I am."

"Is this the deep six here? You sayin' I'm down for the count?" His smile lingers tenuously. "So maybe I got a right to find out about you. I mean you and me being partners and all."

"It's a long story, love."

"I got time."

Two minutes ago a thousand volts wouldn't have jolted it out of her. Suddenly all the old feelings come churning up from some ugly place, like a poison she needs to purge. It's something she's never told anyone—not even Jeannie—and here she is, holding the words back with clenched lips, surprised and uncertain and a bit scared.

For the first time she can remember, a man's looking at her from the neck up, liking what he sees beyond a pair of boobs on a California blonde with a squeaky laugh and a quick smile. Before she knows it, she hears her own words begin to dribble out, her soul like a ruptured spigot.

"Well," Angie says, "it kinda happened like this..."

10:00 PM SATURDAY

"You're done?" Jeff asks.

"I'm done. These books are — they're smoke and mirrors. Like a magic show. But I'm done. Finito."

"You have enough to implicate this guy Logan? I mean, in case Logan's still alive?"

"If the man's still alive," she replies with a tired smile, "trust me, he'll wish he wasn't."

He checks his watch. "Let's get the hell out of here. Tonight. Right now."

"It's late," Jeanne says. "Besides, we promised Angie."

"Yeah, right — Angie." For a moment he verges on anger, but Jeanne's exhausted. She looks almost fragile standing there, expecting nothing more than his promise. Because she's right, they did promise Angie. So he struggles up a weary smile and concedes without an argument. "So — now what? You want to turn in?"

"I'll take a nightcap instead." She realizes they're not going to argue and Jeanne suddenly glows.

"Jeez, babe. Haven't you heard anything I've said?"

"A few drinks won't change anything. I just closed up for the night — and I deserve a little celebrating. We made five thousand dollars, Jeff. Let's go find Angie."

Jeanne walks into the living room, sees Angie and Dwight Manetti sitting close on the couch. She wonders for a moment if Angie's been crying, but her sister looks happy now. Laughing at something Manetti says. They look cute together, she thinks.

"Sweetie," Angie says, standing up. She swipes at a glistening tear with the back of her hand. "You all finished?"

"Yeah. I think so."

"You put in a long day," the Kid tells her.

"I feel like a cold one. No, that's not true. I feel like getting drunk."

"Far out," Angie says. "Let's do it!"

"Remember those Hurricanes you used to make?"

"Oh, yeah. That bartender over at the Crazy Eights taught me."

"They were yummy."

"Rum. I remember lots of rum. And orange juice. Something else sweet."

"Passion fruit," Elvis says, his voice out of nowhere and everyone turns to stare. He's standing by the row of French doors, in his black suit, a white shirt buttoned but without a tie — Elvis' version of casual.

"That's right," Angie says with an odd smile. "And lime juice."

"Got no passion fruit," Elvis tells her.

"Too bad," Jeanne says, ready to ask for a beer instead.

"Got Curacao."

"Oh?"

"Grenadine. Brown sugar. Mango."

"You're a bartender?" Jeanne asks, surprised.

Elvis shakes his head.

"That's what *you* think," Angie smiles. "Because we're about to throw ourselves a party."

As long as Elvis can remember, Micky's kept a glass –
paneled liquor cabinet well stocked, a good host to his
infrequent drinking companions. It's Elvis who lays out
five or six bills every couple of weeks in grocery money,
a Filipino woman named Sadi bringing in several heavy
bags, including Micky's Johnny Walker Blue Label, bringing Elvis his Angostura Bitters or Amaretto or Cointreau.
When Jeanne and Angie move behind the marble topped
wet bar to peek, they find nearly every conceivable liqueur.
Elvis stands there with a crooked eyebrow, watching their
amazement.

"Kahlua. Benedictine. Campari. Oh, look—here's
some peach schnapps," Jeanne says. "Fuzzy Navels!"

"We used to drink Harvey Wallbangers when you were
at SDU," Angie remembers with a giggle.

"Vodka and orange juice," Elvis says. "Galliano on top.
You gotta float it."

They look at him, then at each other, Angie with a sly
smile. "Pink Lady?"

"Gin. Cream and sugar. Grenadine."

"And?"

"Egg. But not the yellow part. An' no ice," Elvis says.

"Incredible," Angie remarks.

"Boston Bullet?" Jeanne poses, because their father used
to drink them.

"Like a martini. Gin and vermouth. You stick a piece of
almond up inside the olive is all."

"I'm getting thirsty," the Kid says, watching them from
the couch.

"Let's do Tequila Sunrises!" Jeanne announces.

Midway into her third drink, Angie says to Elvis, "Lemme give you a haircut."

He's standing behind the bar—he's taken off his jacket, rolled up his sleeves and he's put on a *Hussong's Cantina* apron, an old gift from Micky—slicing wedges of lime and squeezing cut oranges. Angie and Jeanne are sitting on bar stools, Dwight pushing buttons on Micky's expensive sound system, various speakers throughout the house alternately muting and blaring, although Elvis has been glowering at him the last minute or so.

"I went to hair-cutting school and it looks goofy like that," Angie says. It's long and straight in front, with a part near the middle, and too long on the sides, hanging over the scar on his earlobe. Almost a pageboy. Angie takes a chance, reaches up over the bar and brushes it behind Elvis' ear with her fingertips. He stiffens, his first reaction to knock her hand away. But he's aware of Jeanne and the Kid watching him.

Elvis' gaze telling her no fuckin' way.

"I can make it nice."

"Nah, s'okay like it is."

"You got scissors?"

Elvis figures it's time to get the fuck out of there and wipes his hands on his apron, watching Angie and Jeanne head off toward the kitchen. The Kid's eating it up, calling after them to bring more ice. Dwight's in his yellow tank, showing off his shoulders and biceps for the ladies. Baboso, Elvis thinks and grabs a Tecaté—an' maybe they can start chopping on *him*, all that long hair everywhere. Elvis sees Jeff with his own beer, leaning forward on the couch midway across the room, staring at Micky's big chess-board. Elvis wanders over and sits across the table.

"*Esa mujer es demasiado loco,*" he mutters under his breath.

Surprised when Jeff answers, "*Dímelo a mí.*"

"Well, maybe jus' a *little* crazy," Elvis amends in English.

Jeff smiles. "Nice board."

"Yeah, it's Italian."

"You and Manetti play?"

"The Kid, nah, he don' have a clue."

"Tough game to play alone."

"I tried to teach Micky a coupla times."

"He any good?"

"Micky wasn't into concentrating too much."

"Too busy dealin', huh?"

"Yeah, Micky was more—" Elvis closes his mouth, lifts his gaze and stares curiously.

Jeff offers a casual shrug. "With artists, paintings, stuff like that?"

"Yeah," Elvis says warily. "Shit like that." Elvis has a sudden hunch that Jeff knows more about Micky than he's letting on. Man, try to keep *un secreto* in this town — like trying to keep hot water in a paper bag.

Jeff takes a sip of beer. "What about you? You any good?"

Elvis contemplates his Tecaté. Contemplates the sound of laughter coming from the kitchen. He reaches out, nudges his king's pawn forward.

Jeff regards the intricately carved pieces, making his own decisions. "Jeanne and I will be out of here tomorrow."

Speaking to Elvis without looking up. Eventually moving his king's knight. "What happens after that, nothing personal, but I don't give a damn."

Elvis moves another pawn.

"We're taking Angie with us."

Their gazes meet, only an instant before Elvis nods. "That's prob'ly best. Get her outta town, man. Get her safe, huh?" He watches Jeff slide a bishop forward.

"You and Manetti, maybe you should get the hell out, too."

Elvis isn't sure what to say, about to agree but a burst of laughter erupts from the doorway, Jeanne and Angie bustling into the room, giggly drunk, Angie with a dish towel and scissors and Jeanne carrying a pitcher of ice with both hands.

"*¡Cuidado!*" Jeff tells Elvis.

"*Jesucristo.*"

"We're not taking *no* for an answer." Angie moves behind Elvis for an appraisal.

"I don't wan' no one fuckin' with my hair," Elvis says, as gently as he can.

"We're not *fucking* with it," Angie said, already one Sunrise too many to worry. "We're fixing it."

"Get outta Geeksville," the Kid says approvingly. Elvis gives him a squint, but what the hell's he going to do? He looks at Jeff, who moves his queen's bishop forward, concentrating on the game.

"I have to warn you," Jeanne tells Elvis, "Jeff's won a few local tournaments. He's pretty sharp."

Elvis isn't listening. He's thinking about getting shot

and making a million bucks, now getting a haircut, the same fucking day.

She snips it short on the sides, doesn't mention Elvis' crooked ear, the jagged scar across his earlobe and down his cheek. She doesn't mention the bandage, the smudge of blood she sees on the collar of his shirt. Thinking, *not your business, Angelina.*

Elvis tries to ignore the conversation behind him. Jeff captures a pawn, then takes his knight. Elvis is moodily aware of black snippets falling around him, an occasional squeal from Angie or her sister. He tells the Kid to go fetch him another beer, waggling his empty Tecaté, his eyes on the board.

Jeff takes his queen's rook. The Kid returns with a bottle and stands beside Angie, saying, "Hey, lookin' pretty slick there, amigo."

Jeanne tells him he looks a bit like Channing Tatum, in that movie about the wrestler.

Elvis frowns again, feeling naked on top, trading pawns with Jeff, trying to concentrate.

"*Finished,*" Angie says finally.

He reaches up, feels the short brush of hair on his scalp. Feels his ear hanging out there to blow in the wind. Shrugging, like no big deal, but he sneaks a glance at Jeff who finally looks up from the board and nods his approval.

"Who's Channum Tating?" Elvis says.

"A guy with short hair," Jeff replies.

Elvis studies the board a long moment. Runs his hand again over his hair and has to admit he likes the feel. Ponders the board again before moving his queen to take a pawn, boxing the dark king. "*Jaquemate*," Elvis says without emotion, the move out of nowhere and Jeff sitting there with his mouth hanging open.

The Kid's behind the bar with the pitcher of ice. "Yo, Elvis, we're outta OJ."

"I saw some lemonade in the little fridge under the bar," Angie says.

"Tequila and lemonade?"

Elvis thinks a moment, unable to produce with a name. Angie watches him frown. "Hey, we stuck him on that one."

"It's tart," the Kid says, adding a few ingredients. "This is better. Dropped in some Seven Up an' a lime. Oh, an' vodka."

"Shitski," Jeanne says, rolling her eyes.

"We invented something new," Angie announces with a loopy smile. "Maybe we should give it a name?"

"An Elvis Surprise," the Kid offers. "On the rocks."

"On the rocks," Angie echoes. "Just like us." She thinks about the comment for a moment, not sure whether it's funny or not. Giggling finally, too drunk to really give a shit.

Just like us.

The three of them—giddy the rest of the night—eventually finish the pitcher and then another one after that, even Jeff trying a glass and finally Elvis having a taste. Grimacing and shaking his head—although he's secretly pleased to have a drink with his name on it. Maybe something he can serve up in Simone's Cantina one day. *Una Sorpresa Elvio.* Angie puts her head on the Kid's shoulder at one point, everybody kicking back, enjoying the stretch. Somebody scrambles a few CD's on Micky's elaborate sound system—Staind and Neko Case, Black Eyed Peas, Stevie Ray Vaughn and Gloria Trevi. Neil Young. Ely Guerra. Cultures colliding and nobody minding a bit.

The Kid finally breaks up the evening. Nearly midnight and Dwight's a little wobbly, buzzed on tequila and vodka and grinning around the room with a sloppy smile. "I gotta get me some sleep," he says. "Got a feeling tomorrow's gonna be one ball-breaker of a day. Am I right?"

7:00 AM SUNDAY

Renee Torres picks up the red-headed woman in a parking lot near the corner of Pico and 18th Street. Torres is wearing dirty jeans and yesterday's V-neck sweater, her dark hair finger-combed and swirling in tangles around her forehead. The two drive in silence through much of Santa Monica, past the college, until they can see the blue-gray ocean ahead.

They come this way because Gina likes watching the ocean while she talks. She suspects her apartment is bugged and people keep stealing her cellphone, so she plays it safe, maybe feeling normal for a few minutes if you forgot the woman next to you is a fed, and her only interest in you is the guy you've been banging.

She's a small woman, gaunt, barely five feet, with corkscrewing reddish curls to her shoulders, bangs hanging down below her eyebrows. She's already halfway through her second Camel of the morning. She knows agent Torres doesn't like her smoking in the car, but Gina considers it part of the package deal. Like a perk.

"I get you out of bed?" Gina asks.

"Six-thirty on Sunday morning?" Torres gives her a sidelong glance. "What makes you think I'd be sleeping?"

Gina smiles to herself and they chat about innocuous stuff for several minutes, Torres waiting while the woman pulls out another Camel. She glimpses a glint of gunmetal gray before Gina snaps her purse shut again.

They turn right on the Pacific Coast Highway, almost deserted this time of the morning. Gina chews gum with a rhythmic clicking sound and watches a flock of distant pelicans gliding above the waves. "So, like, here it is," she says eventually. "Yesterday I'm drinking coffee at the Bonnie, on account of Danny bein' two hours late. He tells me to meet him at four-o'clock and he's not there. And me with no room key. So I'm stuck in the lobby reading magazines."

"What happened?"

Gina's eyes trace the passing coastline. "Something I told you once before."

"What's that?"

"Something you're not gonna like hearin' again."

"Shit, Gina," Torres says, suddenly angry. "We're not starting this crap, are we?"

"Why would I lie?" She blows a pink bubble, pops it and sucks the gum back into her mouth. "Why call you, take time outta my morning an' tell you something you already gave me a ration about?"

"I don't know. Why?"

"Not outta fuckin' kindness. But I swear to Christ, why would I goof on you?"

"Okay, so you're telling me, what? You saw him again? At the Bonaventure?"

"Yeah, at the Bonnie."

"When?"

"A little before five. And then a little after, when he was comin' out."

"And you knew it was him? For certain?"

"Yeah, it was him. I pay attention. He was in the *Times* a few months ago. Got some award for bustin' up some Asian snow rag. I saw a picture of him way back, a rookie or something at the academy. Not recently, not in the paper, but he's the same guy. I cut out the story, kept it, knowing he was your boss and all. The way he walks, the way he dresses — like he owns the street, what they said about him in the *Times*."

"On the elevator?"

"Like I said, coming off."

"With a couple of Danny's people?"

"Last time, yeah. This time he was alone."

"Not maybe some businessman in a sharp suit? Some hood maybe?"

"Nah," Gina says. "People like Danny, they walk like they want to impress the hired help. Benjamin Roman, he coulda owned the fuckin' hotel, the way he walked. He went up, came out again, maybe half an hour later." Gina pops another bubble and drags on her Camel. "Your boss and Danny's boss, both at the Bonnie at the same time. Why would I tell you, huh, if I didn't see it with my own eyes?"

"For a couple of bills, I think you'd tell me pigs fly."

They drive in silence a moment. Torres checks her watch. "This is the important reason you got me out of bed? Look, I have to cut this short. I'm working today."

"Honey, ain't we all."

Torres makes a disappointed sound with her tongue.

Gina crosses her legs, a few inches of black Lycra smooth and tight across her thighs. She makes sure Agent Torres gets a peek, almost lets her skirt sneak up higher, but she doesn't want to change gears, muddy the waters and have Torres think she's blowing smoke. Coming on, one girl to another.

She knows the rumors about Torres' preferences. Gina's done women before, no big deal. The big deal is that she knows, but Torres doesn't *know* she knows. Gina likes sitting on that kind of information. The same way she knows for certain it was Renee Torres' boss in the lobby yesterday. Gina keeps pace, knows the players and how to keep score. You have to, sleeping with Danny Fortuna and selling this kind of shit to the DEA. It's as important to her as the Beretta she keeps in her purse, or in a clip-on holster under her blouse when she's feeling particularly paranoid. The same reason she makes agent Torres drive way out here before having one of their little two-hundred-dollar chats.

These kinds of precautions keep you alive.

Gina smiles at Torres and sneaks a glance at her sweater, aware of the vague definition of her breasts. Gina wonders if the agent's wearing a bra. Probably a lacy little one, maybe a little pink rose sewn in. Gina reaches down and smooths a wrinkle of mesh stocking along her calf, running her hands up along her knee, guiding the fabric, her hands moving higher, brushing aside the hem of her skirt. She notices Torres' attention drift from the road and Gina smiles. Yeah, she can spill her guts on any number of things, for the right price. Everything in it's own time—because sooner or later Gina knows everything *has* a price.

8:45 AM SUNDAY

The little guy's nervous. Leo Sussman, all five-feet-five of him, weighs in at one-forty, and when he's frightened he sometimes shivers so hard he suspects his bones might rattle out of their sockets and fall in a pile to the floor.

He's shivering now, standing here in Micky's den, Elvis behind Micky's desk and different somehow. Staring at him in a way he doesn't like. Leo doesn't like the way Elvis is making himself at home, either. Micky's desk. Micky's chair. Micky's office.

Leo's come in full of suspicion and false bravado, asking, "Where the hell's Micky? Can't fool me. Micky don't just take off like that."

But he *is* fooled, without a clue as to where Micky might be. And that particular mystery rattles his bones.

Leo and Elvis never had much reason to talk in the past. Probably haven't spoken more than a few dozen times all these years. Leo isn't a part of Elvis' world, nor Elvis part of his. Leo Sussman has been suspicious all morning, Elvis on the phone early and, what, suddenly Elvis is running the show now? Leo's too confused not to come and until he finds out a thing or two, he sure as hell isn't about to leave.

"We got trouble," Elvis says.

"Whaddaya mean we? *Micky's* got trouble? Is that it?"

"You could say that."

"With the law?"

Elvis shakes his head.

"You mean with Teddy Sparks?"

Elvis watches him without a word, letting it sink in.

Leo squints. "Joey never said nothin' to me. Why wouldn't Joey Segal say something, if we got trouble? Wha'd we do, for criminy sakes?"

"Micky's been settin' up some labs in the desert. Not sayin' squat to Teddy Sparks and keepin' the change."

"Shit a brick, I don't believe this."

"Believe it."

Leo exaggerates a myopic gaze around the room. "Where's Micky, huh? Lemme hear it from Micky hisself. When I hear it from Micky, then I believe it."

"Micky ain't here," Elvis says patiently. "Why you think?"

Leo's suddenly silent.

"'Cause Teddy Sparks put the word out on Micky is why."

"I don't believe none of this. Joey woulda said—"

"Joey tells you nada," Elvis says brusquely, and Leo's mouth snaps shut. "Micky's upped his take and who they think's been helpin' Micky count his money?"

The words push Leo back a step. The little man splays a hand against his chest. "Me? You're saying Sparanzano thinks it's me?"

"You're Micky's accountant."

"Whaddaya tellin' me? I'm a *dead* man? That's it? Micky gets fuckin' greedy and they think it's me? Christ almighty, what's Micky got to be greedy about? He's got all the swag he needs, for criminy sake. Why's he wanna hold out on Teddy Sparks? I don't believe none of it."

Elvis pulls a black leather satchel from beside his chair and places it on the desk. A jagged slice of pain shoots up his neck and Elvis feels a warm trickle of blood ooze from beneath the bandage, sticking to the back of his shirt. The crease in his shoulder has been bleeding most of the morning, making him irritable and edgy, Elvis' temper more or less scaring the shit out of Leo.

Truth is, the handful of Tylenol Elvis has been chewing like candy hasn't killed the pain. He doesn't know how much more of Leo's shit he can take. Elvis wonders if it's time to start digging another hole in the back yard.

Sussman stares at the bag, cooling down.

"This is from Micky," Elvis says. He unzips the case. Leo doesn't move. Elvis waits, the satchel gaping. Leo finally shuffles forward and peeks down inside. Opens his eyes round.

"Like goin' away money," Elvis says. He's supposed to say *severance pay*, the way Angie's planned it, but the words don't stick in Elvis' mind. From the look in Leo's eyes, Elvis figures he's made the point anyway.

"Jiminy Christ. You're serious about this?"

"Three hundred large," Elvis tells him. "From Micky to you."

"What in hell I'm supposed to do with it, huh? Teddy Sparks up my ass and what in hell am I s'posed to buy?"

This was all Angie's idea, of course. Elvis reaches into his jacket pocket, unfolds a page and holds it out, columns of numbers and times—an El Al flight itinerary. An e-ticket. First class to Tel Aviv. One way. Charged to Micky's American Express Gold card.

"What you tol' Micky you always wanted," Elvis says.

"Yeah, right," Leo grumbles. "Bunch of wops with guns behind me, bunch of towelheads with guns in front."

Elvis shrugs.

Leo looks uncertain. Looks around the room and makes noises. But he takes the ticket. Takes the satchel. Early the next morning, without another word to Elvio Zapata or a backward glance, Leo will take El Al flight 316 to Tel Aviv.

10:15ᴀᴍ SUNDAY

"Here, put these on." Dwight holds out Angie's sunglasses and gives her a long scarf he's found who-knows-where. A man's camel wool. Probably Micky's. She feels funny, but drapes it around her neck.

"What is all this?" she asks suspiciously.

"Like a costume. We're going for a ride."

"To where?"

"It's a surprise."

Angie frowns. "I don't understand."

"I told Elvis we'd be gone awhile. It's cool." The Kid takes her by the arm, leading her toward the foyer.

They take his ruby red ZX300 convertible, the leather

interior worn and patched, speckles of rust dotting the frame, eating at the chrome. "But she still purrs," the Kid tells her, letting the RPMs gather in second, shifting with a fluid movement by the time they get to Micky's sliding gate. It opens automatically, an electric eye or something, she assumes. The Kid takes the corner with a squeal of rubber.

"You trust me?" he asks her.

"What, not to kill me?"

"Where I'm takin' you," he says, talking above the whistle of wind, his ponytail flipping back and forth. Angie puts on the glasses because he asks her to, tucking her blonde hair up under the scarf.

"Where *are* we going?"

"You'll see," the Kid says. He smiles at her. He's wearing his Armani suit, the one she remembers from Friday night, the night he shot Micky Logan. For some reason the memory brings back a wave of fear.

"Trust that I won't hurt you," the Kid says, aware that's she's not answered him yet. Apparently it's important to him.

She watches the road another moment, calming herself. Finally, "Yeah, I trust you."

The Kid turns on Las Flores Canyon, steep and twisty, but Dwight's having fun and handles the car exceedingly well. Impressing her, she thinks — but slowing enough to keep her from having a bird. He turns south on PCH — sea level, thank God — and takes the 10 to the 405 freeway, traffic uncharacteristically light this morning. Church traffic, the Kid calls it. For much of the trip they don't talk, mostly because the stereo's cranked up — an L.A. band called *The Janks* on the CD player—and the wind's howling. She looks over now and then and Dwight's grinning to himself, lost in thought.

La Cienega over to Culver City. Angie begins to frown, the streets vaguely familiar, bringing back a rushed tingle of angst. The houses they pass aren't quite elite, but a jump up from middle class, older homes with nice, manicured lawns and palm-tree sculpted lawns. Another turn and Angie's heart creeps into her throat.

"Please," she tells him, "I don't want to be here."

The Kid pulls to the curb—fuck the hydrant—and turns off the ignition. Gets out and hustles around to open Angie's door. She's shaking her head, simultaneously hot and cold. One hand clutches the wool knot under her throat.

"No...," she whispers, feeling herself guided and trying feebly to resist. On the sidewalk, he puts an arm around her shoulders and says, "Everything's gonna be okay, Angie. Everything's cool."

She feels her brain leave for that far-away place, nothing real any more. A few tall palms sway beneath a cloudless sky. They walk up a pebbled walkway toward a front door. Like two actors in a Hollywood movie, Angie thinks.

The Kid rings the doorbell. He absently adjusts his tie and picks at lint on his sleeve. Checks for clouds in the sky. Dwight clears his throat and reaches out to push the bell again.

The door opens. Angie's gaze flees to her feet.

The guy standing there is mid-fiftyish, graying hair unkempt around his head. A little bald in front. He wears a bushy, graying mustache flaked with bits of bread or cracker crumbs. Pink jowls hang loosely beneath his cheekbones and he's already acquired a mesh of drinker's veins—gin blossoms—criss-crossing his nose. He wears brown polyester slacks, a polyester flower print shirt over a mound of belly.

Dwight flashes a big grin. "Hey there, Mr. Moody. How you doin'?"

The man's gaze flits between the cocky kid in black, the shy woman beside him. "Huh? Who are you?"

"My sister here—she's got that enrollment money. For your beauty school. Cash is okay, am I right?" The Kid has a hand inside his jacket, already with a foot in the door, pulling out an envelope.

"Hundred dollar bills work for you?"

Moody back steps, the Kid crowding him but Moody's attention distracted by the envelope. He takes it—the Kid pulling Angie through the door after him. The envelope's sealed. Moody rips it open and Dwight shuts the door.

"This is rather unusual. Do I *know* you?" Moody glances again at the woman, frowning because he's yet to see her face. "I don't remember you. Hey, what the—?" He thumbs the rectangular newspaper cuttings wadding the envelope.

Moody's mouth stops working, seeing the Kid's Walther emerge from under the black jacket, the silencer a four-inch cylinder of black steel. The Kid pokes the barrel between the man's eyebrows.

"Oh, holy Jesus!"

"I want for you to do something—"

"I don't have any money here!"

"—to do something for me. It's very important you listen up."

"I swear I got no money."

"This ain't about money."

"A few dollars in my wallet, but that's—"

The Kid frowns, already impatient. "You gonna listen up or what?"

Moody nods frantically.

"Atta boy." Dwight throws a quick glance toward Angie. She's pressed her back against the door and flattens herself. She's hasn't lifted her gaze from the floor. Doesn't matter.

"Here's what I want. Hey, you listening? I want you to drop your drawers."

"My what?"

"Your pants. Pull 'em down."

"You can't be—"

The Kid flicks his wrist. The silenced Walther raps hard against Moody's forehead. A crescent of blood fills the indent and trickles down the side of Moody's nose. The man whimpers and closes his eyes, grappling with his zipper. After a final instant's reluctance, he lets them fall to his knees.

"Now the undies."

Another pause. The Kid presses hard against the man's forehead again and Moody yanks at his yellowish BVDs. He cracks open one eye and seems relieved that the woman by the door had no inclination to peek.

"Grab hold, Mr. Moody."

"What?"

"C'mon, let's walk the ol' pooch. Spank that monkey. Lemme see what you're packing south of the border, eh?"

Moody's eyes grow wider. He throws a panicked look around the room, searching for an out that isn't there. His mouth twitches, beads of saliva working along the corners of his lips.

Another tap with the silenced Walther.

Moody swallows, reaches down and grabs his penis.

"Quite a horse you got there, fella," the Kid says. "I bet you're a regular guided missile with all the ladies. A little sausage monster. An organ grinder. Am I right?"

"What?" Moody says. *"What?"*

The Kid traces the silenced Walther down Moody's nose to his chin. Moody moans, tries to step back and realizes that his feet are mired in polyester. He wobbles. The Kid reaches out and steadies him.

"Careful now. Gotta stay balanced with that monster unleashed. Oh, yeah, that's a real beaut." The gun drops, follows the expanding bulge of belly and drops again to Moody's trembling knuckles. The man's breath hitches. The silencer comes to rest against the side of Moody's manhood and slowly moves along its length. The Kid's paying attention now, nudging the Walther until barely a quarter-inch of wrinkled pink foreskin protrudes in front of the muzzle.

The Kid thinking, yeah, right…about…*there.*

And pulls the trigger.

The gun makes a hoarse cough, the rug puffing up between Moody's feet. A sudden pink spray blossoms from the tip of Moody's penis. He tries to scream—a noise that never escapes his throat. He clutches himself with both hands and drops to his knees, doubling over on the floor.

The Kid backs away, his mouth open, in sudden awe of what he's done. He holsters his gun and turns to leave, surprised to find that Angie has stepped from the doorway, standing directly behind him. She glares at Moody with a furious intensity. Tears stain her cheeks.

"C'mon, let's go," the Kid says. He reaches for her arm, but Angie anchors herself where she stands. She watches Moody writhe and moan for maybe half a minute, blood oozing between his fingers, staining the carpet.

"We gotta leave," Dwight says.

Angie leans forward, her face drawing close to Moody's ear. "There," she says, a fierce whisper. *"There."*

"Time to split," the Kid urges. Angie nods finally. She follows him, closing Moody's front door softly behind her. They walk unhurriedly to the Kid's car, beneath a cloudless sky, like two people in a Hollywood movie.

The Kid peels away, grinding gears and lost in his own thoughts. Angie fingers the knot of her scarf. Pulls it free and shakes her hair loose. She feels the sun's warmth on her face for the first time that day.

"He won't… *die,* will he?"

"Moody?" The Kid gives her a grin. "A dozen stitches and he'll be okay. But it'll be a long time, Angie—a long time before he disrespects another woman."

She nods.

The Kid glances sideways, almost sheepishly. "You okay? Because, y'know, sometimes you gotta stare it down an' spit in its face. Whatever's tearing you apart inside."

She doesn't know what he's talking about, but she feels an unexpected laugh escape. Scared and horrified and at the same moment peaceful in a way she doesn't begin to comprehend. The breeze tosses her hair and she's not sure why but she laughs again, releasing herself into the insanity of it all.

"Yeah, I'm okay."

"Am I right?"

"Yeah, sweetie. I think you are."

10:45 AM SUNDAY

The aroma of brewing coffee beans floods Jeff's senses. The cafe is all polished woods and potted plants, grainy black-and-white posters of a much older L.A. decorating the walls. A smattering of tables catch sunlight through the windows, a half-dozen darker booths lurking farther toward the back. Groups of young women chat and laugh. Closer to the front, Jeff eyes a young family with a toddler and shifts his gaze to another couple — they look intelligent, severe — perusing the Sunday L.A. *Times*. An older gentleman reads a paperback. He glances up and regards Jeff casually.

Jeff orders French Roast and a bran muffin, then finds an empty table. A scattering of periodicals clutter the table, courtesy of the morning's previous guests. Jeff sits. A local newspaper called *The Acorn* headlines a new park playground — there's a photograph of happy kids on swings.

Below the picture, he reads about neighbors establishing a hospital fund for somebody's grandmother. *How blissfully ordinary*, Jeff thinks. *How wonderfully normal*—and here he sits, a world away, surrounded by death, drugs and the DEA. It all suddenly feels too surreal—way too James Bondish for his tastes.

Despite his discomfort with the melodramatic absurdity of it all, he realizes, down deep, he's nervous. He glances toward the parking lot and notices a white Verizon van, no windows, waiting at the curb several yards away. A covert vehicle or phone trouble? He's not sure, his mind throwing shit at him, mixing him up. The man reading the paperback stands up and walks out. A guy about sixty. He looks like a stockbroker.

Jeff sips his coffee and nibbles on the muffin, thinking mostly about Jeanne. Worrying about her, alone with Angie in that big mansion up there in the hills. Crazy. The whole weekend one big—

Three teenage girls come in, chattering and laughing. Jeff doesn't think the DEA can pull that off. The trio, in faded denim shorts and summer T's, order cappuccinos with extra chocolate and cinnamon and whipped cream. Behind them, a black guy in white running shorts—Jeff does a double take, recognizing Terrance Cutter—wearing a sloppy blue warm-up jacket, a blue headband. Cutter doesn't glance his way, waiting in line behind the teenagers, peering up at a wall menu. Jeff looks out the window, trying to act aloof, although his heart's racing.

He's still staring outside when the man with the *L.A. Times* gets up and walks to his table.

"Deputy Russell?"

"That's right."

"How do you do." There's no pretense of a first meeting, no handshake for polite formality. The man sits, the folded newspaper on the table between them. The paper parts, revealing an open leather ID case, the wink of a gold badge. His companion, a younger woman, remains seated, glancing through the Travel section.

"I'm Benjamin Roman. I trust Agent Cutter's told you about me?"

Jeff nods.

"Good. I want to let you know—personally let you know—how crucial you may be to our investigation. What I want to do is determine if your facts gel with ours. Ask you some questions. You have any problem with that?"

"No."

Roman smiles, like a man in a fast car, all the traffic lights green. "You're still a guest at the Logan estate, correct?"

"Yes, we are."

"Occupied by Elvio Zapata and a Dwight Manetti?"

Jeff nods again.

"But still no sign of Micky Logan?"

"Oh, yeah—about Logan."

Roman raises an eyebrow.

"He's dead."

Roman regards Jeff with a dubious expression, then cautiously repeats the word. "Dead."

"Angie told me Logan's buried somewhere under the rose bushes. She swears he was about to kill her on some sort of lark. Mr. Zapata and Mr. Manetti intervened, shot Mr. Logan. Saved her life."

"You're saying that Micky got himself killed over a *woman?*"

"Angie wouldn't make this up."

"It doesn't make sense."

"Tell me about it."

"If that were true—" But Roman lets the sentence hang between them. "You realize Micky Logan is a prime trafficker in this city. We're talking major league narcotics."

"So I figured."

"Strong Mafia ties. If somebody's taken Micky out, I doubt it's over your sister-in-law."

"Angie said it was somewhat spontaneous."

"She tell you when this incident took place?"

"I'm guessing a couple days ago. Not long before she called my wife."

"If Logan's dead and your sister-in-law witnessed the killing—" Roman pauses again. "What concerns me is that apparently nobody's aware of Logan's demise."

"That's a problem?"

They regard each other over the small table. "I'm going to need a favor, deputy."

Something about the tone Jeff doesn't like.

"You're intentions are to return to Jamul?"

"Today, as soon as possible. Yesterday, if I could have. Your man Cutter convinced me to hang out until we talked."

"Then you're not going to appreciate what I have to say."

"No. Somehow I get the feeling I won't."

"Have you told anyone else about Logan's death? Any of my people? Agent Cutter?"

"No."

"Nobody in your own department?"

Jeff shakes his head.

"Intel like this — well, it has a nasty way of leaking out around the edges. Of slipping through the cracks, getting to all the wrong ears. Good, good. If no one knows, I doubt you're in any danger. What I'd like you to do is extend your stay another day or two."

"You're *serious?*"

It's the first time either man has spoken above a whisper. Jeff's aware of the three teenagers glancing over, conscious of Cutter's quick look.

"I'm sorry," Roman says patiently, "but if we can verify Logan's death — well, trust me, this is big news. His absence would change the entire infrastructure of trafficking from Orange County to Ventura. We'll need more information, and we'll need it fast. Your accessibility may be crucial."

"I'm not sure what else I can do."

Roman studies him with thoughtful silence. "You realize there's a chance you're wrong. That you've been deceived. Micky Logan's been bulletproof for a very long time. Your sister-in-law — excuse me, but she's a prostitute, no?"

Jeff feels a hot flush against his cheeks.

"Prostitutes aren't typically considered reliable witnesses." Roman spreads his hands apologetically. "Certain people may be trying to impress her with false bravado. Maybe she's easily confused, even lying to you."

"Angie isn't like that."

"If nothing else, your continued presence insures your sister-in-law's current state of health. You're a deputy sheriff. I doubt anyone at the Logan estate is going to mess with your family, or with Angie, while you're on the premises."

"There's another consideration. I'm not trying to scare you, Jeff—" Apparently they're on a first name basis now, and Roman's pause seems exaggerated. "—but if she's privy to a murder, best case scenario is she's a witness. Worst case, she's an accessory. Here's the way I see it. You want her safe and *we* want her safe. You work with us a few more days, keep your eyes and ears open, and I give you my word, *whatever* her part in this, she's kept clear. Completely out of the stink. Does that sound reasonable to you?"

Despite the man's casual tone, his air of concern, Jeff's conscious of the implication. Roman's throwing out a deal. Call it blackmail. Call it good police work. Jeff isn't sure.

"I need another day to get the ball rolling. I'll square things with your department, let them know you're working with the feds up here in L.A. It'll look good on your resume," Roman says with a wink, attempting a smile, but the expression comes across as flat and humorless.

Jeff stares past Roman, at a trio of swaying palms outside the window. He's confused and hopes it doesn't show. Scared, and trying not to let that slip either. He realizes that he's been traded up, unwittingly into the big game. He's not certain he likes the rules here. Not certain he likes the level of deceit on either side of the field.

"I'm not asking you to snoop. I'm not asking you to risk

any sort of exposure. Don't ask questions. Simply keep your eyes and ears open. That's all."

Jeff's still wary, but what can he do?

"Oh, and one more thing," Roman says. "When I leave you'll find my card underneath this paper. My private number, day or night. You'll report to me exclusively from this point forward. No more nooners at the Federal Building, alright?"

He nods.

"I'll expect a phone check-in sometime tomorrow. At your convenience. You okay with that?"

"I think I can manage."

"Then let's call it a wrap." Roman gives him a final appraisal. "Hang around another couple of days and you might help us bring down one of the biggest crack operations in the state. Not bad for a weekend in L.A., is it, Jeff?"

11:15 AM SUNDAY

"Hurry up, Teddy, I'm late for Mass. What's this nonsense I'm hearin' about Micky wantin' to retire?"

"That's not entirely true, Mr. Capriccio," Sparanzano says into the phone. He stares absently past the glistening L.A. skyline, gazing at nothing.

"What part ain't true?"

"Micky's dead."

"You say *dead?*"

"Yes, sir."

"How do you know this thing?"

"A call from a friend of mine, the one with ears in the DEA. Told me Micky's been put down."

"Whacked?"

"By his own people."

"*Schmucks!*" Capriccio shouts, his voice crackling with intensity. Sparanzano understands his rage, understands the paranoia of a man who's spent sixty years glancing over his shoulder, spooked by shadows.

"And what?" Capriccio says. "Now these fuckers want to negotiate with us?"

"They're scared enough to try."

"Schmucks," the Duke says again. "Whadda the bums askin' for? Whadda they what?"

"Strictly cash. They want to cut and run. Four mil."

"Wha'd you say—*forty?*"

"Four million. As in one, two, three, *four.*"

"That don't hardly buy off Chinatown. This some kinda joke?"

"I don't think they know what they're doing. They got balls for asking, but it's chump change. The way I see it, this is between Micky and his own. I'm thinking we low-ball their offer, give them an even million and take over Logan's entire operation. We bring in—"

"Slow down, Teddy. Slow down. I'm all discombobulated here. You're saying give 'em the money?"

"I'm saying we don't have the entire story. Maybe they're backed by muscle and maybe not. If they have Micky's street people in their pocket, we'd be hard pressed to find new distribution without a war. But we can pay these people and make a smooth transaction, move Segal and maybe Ernie Parmucci into running Logan's end. In two months we'll have made back our entire—"

"What you don't see here is Logan's people selling us what ain't theirs to sell."

"This is true, Mr. Capriccio."

"And you wanna pay 'em a million bucks—why? Tell me again why you wanna throw 'em money?"

Sparanzano exhales slowly and closes his eyes. "To keep the peace."

"Logan, he was a good mick. Played straight with us. If unnatural harm came to him, I owe his *madre* to make it right. I'd do no less if he was Sicilian. *Capisci?*"

When Sparanzano says nothing, Capriccio adds, "It's a principle that's involved here."

"The principle may get expensive."

"Principle's got no earthly value. It was you once who tol' me that. You remember?"

"Yes, sir."

"You remember sayin' those very same words to me?"

"Yes, I do."

"I want vengeance, Teddy. Make an example of these people. Do it quick. Let these motherfuckers feel my anger while *I* feel my anger. Show 'em out on the street we don't put up with no bullshit from nobody. Make it bloody. Make it obvious."

"Yes, sir."

"Now go, do what you gotta do. You're a good boy, Teddy. Go an' make me happy."

11:30 AM SUNDAY

"Scratch him," Ben Roman says to the agents milling in the parking lot beside the Federal Building. Agents Torres and Cutter, a few others, stand around a Verizon van with expressions of quiet frustration.

"What do you mean scratch him?" Torres says.

"I mean that Russell wants out."

Trip Cutter, still in his blue warm-up, looks surprised. "What happened?"

"I told him the truth," Roman says. "That if Logan finds out he's been to the DEA, he and his wife might likely end up dead."

"You told him *that?*" Torres says.

Roman shrugs. "It's a fact, Renee. I'm not going to pull any punches with the guy. He's a citizen."

"Jesus. He's a deputy sheriff."

"And out of his league. He's got a wife and sister-in-law in a precarious situation and he's spooked. If he can't give us one hundred percent, then he's a liability. He's leaving this afternoon, taking his wife back to Jamul."

"With*out* Ms. Breusser?" Torres asks, frowning.

"He's taking her along as well."

Cutter shakes his head. "Look, maybe if I—"

"Finito. End of story," Roman tells them. The discussion ceases. He gives both Torres and Trip Cutter a sullen gaze. "Tomorrow's another day. It's not the end of the world. We tried and we'll try again. Go home, get some rest and enjoy the remnants of your weekend. Have a couple Bloody Marys and shake it off. That's an order."

12:15 PM SUNDAY

"Are we leaving?" Jeannie asks with visible apprehension.

Jeff blows a rush of air out his nose. "Not exactly. Not yet."

"But you said—?"

"The DEA wants us to stay."

"*Stay?*"

"Maybe another couple of days."

"We already told—"

Jeff raises his hands, a gesture of surrender. "We'll have to find a reason to tell them—I don't know, that somehow you made a mistake. Maybe you didn't have access to all the information you needed. Convince Mr. Manetti that Micky—that his stepfather, hell, *whoever* it is—was worth a whole lot more. Maybe a whole lot less."

"I'm not sure I can do that," Jeanne says.

"Up until now we're the only ones not lying through our teeth. It's time we played catch up."

"I don't like this."

"I'm not particularly thrilled either, babe."

She nods, absently biting on her lip. Jeff thinks about the Smith .38 locked in his duffle bag. Suddenly wanting it closer.

"And Angie?" she asks.

"Yeah, about Angie—" Jeff glances up, his sister-in-law's absence suddenly conspicuous.

"She went for a drive with Dwight."

"A drive?"

"They'll be back in an hour or so," she says impatiently. "So what *about* Angie?"

"There's a chance Angie could be in serious trouble. If we stay another couple days, help out the DEA, the agent I talked to, he says he'll keep her safe. He made some insinuating comments about Angie being an accessory to murder."

"Jeff?"

"Don't worry. I told him we'll hang around. They want more information. Didn't ask me to spy or anything, only to keep my ears open. Whether we stay or go, it's up to you. Jeannie, you want to get the hell out of here, we're out of here. This minute."

"Not without Angie."

"Yeah. That's what I figured. We pull her out now, maybe all the wrong people follow us home."

Jeanne's stunned into silence.

"The thing is, if Angie's in over her head, I pretty much put her there." His gaze drops and then reluctantly meets Jeanne's, searching her face apologetically. "I went to the DEA because I thought I was making the right decision. I'm a sheriff, for God's sake. Except the things I told them — well, suddenly they're telling me Angie might be an accessory. Whatever Angie is, she's *not* an accessory. That much I know."

"We'll be okay," Jeanne says. "Angie will be okay. We'll do what the DEA wants and then we'll get her as far away from here as we can. For now, we do what we have to."

"Which means we lie," Jeff tells her.

She nods. "Like a goddamn rug."

12:45 PM SUNDAY

Jeanne meets Dwight and Angie in the doorway, her sister with an oddly tranquil expression and the Kid looking somehow self-satisfied. Swaggering a bit, it seems to her. Not quite smug, but content.

"Nice drive?" Jeanne asks, trying to keep the worry out of her voice.

"Yeah. Not bad." Angie looks at Dwight, the two of them making some sort of secret connection.

"I hate to spoil the party."

"What's up?" the Kid asks.

"We might have a problem."

"Yeah? What's that?" The Kid remains brazen, at the moment able to handle anything. Giving Jeannie an easy smile.

"I've may have made a mistake with the books. Not a mistake, per say. I think — " But the Kid holds up his hands, the smile gone, a sudden panicked glaze in his eyes. He takes a few jolting steps into the living area, "Elvis! Hey, Elvis!"

"It's nothing to worry about," Jeanne tells Angie. "Trust me. I just need some more information."

Another *trust me*, Angie thinks. Her day for surprises.

Dwight comes back in a few moments with Elvis tagging behind. Jeff watches from a corner. All the players assembled on the field, Angie thinks. Elvis appears disheveled, like maybe he's been sleeping all morning, and actually kind of handsome, she's surprised to realize, in his new haircut. He's wearing baggy surfer's shorts to his knees and a ratty sleeveless sweatshirt that reads *Los Perros Aztecas* in faded letters. Angie realizes that she's never seen him out of his suit before. He looks muscular—like a bear.

"There's something I've overlooked," Jeanne tells them. "Something your, um, your stepfather's books don't show and I'm a bit concerned. It's about the debit column. Non-reimbursable business purchases that can affect your P&L by a significant margin. Those figures don't show up anywhere and I think they're important."

Jeanne's not comfortable lying. If Jeff hadn't been standing there she wouldn't have pulled it off. She can't bring herself to look at Angie and keeps her eyes focused on Dwight.

"You mean what you told us last night? It might have been too much?"

"I'm afraid so. Those numbers aren't anywhere in the ledgers. And unless we can find them—?" She waits a moment while both men ogle empty spaces around the room. "Could there be any *other* records of transactions, checkbooks, anywhere else your stepfather might have kept private figures or notes?"

The Kid looks at Elvis and Elvis thinks about Micky's floor safe again, the one in the den—all the shit Micky's stuffed down there over the years. Envelopes and paperwork that Elvis never much thought about before, other than all that money, a good chunk on its way to Tel Aviv with Leo Sussman.

"Gimme a minute," Elvis tells her.

"You know what she's sayin'?" Dwight's like a gnat at Elvis' ear, the two of them midway down the hall, the Kid bouncing off the walls, annoying the shit out of him.

"She's sayin' we maybe asked for too much money. Jesus Christ, man. We're dealing with the fuckin' Mafia, man, and maybe we asked for too much money!"

"Yeah, I know wha' she's sayin'."

"Shit, man. Maybe we shoulda bailed outta here when we had the chance."

Elvis puts a hand out and palms the Kid in the chest mid-stride, halting him with an "*Oomph*" in front of Micky's door.

"Wait here."

Elvis locks himself in the room and fingers the safe's release mechanism from behind Micky's desk. He jerks back a floor rug and pulls up the false block of floorboard. Elvis stares down into the gaping hole where Micky's mad money had been—close to five hundred large still zipped inside a duffel bag because he wasn't stupid enough to give it all to Leo. Elvis ignores the bag and sifts through a pile of plastic accordion folders, finds a third leather ledger that he's seen Micky use only once before. He blows a light dusting off the cover and sticks it under one arm. He closes the safe and spends another minute putting the room back in order.

Midway to the door, Elvis wonders if it had been a mistake, giving Leo the boot. Wondering if it should have been *him* on that airplane to Tel Aviv.

1:15ᴘᴍ SUNDAY

Danny Fortuna calls Shep Boco and tells him to get Richie Moya and Al Liola—Liola a guy who's done freelance jobs with Danny's crew in the past and can handle an automatic. Can take out an alarm system or blow a breaker panel quicker than anyone else he knows. Danny tells Shep they'll need some heavy artillery for this one—get Moya to round up some hardware and have everyone together by seven-thirty, the usual place. Sit tight and wait for his call.

Then, because Danny Fortuna always gets amped before a hit, he calls Gina and tells her he'll be over in half an hour, saying he doesn't want no fuckin' phone calls while he's there and make sure there's no crud on the sheets.

Danny pours himself a tumbler of Jack Daniels over a wedge of lemon and sits with his feet on the couch, listening to Chris Isaak with his eyes closed. Thirty minutes later, a second tumbler gone, he figures *fuck it*, swaying a bit when he stands up. He finds a leather belt in his bureau, a brass buckle dangling with sufficient weight, and staggers off to find Gina.

The wound hasn't closed, the trash can in his bathroom overflowing with bloody gauze. Elvis figures he's going to bleed a slow death if he sits around doing nothing much longer. He knows of a few clinics in L.A.—get in, get stitched, get out again—but most of those places have eyes and ears he can't trust. One thing about LeRoy Beers, he knows all the same people Elvis knows.

He patches his shoulder and walks into the living room but can't find a soul. Maybe everybody's halfway out of state by now. Elvis wonders if he should hop into his Caddy and drive until the road ends, no particular destination in mind.

But there's maybe one place he *can* go.

Micky bought the silver Bentley Mulsanne on a lark a few years back, but then had second thoughts. He quickly realized the car was too pretentious for a dealer, even in L.A. "I get enough fucking attention," he told Elvis, Micky suddenly with buyer's remorse.

They'd occasionally taken the Bentley up north, those few times that Micky wanted to go wine tasting in Napa, or that weekend in San Francisco when Micky paid fifteen hundred bucks to see Celine Dion—third row center—in concert. They'd put a few miles on the car since then, but not many, Micky with no inclination to head out of town come lately.

Elvis doesn't take his copper Fleetwood this afternoon. Too many people know the car and he doesn't want somebody catching his trail out of town. Elvis points the Bentley north, driving in pain as he snakes his way up PCH into Malibu and toward Point Mugu. A few times he pulls to the side of the road and waits a minute or two, eyeing the rearview. By the time he makes Camarillo—Pacific Coast Highway jutting inland, merging with the 101—Elvis pretty much figures he's alone.

He's in Oxnard fifteen minutes later and turns west on Rice, picking his way past Del Sol Park, the Bentley glaringly out of place among the pickups and old Hondas, the Chevy low-riders and primer-patched Mazdas. Elvis drives with the window down and smells flame-roasted *pollo* and *chorizo* along the narrow streets of closely situated, wood-frame houses. English might not be spoken for days in these neighborhoods—the kind of place LeRoy Beers might find as alien as the dark side of the moon. For the first time since Micky Logan died, Elvis feels safe. A moment later he spots a small house, dark brown, the shades pulled, the door and window trim painted a dull, fading red.

A few years back, Tomas Ruiz dated Elvis' sister, Rosa. He's a thin guy with a big gut and a bushy, black and white mustache. Tomas is an unlicensed veterinarian who raises and sells gamecocks. He stitches birds back together again on Saturday nights after the bouts. Because Tomas had been good to his sister, Elvis squared a gambling debt for him the previous year. Tomas would have happily married Rosa, except she wanted him to go to Mass on Sundays and Wednesdays and give up cockfighting, weed and alcohol—and even Elvis agreed that sometimes the woman asked for too much.

Elvis knocks on the red-trimmed screen door. Tomas appears from a back room. He's shirtless, wearing torn jeans and carrying a bandaged rooster under his arm. He clutches a perspiring Modelo Especial in one hand.

"Come in," Tomas says, in Spanish. His expression sours. "You've lost blood."

Elvis follows the man through a hallway devoid of out-side light. Chickens cluck and run from the intrusion. Elvis glances into a room, sees a fat hen nesting atop a TV set.

"Rosa fears you'll be dead in a year or two," Tomas remarks over his shoulder.

"Maybe sooner," Elvis admits.

"Knife," Tomas asks, "or gun?"

"Bullet. A graze."

"Good. You won't need a tetanus. Sit."

Elvis does so, on a small white bed in a small white room, metal cabinets lining the walls and a glaring light overhead. He's surprised to realize that the room looks remarkably like a doctor's office. Maybe some rooster shit here and there on the floor, but otherwise clean and orderly, smelling of disinfectant. He removes his shirt and Tomas peers at the wound.

"Thirty-eight, eh? I think maybe nicked the *supraspinatus*, what they call the right rotator cuff muscle in your shoulder. You may lose a little strength, a little movement over time. But you're lucky."

Elvis, a lefty, nods indifferently.

"This is your axillary artery." Tomas pokes gently at a spot half an inch below the wound. "Bullet hits here, your whole body pours out in less than a minute."

He moves to one of the metal cabinets and rummages, finds a hooked needle and a coil of thick black thread. Tomas says, "*¡Un momento!*" with sudden inspiration and leaves the room, then returns with three yellow tablets and a bottle of *4Copas*. Elvis washes down the pills with the tequila and feels an immediate burn inside his stomach. Tomas waits until Elvis has taken several more swallows, then sucks in a breath and began to stitch. Elvis winces, every nerve in his neck screaming. He thinks longingly about Simone's pink and blue cantina on a sun-drenched hillside in Baja. The illusion suffices.

3:30 PM SUNDAY

She picks at a Chinese noodle salad with non-fat sesame dressing, reading *Elle*. Torres' stocking feet hang off the end of the couch, her toes subliminally keeping time to Thalía's *Gracias* turned low in the background. The phone rings. Her office line is forwarded here, so she reaches over and answers.

"Y'ello?"

Silence. Torres hears breathing, a ragged, scratchy sound. On a hunch she says, "Gina?"

A small sob hiccups against her ear. Gina's never before called on a weekend. A chill creeps along Torres' spine.

"Gina?"

A whisper. "He's a fuck. A lousy *fuck*."

"What's wrong?"

"I don't care anymore. I don't fucking care."

Torres waits.

"It's Danny," the voice tells her. "Danny Fortuna just left."

"Where are you?"

"My apartment."

Another chill. "Your apartment?" Gina phones from a pay booth off of 29th Street because she swears her line's bugged. Swears Danny has an ear to her place.

"Fuck 'em," she says. "Don't care if he's listening or not. You *hear* me, Danny? *Fuck you to death!*" She takes a deep breath, lets it out in a shaky rattle. "He hurt me. Did... *things* to me. I don't care any more."

"I'm coming to get you."

"I'll be gone. I'm buying a bus ticket out of this shit hole. I swear to God, five minutes from now, I'm already gone."

"Gina?"

"Before I go, I gotta tell you something. Danny Fortuna's gonna fuckin' kill somebody. Last time he went this kind of crazy on me, they found Aldo Tuccini in the bay, sucking his pecker."

"Who, Gina? Who's he going to kill?"

"Dunno. The street says Micky Logan's collectin' worms. Somebody's gonna pay for that. But maybe someone else. I don't know."

"Logan?" Torres asks, startled to hear the name.

"Consider it a freebie. You see Danny Fortuna, shoot the bastard in the fucking nut sack. This one's on the house."

"Gina, wait a—"

But the line's already dead.

4:00 PM SUNDAY

Gina empties three drawers of jeans and sweaters into her suitcase. She leaves her working clothes hanging in the small closet—eight hundred dollars of gaudy fabric for the next working girl to claim. Gina's already on her second glass of Charles Shaw Merlot and eighty milligrams of OxyContin, and Danny Fortuna doesn't seem so goddamn tough anymore. She decides to shower—long and hot—because her Korean landlord busts her balls for taking long, hot showers, but fuck *him* too. She dresses in brown corduroys and a white long-sleeve Oxford that covers the bruises on her arms and back, her hair combed nice and braided. She's done her best with her makeup, dabbing at the marks Fortuna's left on her face.

She knows she has to hurry, but the Oxy-cocktail is distorting time. She knows she's running late for the bus, but then decides to call her mother. She tells the old woman, "Mama, I'm comin' home."

Her mother cries and praises Jesus, then starts in about her brother's parole hearing up at Lubbock and how she planted chrysanthemums last Sunday atop her sweet daddy's grave. Oh, and cousin Maxine's given birth to twin boys down in Austin. Cute as buttons.

Gina bounces on one foot, then the other, going buggy listening to her mother prattle on. Finally she says, "Look, I gotta run and catch the Greyhound. Be there tomorrow morning." Her mother tells her how her bedroom's still the same, not a thing out of place. Gina visualizes the pink flowered wallpaper and the Micky Mouse quilt and the lace pillows they'd bought at Bible Patch Village over in Gran-geville. Gina's acutely aware of the time now, the seconds ticking while she listens to the old lady fuss. "Ma, I really gotta go."

Shep Boco knows how to jimmy a door and enter a room without a sound—suddenly there he is, in your face. The lock on Gina's door clicks in about three sec-onds. Boco stands in the doorway, listening. He hears a voice—somebody on a telephone. He glimpses a half-kitchen off to the left, a living room the size of a post-age stamp. There's a bathroom at the end of the hall, a bedroom doorway to the left. He hears Gina say, "*See you soon, Mama.*"

Boco moves forward, his big Browning out, the six-inch Martoni muffler fitted in place. A couple more steps and he's able to peer around the corner.

Gina pushes the last few items in her suitcase, locks it and drops it to the floor next to the bed—fear beginning to creep in around the edges of her pleasant buzz. She's about to grab her jacket and head for the door when a shadow moves against the wall. She turns.

"Shouldn't go 'round saying things about your boy-friend, honey."

She opens her mouth and Boco shoots her, the gun making a dull ping. A tongue of blood spits from beneath Gina's collarbone. The momentum flings her back against the dresser, hanging her up for a moment, her eyes wide, her face ashen.

"You ugly *fuck*," she screams.

He shoots her again, low this time, the bullet cutting

into her stomach, doubling her over, not killing her out-right because she's pissed him off calling him names and he's not about to let her slip away so easily. She goes down on all fours behind the bed and Boco rises on his tiptoes, trying to sneak a look. He hears her moan and sob. Boco smiles to himself, taking his time stepping around the foot of the bed, the Browning's silenced snout making lazy cir-cles at the ceiling.

He sees the gun in her bloody hand—not at all expecting it—the barrel barely the length of her fin-ger. The Beretta makes a pop. A blinding agony stitches through his left eye, punching him backwards against the closet door. Boco claws at his face, his hands sticky wet, his head exploding in such terrible pain. His heart thuds and jerks in an angry place between his eyes, pound-ing, searing his brain until all thought succumbs to the agony.

The little gun slips from Gina's fingers, her only thought the door across the room. She grips the side of the bed frame and pulls herself to her feet. The pain in her gut radiates through her body in churning waves. She clenches one fist against her belly, guiding herself with her other hand, leaving a smear of blood across the sheets. Three more steps to the bedroom door—but somebody's standing there, watching her.

"Need some help, hon?"

She's aware of the pistol, of the pearly whiteness of Richie Moya's smile.

Moya shoots her in the forehead, the impact flinging her spread-eagle onto the bed with a grunt, her arms flung wide. Moya steps forward and, because he wants to, he shoots her three more times, slowly, each shot rocking Gina up and down on the creaky springs, up and down, up and down, her blood coloring the sheets.

Moya turns and sees Boco huddled against the wall, both hands cupping his face. He's whimpering, blood oozing bright red through his fingers, drooling to the floor. Moya doesn't mind the sight of it, but the leaking bits of greenish-gray stuff trouble him.

In the closest gesture he's ever made toward human compassion, Moya points his gun above Shep Boco's right ear and squeezes the trigger.

5:15 PM SUNDAY

"I don't like it, Danny."

Sparanzano presses his fingers against his temple, soothing away the swirling colors of his displeasure. "Shep was family. That some two-dollar whore could take him from us? It's an omen."

Fortuna says nothing. Boco's death doesn't bother him as much as that it was Gina who pulled the trigger. She should have been *his* hit. Shep would still be alive and the whore would have died screaming his name.

"She got off easy," Fortuna replies with a shrug.

"She was ratting us out to the feds, Danny. Maybe a long time and we never knew. Benjamin never knew or he'd have told us. I don't like it."

"Couldn't have told 'em much."

"The point is — I don't appreciate surprises. She fingered you for the hit tonight, Danny."

"She don't know who."

"Does it matter?"

Fortuna shrugs again.

"We're losing our peace, and for what purpose?"

Fortuna's not sure if Teddy Sparks expects an answer or not. He waits patiently.

"Have you had any dreams recently, Danny?"

"Dreams?"

"Dreams about water? Or winged insects?"

Fortuna slowly shakes his head.

Sparanzano spends a moment in thought. "If I had my way, I'd pay Mr. Zapata his money. I'd wish him well and offer my condolences for whatever fate befell Micky. I'd walk in tomorrow and it would be business as usual. In a few months our debt would be gone and we'd have Logan's entire interest in-house. One less outsider. One less cut. But Mr. Capriccio says it's about honor. So for the sake of honor, we muddy the waters. We cause our own problems to erase those made by others."

Fortuna's never felt comfortable around his boss's esoteric meanderings. When he's sure Sparanzano is finished, he says; "How you want it done?"

Teddy Sparks sighs. "Make it look like gangs, Danny. Hell, I don't care — make it look like Mormons if you want. But you stay out of it. The whore said your name to one of Roman's people. So tonight, you and I dine at Valentino. We stay late, so when the feds find Mr. Zapata dead and look around to point a finger, it won't be at us. A dozen waiters will alibi our presence."

Fortuna nods.

"Have Richie take over the hit."

"Yeah, him and Al Liola. But what about Shep?"

"Use Tommy the Shark."

"He pulled three years at Atascadero a few weeks back."

"Tommy did? That's too bad. What about Nick Whasis-name?"

"Nick Garbianni? He's in a fucking Winnebago with his wife and kids for a month. Went up to Canada to fish."

"Then use Vinnie."

"Man, I dunno," Fortuna says cautiously.

"Vinnie's been asking me—" Sparanzano pauses, having second thoughts, then waves them away. "Use Vinnie," he says again. "He's available and the Duke wants this to happen tonight."

"If you're sure that's what you want."

"Get it done, Danny," Sparanzano says quietly. "Bring Mr. Capriccio his honor. Bring me my tranquility."

Fortuna silently eyes the half-empty bottle of Chianti on the table and shakes his head; all this talk about insects and omens and shit, and now this—using Vinnie on a hit. Vinnie, who can't find his ass with both hands in the dark. Jesus.

Midway down the elevator, Fortuna wonders if maybe he should have mentioned the giant blue grasshoppers. In his dream last night dozens of them tapped and bumped against his bedroom window, mewling at him like baby kittens, their faces morphing into those of dead men—men who Fortuna remembered killing over the years. Pretty fucking spooky.

5:45 PM SUNDAY

"It's not so bad," Jeanne says. "I have a feeling about Angie."

Jeff offers her his usual look.

"This time, I think she's ready."

"You've been saying that for, what—almost a year?"

"She's scared enough to come home. I think the fact that you've—" Jeanne stops.

He's curious. "I've what?"

"You've listened."

"I haven't before?"

"You were too busy being a sheriff."

"It's what I do, babe."

"But it's not who you *are*. It was always your badge talking to her, not your heart. Last night you were family. Someone who cared."

"I've always cared about her."

"Because of me," Jeanne tells him. "Because she's my sister."

Jeff wonders if that's true.

Jeanne puts her arms around him. "Last night, you cared about Angie because she was *Angie*. I noticed it, and she did too." Jeanne gives him a look. The kind of look he doesn't always understand.

"I wonder if you truly know how much I love you?"

Kissing him hard then, before he has a chance to answer.

Elvis had gotten back from Oxnard an hour before, parking the Bentley at a crooked angle in the garage, stumbling from the car, the driver's door still partially open. He
enters through the kitchen, past the laundry and exercise
rooms, pausing to listen to the silence inside the house.
He'd choked down a few more Demerol in the car — Tomas
had given him several dozen pills, also penicillin, warning
him to go easy on the meds. Too late, Elvis already sloppy
stoned by the time he reached Malibu.

He staggers upstairs and into his bedroom with its
king size bed of rough hewn, hammered pine — extra long
because so was Elvis — a pine bureau and dresser with copper pull handles, expensive prints of bullfighters and bull-
fights on the walls. Elvis could have picked up the furniture
in TJ for a couple of bills, but Micky had dropped eight
grand in a boutique shop in West Hollywood, expensively
replicating Mexican shabby. Elvis locked the door behind
him and stumbled into bed.

He fumbles for the remote on the nightstand, flipping
until he found *futbol mexicano* on his wall-mounted wide-
screen HDTV with 230 channels. For a long moment he
watches brightly jerseyed players — green and yellow, red
and white — swim back and forth until the colors blur. The
next thing he knows he's standing behind the bar in Simone's cantina, making strawberry margaritas for a bunch of
happy gringo *turistas* in skimpy summer clothes. Even his
gran'mama is there — standing outside El Culo Perezoso of

course—looking at him through a window, flashing a big toothless grin.

"Hey, bartender," somebody says and Elvis glances back, but the happy ladies are gone. Instead, Danny Fortuna and Teddy Sparks wait at the bar, wearing Hawaiian shirts and big-brimmed straw hats. He searches frantically for his *gran'mama* again but she's not there. Instead, LeRoy Beers gives him a crazy smile through the window—Beers with a shotgun suddenly pointed, the barrel tip up against the wavy window glass. The gun goes *boom, boom* and *boom* again. Boom, boom, boom—

Elvis wakes to a knock at the door, hearing Angie's voice above the vague mumble of the TV, Angie saying, "Elvis? Are you in there?" Her knock persistent.

"Elvis? Hey, Elvis?"

He works cotton from his mouth and says, "Yeah?"

"Jeannie's hungry. She's taking an hour off to eat. You want to join us?" Elvis blinks several times, aware of a yellow hue outside the window and glances curiously at a clock, surprised to find a few hours gone. He grabs the remote and turns off the TV.

"Elvis?" Angie asks.

"Yeah," he says again, still light-headed, but not concerned because Micky always keeps plenty of food—Santa Fe chicken and Gorgonzola salad, roast beef slices and baked beans, teriyaki chicken wings, bacon-wrapped feta cheese bites, veal-stuffed mushrooms and egg salad with bits of Canadian ham and black olive. A smorgasbord of foods swirl dizzily inside his head.

"You want to join us?" Angie asks patiently.

Elvis tells her *gracias*, he's not hungry, and closes his eyes again. Colors swim behind his eyelids. But Elvis finds himself oddly alert—the hazy remnants of LeRoy Beers' grin fading from his memory. And here he is, napping like some old *abuelo*—something he'll never be if he doesn't get his ass in gear.

He moves slowly to the bathroom and splashes water on his face, then spends a moment admiring Tomas' sutures in the mirror before he dresses—white shirt, black suit, shoulder holster, polished Florsheims from his closet—and wanders downstairs. He hears Angie's distant laughter but turns the other direction. He walks to Micky's library and closes the door behind him.

He passes Micky's desk, the humming computer, all of Jeanne's papers and printouts strewn about. Elvis steps to the bookshelves—two entire walls filled with books; art books and computer manuals, reference stuff that Elvis never understood why Micky collected. Travel books on Ireland and Wales, Tahiti and Singapore and the Canary Islands—and chemistry books, which at least make sense, Micky being a chemist of sorts. His gaze skips over the leather-bound classics like *Moby Dick* and *Tale of Two Cities* and *Of Mice and Men*, a bunch of Shakespeare, books that Micky once told him were, like, an integral part of any dude's fuckin' library.

Elvis finds what he wants and begins to pull volumes down. He's sitting at Micky's desk when the Kid opens the door and pokes his head in. "Elvis, hey, there you are. Been looking all over. Angie wants to know if you're—"

The Kid takes a few steps into the room, holding a half-empty bottle of Corona. "What, you're *readin'*?"

Elvis feels like he's been caught somehow, uncomfortable, the Kid coming toward him with a curious expression. He picks up a book from the stack in front of Elvis. "*Magic and Sorcery?* You're shittin' me, right? Abracadabra, alacazoom?"

"They're Micky's," Elvis says.

The Kid pokes at another book. "*The Ways of Tarot?*" Pronouncing the last T, like *carrot*. The Kid gives him a wide grin.

Elvis feels a hot throb of embarrassment.

"*Mysteries Of The Occult,*" The Kid says, still reading titles.

"You *wan'* somethin' here or what?"

"My karma ran over your dogma," the Kid tells him, taking a swig of beer. "You ever see that on a bumper sticker?" He smiles but gets nothing out of Elvis.

"Hey, Angie wants to know if you want a beer. They're already chowin' down. But I'll tell her you're too busy studyin' for final exams." The Kid waggles his bottle, leaving Elvis with a good-natured smirk.

Elvis wonders what he means. *My karma and your dogma?* Maybe something Sparanzano would know about—and why he's sitting here with all these books, feeling stupid.

5:45 PM SUNDAY

Ben Roman's phone rings. Peggy knows not to answer; she lets it ring seven times until she hears the bathroom door open and her husband's footsteps in the hallway. A moment later the heavy den door clicks shut.

"Yes?"

"I thought you should know," Sparanzano says, "We're about to clean house."

Roman says nothing.

"I'm telling you because one of your people might have been tipped. A female agent of yours."

"One of mine? I've got four, five women in the field," Roman says. "You have a name?"

"I'm afraid I don't. But an acquaintance of ours, a girl named Gina, had a big mouth. I wanted you to be aware," Sparanzano says. "Should questions arise."

Roman suspects immediately, of course. Renee Torres. He fidgets in this chair. "Teddy, listen to me —"

"We're doing this tonight. My employer wants immediacy."

"Tonight? No, wait. That deputy cop's still over there."

"Of course. What did you think?"

"Christ almighty, I wanted him *isolated*, not dead. He's not part of this."

"He knows that our celebrated friend has left town. What additional information from him do we need? Perhaps he knows far more than he's telling us. If we do this now, it saves us from doing it later, attracting more attention."

"For Chrissake, his wife's with him. They're fucking tourists."

"I'm sorry, my hands are tied. I'm running late. I have reservations at seven-thirty. You understand, of course."

Roman rages silently.

As if aware, Sparanzano sighs into the phone. "Every once in awhile—you know the game we play. This is the life we've chosen, Ben. These people will depart for a better place. Sooner or later, we all do."

Torres is going bat shit crazy. She's dialed Gina's number a dozen times over the last few hours before she finally relents, assuming Gina's on a Greyhound bound for obscurity. She knows Trip's not in a good mood—having dinner tonight with his brother up in Agoura Hills, with his wife and two young daughters and trying to forget the morning's fiasco.

But her conversation with Gina continues to rattle and hum inside her head. She tries to convince herself that the woman's been wrong numerous times before, too eager to embellish the facts in exchange for the cash Torres throws her way. Occasionally outright lying for rent money, or simply with a need to chitchat. *This* time, Gina's words eat through Torres' brain like a cancer. She needs to know for sure, and she also knows it's a conversation she won't be able to pull off alone.

She can't wait any longer. She finds the courage to call

Trip's cell. He's a few beers into the evening already, on the verge of petulance when she tells him it's important. No, she can't explain yet, but she reiterates. It's important.

The thing about Cutter—he's the best friend she has. And angry enough to be curious. He tells her he'll pick her up in about an hour.

When he pulls up in front of her apartment, it's closer to ninety minutes. She doesn't mention it, even half in jest.

"So how long you gonna keep me in the dark, girl?" Trip Cutter asks from behind the wheel of his big silver Ford Aerostar, the family's toy-cluttered utility vehicle.

Riding shotgun, Torres keeps her eyes on the road. They've already made PCH, the ocean a velvet sheen against the horizon. Twilight casts the mountains in a chalky purple shadow, the sky ahead already a dark cadmium blue. The crescent moon glows high against the ocean. "A few more miles, Trip. Turn left up here, at the light."

She knows if Micky Logan answers the door, alive and well, she'll apologize and walk away, and tomorrow morning Gina's *persona non grata* in her little black book. If not? Hell, whatever they find at One Barranca Vista will be more than they know now.

They drive several minutes in silence, until Cutter says, "Okay, so tell me this isn't one of those we're-in-deep-shit instincts of yours."

"You're a love."

"And don't start talking goofy at me. Yvonne thinks you're sweet on me as it is."

"You still haven't told her, have you?" Spoken almost tenderly, with a smile.

Cutter shrugs. "No need."

"I don't mind, you know. Her knowing."

"It's good for her," Cutter tells her. "Keeps her sharp, thinking about all these pretty *white* women maybe after my bones. Keeps her on her toes."

"Uh huh. Take a right up here."

Cutter nods, assuming that whatever's eating her up will eventually wiggle its way out. He's used to her moods. He turns the van into the foothills. The night is immediately darker here, far more ominous as they leave the frivolity and colorful lights flanking the Santa Monica beaches.

Another few miles up the winding canyon road and it dawns on him.

"Shit a brick. We're going to see Logan, aren't we?"

"Give the man a five cent cee-gar," she says softly.

"And the *reason* for this particular excursion?"

"Because I'm pissed about always being one step behind. I'm tired of getting the cold shoulder, every time I mention Teddy Sparks. Tired of people running out the back door, every time I think we can get close to the man."

Cutter shoots her a look. "You're talking about Russell, aren't you?"

"He's the tip of the iceberg but—okay, yeah, I'm talking about Russell. Ben cut him loose too quickly. We could have used him somehow. You talked to him, Trip. You think he was a jelly sandwich?"

"Nah, Russell seemed pretty cool. A little spooked for his family maybe."

"Spooked enough to bail on us?"

He gives her another curious glance. "So why *are* we coming up here?"

"To take a look at whatever's hiding in plain sight. At whatever Ben couldn't see. Whatever Russell couldn't stick around for. I want to check for myself."

"And this couldn't have waited until tomorrow?"

"I want to rattle some cages. Besides, tomorrow might be too late."

Cutter's silent a moment, mulling her words. *Tomorrow might be too late.* He suddenly wonders why. "There's something else, isn't there."

Torres' mouth forms a thin, troubled slash. "It's time we find out once and for all if Logan's alive or dead. And if he's alive, find out why someone wants him dead enough to put him in hiding."

"Whoa, girl! Who wants Logan dead? What are you talking about?"

"I think Sparanzano's orchestrating a hit."

"Man, you got Teddy Sparks on the *brain*, you know that? We don't even—Wait a minute, what do you mean a hit? You're tellin' me *now*? Where'd you get this kind of intel? Jesus Christ."

"It's a feeling, Trip. Just something I overheard."

"So you and I are gonna waltz right in? And do what?"

"And blow smoke," Torres says.

"Roman doesn't know about this?"

"Not yet." Several seconds tick by. "I have my reasons."

"Maybe it's time you told me?"

"I don't think you'd believe me. I'm not sure I believe it

myself. After we talk to Logan, ask him a few questions — I promise, Trip. I need to see Logan. I need to be sure. Then I promise, I'll spill my guts."

8:45 PM SUNDAY

"This is way too bizarre." Jeanne takes a tooth-marked pencil from her mouth, yellow-orange slivers dotting the front of her Charger's sweatshirt. She taps the pencil on a page filled with rows and columns of precise, hand-written figures. "It's like — I don't *know* what it's like." The three ledgers, leather straps neatly sliced, lay open in front of her. "It's almost as if he's trying to keep certain assets from himself."

"Who, Logan?" Jeff asks. He's been sitting on the couch, massaging Angie's neck, Angie barefoot on the floor in front of him reading a *Cosmopolitan*. Every few minutes they trade positions, Jeff and Angie, keeping Jeanne company and mostly killing time. Jeff gets up and moves stiff-legged toward the desk, hovering near his wife's shoulder.

"What's it mean?" Angie asks. She's been taking an *Unforgettable First Date Quiz* and failing. She wonders if this morning's experience with Dwight constituted a first date of sorts, remembering Mr. Moody bleeding all over the floor. Now *there's* one for Cosmo.

"I wish I knew," Jeanne says. "You can't believe what this man was doing with his money. It's all over the place. The way he shuffled millions of dollars at a whim. Half of these figures seem like payroll numbers, but I don't know what's going to turn up or where."

"Like a scavenger hunt," Angie says.

"Exactly. I mean, see these figures here?" Jeanne points to a column with her pencil and Jeff stares at the page, lost in a fog. "If I didn't know better, I'd say he was stealing from himself. No, not really stealing. More like he's hiding assets from himself."

A six-toned chime sounds somewhere in the house.

"What's that?" Jeff wonders.

"The front gate," Angie says with a frown.

"Isn't it getting late?"

"I better go check."

"What, Manetti can't find his way to the front door?"

Angie swats him with the magazine as she passes, her mind already elsewhere. "I'll be back in a sec."

"Logan's like a magician," Jeanne says, shaking her head.

Jeff looks at the empty doorway and, despite Angie's absence, drops his voice to a whisper. "Something we can take to the feds?"

"I'm not sure they'd be able to understand this any better than I can. It's all smoke and mirrors, darling."

Elvis stands in the tiled foyer and fingers a console. A video monitor blinks, revealing a silver van under the front gate's Halcyon-lighted glare. He stares at the image for almost half a minute, then thumbs the speaker key and says, "Yeah?"

"Mr. Logan?" A woman's voice. Pleasant.

Elvis hesitates. "He ain't home."

"Mr. Zapata?"

"Who's askin'?"

"We met once before, Mr. Zapata. The Federal building on East Temple."

"You a fed?"

"My name is Renee Torres, DEA. Do you have a moment?"

"Micky ain't home," he says again.

"But you *are*."

Elvis absently rubs his earlobe, trying to think this through. "You got a warrant?"

"It's not that kind of visit. My partner and I would like to have a little chat. Off the record. It may be important."

Elvis wonders what Micky would do. He figures Micky would have been curious enough to listen.

"Mr. Zapata?"

"Five minutes," Elvis tells her and thumbs the front gait switch. He watches the van crawl up the driveway, Elvis with a bad feeling burbling in the pit of his stomach. He unsnaps the holster under his jacket and meets them at the front door.

"Mr. Zapata, I'm Agent Torres." The dark haired woman extends her hand and Elvis shakes it, engulfing her small fingers. "This is Agent Cutter. I appreciate your taking time to see us."

"Uh huh." Elvis studies the black guy with his ID out, flipped up so Elvis can see the badge, a little gold eagle sitting on top. The guy's expressionless.

Elvis backs away from the door and the two agents step inside, looking around like most people do, ogling Logan's home, getting used to the opulence.

"Mr. Logan has good taste," the black guy says.

"Yeah, Micky's got some bling."

Torres smiles pleasantly. "I take it Micky's not in this evening?"

"Nah, out somewhere."

"When's the last time you saw your boss, Mr. Zapata?"

"A few days, give or take."

"He always stay away so long?" This from Cutter, making Elvis glance away from Torres.

"Now an' then."

"On business?"

"Yeah, tha's right."

"You got a number, maybe, where he can be reached?"

Elvis looks a couple times between the black guy and the female agent, giving nothing away. He finally says, "You're wastin' your five minutes."

"After you hear what we have to say," Torres tells him, "you might want to extend our invitation."

Angie arrives a moment too late and tries to eaves-drop from a corner of the living room, not daring to peek around the archway into the foyer. The Kid gets there too, peering over her shoulder. He would have gone straight to the door but Angie grabs his arm. Better to let Elvis handle this solo. The Kid's wearing a dazed guppy look, whispering in her ear, "The feds are here? The fucking *feds?*"

Angie hears footsteps on the tile and realizes that Elvis

is escorting them into the house. She didn't expect that, barely has an instant to paint her smile, the two agents coming through the foyer, her expression caught somewhere between concern and distracted politeness.

Agent Torres doesn't react, but the black guy's expression changes. He hesitates a half step. Neither of them appears interested in further introductions.

"You mind if we have a seat?" Torres asks because Elvis has stopped walking—far enough—the five of them forming an uneasy knot in the middle of the living room. "Maybe talk a moment or two? What we have to say, well, we think you'll find it educational."

"Can we ask what this is about?" Angie asks.

The woman smiles with faux cordiality. "It's about the state of your collective health, Ms. Breusser." Dropping her name—*wham bang*—without a second's hesitation.

"We'll take a couple aspirin," Elvis says, "call you in the mornin'. "

"No, wait, what's *wrong* with our health?" Angie asks.

"The real question is, how's Micky's health? Because at the moment, I'd say yours very much depends on his." Torres lets them mull that one a couple of seconds, gauging reactions. "If Micky's alive and well, I suggest that he contact Duke Capriccio at his earliest convenience. I believe you're aware of the name?"

"Yeah, maybe heard of him," Elvis says.

"Because it seems Mr. Capriccio's got this notion that Micky isn't well. That he might be so unwell as to possibly be dead. Thing is, I know for a fact that Micky's demise would greatly disturb Mr. Capriccio"

She glances at Cutter, the big man nodding on cue, saying, "Would really tick 'im off."

"And Mr. Capriccio does not work well with angst. Last time that happened, I believe LAPD had four or five unresolved homicides, Mr. Capriccio working through his problems."

"This is—what, like a threat?"

"We're letting you know there's backfield motion in Capriccio's camp, Mr. Zapata. Does the name Teddy Sparks mean anything to you? Because we think there's a hit going down sometime soon. Somebody's pissed off The Duke. We really hope it wasn't you."

Elvis is about to tell them it's none of their fucking business—but that's when the lights go out.

Ben Roman glances at the clock every few minutes, restless, thinking about Deputy Russell—a man he's essentially set up to die. He tries to rationalize the necessity of Russell's death but can't make sense of it. He stares at the phone for a long moment, feeling the cold emptiness of the house, Peggy off now to her tai chi class and Roman alone, brooding, suddenly edgy.

He tries Torres' cellphone—but she's not answering. She's not picking up her home phone either. Roman gets her machine but doesn't leave a message. It's not like her to be out of reach. He fixes himself a J&B over ice and returns to his desk, standing there, staring at the phone again. Wondering, *So what if it's not Renee?*

Roman tries Trip Cutter's cell and gets nowhere. He calls Trip's home number and Cutter's wife answers. Roman speaks with self-imposed calmness, enduring a few seconds of polite chatter about Trip's daughters and his own daughter away at Skidmore. Finally he asks, "Is Trip around? I just have a quick question."

Yvonne tells him her husband left to pick up agent Torres about forty minutes ago—didn't he know?

"Oh, that's right," Roman says, placating her sudden concern with feigned nonchalance. "Nothing that can't wait until tomorrow."

Roman hangs up, tension knotting the muscles in his neck. He looks at his watch again—coming around to nine o'clock already—and calls Henry Marx, hears classical piano tinkling in the background.

"Sorry to bother you so late, Henry."

"Not a problem."

"Listen, did Renee mention anything about working OT tonight?"

"Not a word."

"What about Trip?"

"Nada. What's up?"

"Probably nothing," Roman says. "Any chance you know if Renee has a street source named Gina?" He's aware of his agent's sudden silence. "Look, Henry—I'm worried is all. This might be important. Off the record, okay?"

He waits another moment before Marx says, "Well, uh, yeah. I think she might have once mentioned a Gina somebody. This was a few months ago. A prostitute, I believe. I don't know if I'm—"

"Thanks, Henry. I gotta run." Roman hangs up, an electric fear sizzling through his chest.

In the dark, simultaneous motion.

Somebody says, *Oh, fuck.*

Somebody runs.

Elvis instinctively reaches for his Glock, thumbing the safety snap and bringing the big pistol up into position. Cutter, a couple steps away, hears the safety click. He cross-draws his own sidearm from its belt holster.

"Hold on, hold on," Torres says, aware of the subtle *swish* of gun sounds. "We've got weapons drawn here. Everybody calm down." Her voice is firm, sensible. Through the room's west-facing windows, she's aware of the slimmest ribbon of deep cobalt on the horizon, but little of the light bleeds in around them. She can hear the in-and-out echoes of heavy breathing.

"What we have is probably a power failure," Torres says—saying it but not believing it herself. She realizes with a numbing dread that it's happening, and here they are, unprepared, having bumbled their way smack into the middle of a potential kill zone.

"Yeah, let's all chill out, people," Cutter says. His voice floats nearby. Torres feels his presence grounding her own fear. She's aware of shadows moving tentatively around her, as if the night itself is coming alive.

It's Angie who freaks in the sudden darkness, explod-ing blindly into motion. She careens into Dwight's shoulder. He reaches out, but she claws away. "Let me *go!*" she moans in a strangled voice strangely not her own.

"Angie, wait—" Dwight says, but she's already gone, crashing into a lamp table and knocking things to the floor. She stumbles up the living room steps and bolts for the kitchen, drawn by a filtered haze of moonlight. But uncertain shapes loom and she flees to a hallway, past the pantry, the unused maid's quarters filled with life-cycles and exercise equipment, pitch black inside. Angie stum-bles against the wall and keeps moving, arms flailing. She glances through another doorway, another room—there's a bubbled skylight overhead and the crescent moon glows, its chalky brightness enticing. The laundry room swallows her. Exhausted by her own fear, she slides to the floor, her back against the cool metal front of a washing machine. She smells soap, the room's scent soothing. Angie thinks of her mother and begins to sob quietly under the moonlight.

Elvis wonders who's out there, LeRoy Beers or Danny For-tuna. Take your pick. Wondering if he has a preference, but since the DEA's here he figures it's gotta be Sparanza-no's people.

"A blown transformer?" Torres wonders. "Maybe half of Malibu's out."

Elvis doubts it. "Wait a sec," he says and moves with

remarkable stealth, stepping around furniture and impos-
ing shapes, his eyes adjusting. From a table beside the
couch he gropes for the phone, finds it and listens to dead
silence.

"Line's been cut," he tells them, his voice a rumble drifting through the night. "Means we got company."

"I've got my cell," Cutter says.

"No good in here. Micky's got a damper. Can't get no
reception, even with the lights out."

Cutter tries anyway, his face briefly bathed in a faint
blue glow. "Shit," he tells the room.

"Micky doesn't want nobody makin' no private calls,"
Elvis says with a shrug that nobody can see.

Torres unsnaps her shoulder purse, withdraws her Ladysmith from its quick-release compartment and thumbs the
safety off. "What about outside reception?"

"Halfway down the driveway maybe."

"Trip? You up for a stroll?"

"They'll hit us from the back patio," Elvis says, "but if
it's me comin' in, I'd keep someone out front. An easy kill,
anybody tries to come runnin' out the door."

It makes sense and Torres swears to herself. She knows
she has to keep it together, think things through. People
with guns on the outside, people with guns on the inside.
If they're not careful, she realizes they could end up shooting each other before the night's over.

"It's a chance we gotta take," Cutter says.

"Another door out front, near the garage," Elvis tells
them. "Grocery lady comes in that way. Keep in the shadows an' maybe nobody sees you."

"Yeah, that'll work. Renee? You gonna be okay here for a minute or two?"

"Just ducky," she supposes, reassured by the dry tone of his voice. She watches his silhouette move through the room. Cutter hesitates and she thinks she detects a backward glance.

"Great sense of timing you got yourself there, girl. You know that?"

Trip Cutter recalls a sketchy design of Micky Logan's home. Ben Roman had procured the blueprints a few years back, his agents having numerous opportunities to scour the place on paper. *So many goddamn doors,* he remembers. He gets midway through the hall, feeling vulnerable because he's left his 18-round Sig Sauer locked in its bureau drawer. He's carrying his "polite" piece, a six-shot Smith & Wesson revolver—and he swears the next time Renee drags him out for a ride he'll make her fill out an affidavit first.

A phantom glides against the darkness in front of him. Cutter swings his gun into firing position.

"It's me," Jeff whispers.

"You *who?*"

A pause. "Mr. Zapata?"

Cutter places the voice. "Deputy *Russell?*"

Another pause. "Yeah?"

"Jesus Christ. It's Trip Cutter, DEA. What the hell you doin' here, deputy?"

"Me? Where the hell should I be?"

"Back in Jamul."

"Jamul?" Each man wades through a muddled silence before Jeff says, "Don't you people ever talk to each other? What happened to the lights?"

Cutter doesn't have time to fit the pieces together at the moment. "We, uh, seem to have a situation here, deputy. You got your wife with you?"

"I'm right here," Jeanne says.

"How do you do, ma'am. I'm Agent Cutter, DEA."

"Hello."

"We're having a frigging conversation in the dark," Jeff says incredulously. "What's happening?"

"Whatever it is, it isn't good. You have a piece on you?"

"Service revolver."

"Do me a favor. Go back to your room and stay there. I'm not trying to pussy-whip you, deputy, but we got too many people wandering around this damn house with guns. The lights come back on, then you an' me will have a talk. But the best thing to do right now is keep your wife safe."

Torres sees the hulking shadow of Elvio Zapata crossing in front of her. "Any chance you have a back-up generator on the grounds, Mr. Zapata?"

"Yeah. Switch is in the kitchen."

"You have outside floodlights?"

"Some. Not enough. We light up the outdoors, we light up inside, too. They gonna see us before we see them. We maybe should sit tight a li'l bit."

Torres peers into the chalky wall of moonlight-tinged foliage beyond the patio. A dozen people could be lurking back there, but she can't see more than dancing shadows. Zapata's right—light up the place up and they're all illuminated, easy targets for anyone waiting.

"You hear that, everyone? It's going to stay dark a while." She pauses, listening to the silence. "People? Anyone? Hello?"

"Jus' you and me," Elvis believes, not quite certain himself.

"Christ," she says and wonders how long she's been talking to herself. She squints around the room, trying to get her bearings. The shape she assumes to be Dwight Manetti is a lamp.

Torres takes in a ragged breath and let it out slowly. "I'm going to have to rely on you for information. Places of access. Weak areas. You have any suggestions, Mr. Zapata?"

"Stay here, see what their plan is. If they don't got no grenades or plastic, maybe we'll be okay."

Torres eyes the inky foliage again, a sudden tapestry of motion in a passing breeze. *Grenades?* she thinks.

"Angie?" A whisper.

Angie's breath hitches in her throat. She whimpers.

"That you, Angie? It's me," the Kid says. He's already searched a half-dozen rooms, moving cautiously, listening to silence. He hears sounds now, barely able to make out a silhouette, Angie with her arms wrapped around her knees, on the floor in front of the washer.

"Dwight?" Sounds scrape in the darkness as she reaches out for him.

He moves toward her, feels her hands groping, pulling

him to the floor. "It's okay, Angie. Hey, it's cool. I'm here. It's okay."

"Shit, shit! I don't like it dark."

"It's okay. I'm right here."

Angie wraps her arms around his shoulders. The Kid puts his Walther on the floor next to his leg. Takes her in his arms.

"Don't leave me."

"I won't."

"I'm so scared, Dwight. I'm just *so* scared."

Jeff closes the bedroom door barely an instant before Jeanne, clutching his arm, squeezes tightly enough for him to grimace. "What about *Angie?* She's terrified of the dark, Jeff. She's going to be hysterical."

"I know." He finds the bed frame with his shins and grunts, gropes left-handed for his canvas jacket draped over one of the ornate foot posts — and feels the two speed loads zipped in a pocket. "I'll find her."

"But that agent told you — "

"The DEA's told me a lot of things," Jeff says with a dull throb of anger. He feels for her hand and tugs Jeanne gently behind him, recalling the big bureau against the wall, a meager space in the far corner, concealed from the doorway.

He plants her on the floor behind the bureau. "Stay here and keep low. I want you to hug the wall and wait for me. Don't move, don't say a word. No Supremes medleys," he says, trying unsuccessfully for levity.

"Jeff?" She's breathing in fierce little gasps, her voice high and unnatural. She squeezes his hand until it hurts.

"Don't worry, I'll get her."

"Please, Jeff—"

"Shhhhh," he tells her. "It's okay. You'll be okay. I love you, babe." He bends forward, his lips brushing her ear, and then he's gone, the sudden intensity of darkness suffocating her. Jeanne balls herself against the bureau, her spine pressing against the wall, her arms wrapping her knees. She jams her mouth against the side of her wrist, listening to the silence, biting down until she tastes blood.

9:00 PM SUNDAY

Richie Moya peeks over a stone wall and sees only blackness, Moya beginning to have second thoughts. Al Liola's been gone a long time and fucking Vinnie's crouched beside him, giggling like a school girl every few seconds, too coked up to know shit from Shinola.

Moya knows it should have been Shep or Danny with him out here in the dark. But Shep's dead, and Danny Fortuna's sucking down fifty-dollar vino with Teddy Sparks. Sparanzano wants it messy, something bloody and hard to forget. Scatter some tongues, some eyeballs—maybe a severed head inside the fridge chewing on a piece of celery. Something to razzle-dazzle the street people. *"Remember Charlie Manson?" Danny'd told him earlier, over the phone.* "Make it look like that."

And if there's one thing Vinnie knows well, it's how to be a fuckin' psychopath.

Beside him, Vinnie's giggling again and Moya's heart begins to beat a quick rumba inside his chest. It's okay being *in* the dark but, man, staring *at* the dark — that's different. That's when you start seeing ghosts and crazy shit.

"Will you calm the fuck down," Moya whispers at Vinnie, for maybe the third or fourth time already.

An hour before, Al Liola had jumped the Ford pick-up in the back lot of some dive bar over on Lincoln, a beat-up 4x4 with wooden ladders strapped in the back — *Malibu Ed's Painting* stenciled on the doors. The way Moya figured, they'll have returned the truck before Malibu Ed ever staggered out and realized they'd jacked his wheels.

The three men crammed themselves into the cab and drove north — Christ, Vinnie smelling like wet socks — the 4x4 tailing a silver minivan halfway up Las Flores Canyon. But Liola got confused, made a wrong turn on Yucca Trail and drove a mile in the wrong direction. By the time they got turned around, back on Las Flores, the road ahead was black, the minivan long gone.

Logan's place hadn't been hard to find — the only house on Barranca Vista and two big stone veneer lampposts marking the ornately gated driveway. Liola put fifty yards between them and the lamp light, then pulled off the road into darkness. They fumbled the ladders off Malibu Ed's truck, heaved one over the fence for getting back out, then jockeyed the other ladder into position against one of the stone posts. The funny thing about an electrified fence, Al Liola told them — it don't work so well with million dollar landscaping.

They lowered a couple satchels to the ground—three silenced Heckler MP7's; high velocity, large calibre submachine guns stolen from a Long Beach pier a few months back, with close to eighty pounds of extra clips and ammo. Also six cans of Liquitex to tag the walls with gang signs and fuck with the cops afterwards. They climbed clumsily but carefully over the post—a hundred thousand volts an accidental slip away—and jumped down with grunts and curses into the shadows.

Midway up the driveway, Moya signaled to split up. Liola made his way to the garage, found the electrical and switchboard panels where promised and, dangling a penlight between his lips, re-routed the alarm and shut down the surveillance system. He cut the phone line and rigged a three-minute delay fuse. Liola jogged back to the driveway that eventually circled toward the front of the house—*hey, whose Minivan?*—and ducked behind the vehicle where he could keep an eye on the door. Moya had told him to wait a little while after the power blew. If nobody came running out, find a way in.

Moya crept around back, Vinnie at his heels, the two of them moving quickly behind the garage and past the big pool, barely to Micky Logan's patio when the fuse ignited, melting the circuits and plunging Logan's house into darkness.

"Give 'em a minute or two after it goes dark," Danny had said that afternoon. "Enough time to crank up the generator, or maybe come wandering outside, wondering what the fuck. The whole friggin' house will light up like a Christmas tree—be like shooting turds in a toilet." Telling Moya it would be over before the fuckers realized they were even dead. Oh, yeah, and if they should find a couple of women there at the house—pop them too.

However, Danny's two minutes are long gone, and still no lights. Moya can't see shit.

"It ain't happenin'," Vinnie whispers.

"Shut up."

"Ain't fuck'n happenin'."

Shit, Moya thinks, the bug-chirping blackness crawling under his skin. His gaze twitches at shadows and sounds, Shep Boco poking around his brain like Marley's ghost. Stuck here with a asshole like Vinnie and not even—

"This is dog shit," Vinnie announces. He climbs to his feet, the Heckler's long, sausage-like suppressor tilting toward the glass wall, and before Moya can say *No!* Vinnie squeezes the trigger.

Inside the house, the darkness screams in a cacoph-ony of exploding glass. Torres stumbles sideways and loses her balance, goes down hard against the side of a coffee table. She manages to keep her gun and gathers herself into a crouched firing position, her breath coming in hot rasps. She feels an angry bruise throb against her thigh but doesn't dare pull her gaze from the surrounding blackness.

Elvis sidesteps against the wall and hears something like an angry bee whisper past his ear. He catches a muted muzzle flash on the patio, raises his Glock and puts two hollow points into the rhododendrons. In the confines of the room, the gun's report sears his eardrums, dizzies his brain.

Teddy Sparks, Joey Segal and Danny Fortuna are midway through a large plate of aragosta primavera, already on their second bottle of Barolo Riserva. A small electronic chirp stops the conversation mid-word, the three men instinctively reaching inside their jacket pockets.

"Mine," Sparanzano tells them.

Ben Roman's words tumble into his ear. "Call it off, Teddy."

"Ben? What a pleasant surprise."

"Call it off."

"Oh?" Sparanzano hesitates a moment, his gaze instinctively searching the restaurant. "Your realize this is an open line."

"I don't care if it's a fucking megaphone. I've got two shields at Barranca Vista."

"You're certain?"

"Shut it down *now*."

Sparanzano glances at his watch. "I'm sorry, but even if I knew what you were talking about, there's nothing I can do. It's too late. I'm in the middle of dinner. Good night, Ben."

Sparanzano pauses for several seconds, thinking, then leans toward Danny Fortuna. "There may have been two DEA's at Micky's place. Might that be trouble?"

Fortuna shrugs. "Not if everyone keeps their heads."

Sparanzano nods to himself and reaches for his glass

of Chianti, both he and Fortuna with the same brooding concern.

Vinnie.

Elvis' two rounds sizzle past Moya's jaw, a hot smack of air against his cheek. He drops behind the stone wall and feels Vinnie hit the ground beside him.

"Rock n' roll!" Vinnie shouts into the darkness.

"You fuckin' idiot!" Moya yells, wild-eyed and frantic in the dark. "You friggin' moron!"

Moya's first impulse is to get the fuck out, turn and run, but Danny'll be mad as hell if he botches this one. For a second he considers sticking his gun in Vinnie's face and pulling the trigger, then reluctantly pushes the thought away.

"You fuckin' toad. You stupid piece of shit. Stay the fuck here. I'm gonna go, find a way inside." He listens as Vinnie releases his empty clip and jams home a reload.

"I'll cover you," Vinnie says with another insane giggle.

"Yeah, you do that." Moya feels a crazy adrenaline surge, then scrambles off into the darkness—moving quick before Vinnie can accidentally blow him a new asshole. If there's any fairness in the world, Vinnie Sparanzano will get spammed tonight, and Moya doesn't particularly care by who.

Trip Cutter hears the tinkle of glass, a delicate sound that flutters through the darkness. The corridor forms a T in front of him, doorways everywhere, bathed in black. He holds his breath, peeks over one shoulder—behind him, a sudden presence sends an icy jab up through his testicles.

"Hey, it's me. Russell."

"Fuck it almighty, deputy," Cutter whispers. "You gotta stop sneaking up on me like that."

"You hear it?" Jeff asks him.

"Glass?"

"Yeah, came from the left."

"You sure?"

"From the left," Jeff says again.

Guest rooms, if Cutter's memory serves. Another hallway leading to a laundry room and garage. The other end leads to another patio and a big, bean-shaped pool out back somewhere.

"Your wife's okay?"

"Yeah."

"Look, deputy—Jeff—we're gonna plug this thing up. Can you stay right here, watch my tail?"

"You trying to keep me safe, Agent Cutter?"

"I'd say you're *way* outta your safety zone at the moment. To the left, huh?"

"Yeah."

"Anybody who's not me, you nail the bastard, okay?"

Cutter's an abrupt jolt of movement, staying low, reaching the first doorway. He pokes his gun into the darkness, listening and waiting.

Jeff casts a series of quick glances behind him, then sees Cutter's silhouette moving to another doorway. Jeff chances a glance to his right, then back toward Cutter and—

Wait. Something?

He peers intently, trying to discern a subtle motion in the hallway. Somebody moving—or only his imagination,

tricking his senses? Jeff squints. His mind fumbles and—
oh, *fuck it*. He swings his revolver and points at the hint of
motion, maybe four, five steps away.

He pulls the trigger, four quick jerks. In the muzzle flash,
a dark-haired man dressed in black looks surprised, then
swings a fat-muzzled gun toward him.

Trip Cutter empties his revolver from the hallway, quick
strobes of yellow-white light painting the walls in screaming, stopgap fragments of time. Acclimated now, Jeff fires
again and glimpses the guy already spurting blood, stumbling backwards. The guy in black merges again into the
still of the night, echoes pounding and no way could he be
a threat, no way in hell—Jeff's gun dancing in little cir-
cles and no way—

A hand touches Jeff's shoulder and he nearly leaps out
of his skin.

"He's down, deputy." Cutter's hand is firm, quelling the
whirlwind spin inside his brain. "But your sense of direction really sucks. Hold on. I'm gonna make sure."

Jeff takes a breath, in control of his nerves again, pluck-
ing a speed load from his jacket pocket, ejecting the spent
shells on the carpet.

"He's toast," Cutter says. Jeff can see the faint outline
of the man's automatic in Cutter's grasp. "How you doing
for ammo?"

"Two more loads," Jeff told him.

"Yeah, well, I'm flat out. Didn't come huntin' for bear
this evening. Think I'll keep ahold of this here sissy piece."
He waggles the long-snouted submachine gun. "A lousy
time for Micky's pals to show up, huh?"

"With friends like these," Jeff says absently and snaps the chamber closed.

"Everyone looking for a piece of Logan's ass," Cutter supposes, "same as us. Are you ready to—"

"What? Wait a sec."

Cutter waits.

"I mean, didn't Roman tell you?"

"Tell me what, deputy?"

"About Micky Logan? I explained it this morning at the coffee shop. Logan's dead. I'd assumed Roman would have said—" Jeff closes his mouth. Both men contemplate the implications in the darkness.

"You're sure about that?"

"Of course I'm sure."

"That Logan's *dead?*"

"That's what I told Roman."

"No way he might have con—"

"Logan's dead. I told your boss at the coffee shop. I told Ben Roman."

Cutter moves back beside Jeff, crouching for a second in the dark hallway. Both men are uncomfortably silent, Jeff with a sudden inkling that, whatever's happening here, *nobody* knows the hell what it is.

The Kid holds Angie, stroking her hair, listening to the sporadic gunplay and wanting to be in the middle of it. Angie's trembles gradually subside, her breath slowing— the house silent for the last minute or so. The Kid's eyes have adjusted to the quilted patches of moonlight on the floor. He can see her clearly now, the way her hair falls, the definition of her face. He decides she's beautiful, sitting there next to him. Decides that, yeah, he could live with a girl like Angie. Maybe even forever.

"You okay?"

"I think so."

"I gotta go give Elvis a hand. Bunch of fools tryin' to whack us, Angie. Time for me to earn my million bucks. Am I right?"

She doesn't want him to leave, but she feels him pulling away.

"You'll be all right," he says. "Wait here for me."

"I'm scared, Dwight."

He kisses the top of her head, aware of the scent of her shampoo, and picks up his Walther. "Just stay put. I'll be back before you know it."

"Okay." Her voice is small and accepting.

The Kid stands and moves toward the darkness of the doorway. The night closes around him and he blinks, his eyes attempting to readjust. In front of him, maybe a hint of motion. Dwight squints, cautiously says, "Elvis?"

The blast takes him off his feet, a staccato burst of muzzle flash and noise and the last thing he really feels is an ice-cold vise grip his chest, squeezing the breath from his lungs. Dwight is flung backwards, falling into the pool of moonlight, spread-eagle across Angie. His spine arches across her knees. "Ow, ow, ow, ow, ow," he says, a choked gasp of sound that dribbles from his lips. She sees the angry black welts stitched across his chest, fluid pools expanding together in an inky mass. She wraps her arms around his neck, tilting his head toward her. Under the sliver of moonlight their gazes lock — something gentle, apologetic in the expression behind his eyes and then it's gone, the Kid's eyes still open, but with an empty, vacant look, and Angie instinctively knows there's nothing more he can see.

"Oh, Dwight," she whispers, cradling his head against her breasts, feeling the warmth of his blood spill across her. The darkness steps forward and Angie looks up, sees what Dwight had never chanced to see, a glimmer of a smile against the hint of chalky moonlight.

"Need some help there, hon?"

Vinnie's idea of death is a video game. He has Xbox, he has Nintendo. You sit on the couch with a few drinks in you, killing everything you see. Vinnie has the giggles bad but he can't help himself; he's sniffed up a couple of toots waiting here behind the stone wall — and oh, man, he's *flyin'*.

He's empties his gun toward the house, then pulls another 40–round clip from the satchel. Teddy Sparks wanted a bloodbath, Danny Fortuna telling them to blow the place all to hell. This is show-and-tell after all, a demonstration of power and, oh, yeah, Vinnie's got the power.

Every now and then he expends another magazine, the gun uttering a quick hiss of staccato bursts — only a few seconds to unload a full clip, Vinnie hearing things crackle and burst inside the house, getting a kick out of it. Giggling again.

This is Vinnie's night. He'd been on hits before, but always as a tag-along. Until now, always behind the wheel, sometimes hearing a muffled pop-pop-pop before driving a couple guys off into the night. This time it's for real, and man, he's *jammin'*. The time of his life. He doesn't realize it yet, preoccupied, but Vinnie's sporting a raging hard on.

Inside Micky's house, Elvis takes a series of crouched steps, Torres still hugging the floor behind the stairs. After the third barrage, Elvis chances a couple more paces, nearing the foyer, another half-dozen steps to the front door.

"Mr. Zapata?" Torres whispers. "You have a plan?"

"Yeah, I'm goin' out the front."

"But you said—"

"Anybody out there woulda come around by now, joined the fight."

The darkness outside utters a harsh metallic burp, the room suddenly full of angry whispers, plaster and wallboard disintegrating in stinging puffs. Remnants of glass rain down from the foyer windows. Elvis waits patiently and says, "Gimme two minutes. Then make a noise."

"A what?"

"Get his attention."

Elvis doesn't wait for her response. Torres watches his shadow disappear around the corner and merge with the night.

"A noise," she mutters, ticking off the seconds inside her head. Not quite certain what he means but she dutifully counts past one hundred—almost an eternity waiting there alone in the dark—getting ready, pulling her gun up close to her face. She hits the magic number and swallows hard. Still pressing against the floor, she yells as loud as she can, "Hey, *asshole!*"

And then, because she isn't sure he heard her, she fires two shots toward the patio.

Vinnie thinks, *who, me?*—amazed that somebody might still alive inside, then a flash of light and a couple rounds slash through the tangled branches over his head.

"You can't shoot worth a damn!" A woman's voice, taunting him from inside.

Vinnie's not stupid enough to answer, but it does piss him off. He waits a moment, then scoots the gun's snout a tad to the left, pulls the trigger and listens to the resulting carnage. Listens to the following silence and—

"You call that *shooting?*" The same voice, but stressed up a notch. He giggles again and thinks about the half-empty vial of coke in his pocket. Time for another snort. He hears a sound and glances up, catches the barest flash of motion—

Elvis muscles the gun across Vinnie's face and feels the crack of bone, the sudden warmth of blood against his knuckles. Vinnie drops like a sack of shit.

Richie Moya stares down at the woman, the dead punk in her arms. Angie lowers her head. Scared. Trembling. The gun's long snout brushes a swirl of hair above one of her eyebrows.

"Hey?" he whispers, wanting another look before he pulls the trigger. "Hey, darlin'?"

Angie gazes up.

His trigger finger tightens—then abruptly eases off. Moya with a heartbeat of awareness, the darkness around him devoid of sound. He cocks his head and listens.

The last few minutes have been a skirmish, gunfire echoing all over the fucking place. Moya's been aware of three, maybe four small guns, a shit storm of returning gunfire they sure as hell weren't expecting. And now only silence. A spooky sort of silence.

"One sound and you're fuckin' hamburger. Understand what I'm saying, hon?" Moya presses the muzzle against her temple, making his point, then bends close and tells Angie in a whisper what he wants next.

9:30 PM SUNDAY

The smiling man keeps the gun pressed hard against her ear, his other hand tangled in her hair, tugging her in one direction or another. Angie's numb—she doesn't remember much of their trek through the dark hallways, eventually into the dry night air. She vaguely remembers passing the swimming pool, the still water an inky sheen. They move down a stone path and into the rocky desert terrain. She trips several times, her ankles and calves whipped by bits of sage and bramble. She's aware of being pulled away from the looming shadow of Micky Logan's house and wonders if she should scream. But she instinctively knows the consequences. Angie closes her eyes, stumbling forward, the man's hands gliding her through the night as if in a dream.

Past the garage, Moya angles toward the sloping driveway, tired of tripping over rocks and having to drag the blonde bitch around by her hair. He looks back, the house still dark, and notices a minivan sitting under the moonlight. Al Liola must have seen it and—what? Didn't think it might have been important enough to give them a fucking head's up? The girl moans. He digs his fingers into her hair and pulls hard. Another sound, swear to Christ, and he'll pop her, leave her splayed on the driveway for someone to find in the morning. Unless the coyotes find her first.

Fuckin' Al, he thinks again, pushing the blonde forward. He hopes the motherfucker's dead. Hopes to hell that Vinnie's dead too. The silence scares him. The inky, looming shadows scare him. Even this fucking blonde scares him—because she's not part of the plan and man, Danny Fortuna's going to go ballistic. He thinks about killing the blonde again, but the truth is he's too scared to be alone.

Fuckin' Vinnie.

Torres waits, listening to the silence, aware of the sound of her own heartbeat pulsing in her temples. She sees motion and steadies her aim, waiting. Elvis whispers, *Don' shoot, don' shoot,* dragging what she assumes to be a body. A moment later Cutter emerges from the hallway and says in her ear, "You're never gonna believe who I found around back. Deputy Russell and his wife." The house full of surprises. They listen to Elvis drag the limp form toward the foyer.

"Renee? Did you know Russell was still here?"

"No, I didn't," she says, truthfully.

They wait another moment in silence, their eyes pretty much acclimated now, the darkness no longer foreboding. She says, "You think they're gone?"

"We nailed one around back. This one makes two. It was me still breathing out there, I'd sure as hell be halfway down the hill by now. They wouldn't have expected a crowd."

"What do we do now?" she wonders.

Cutter exhales a slow, thoughtful breath. "I suppose we find out for sure, huh?" He glances up, locates Elvis' hulking silhouette amid the shadows.

"Mr. Zapata? What say we get that generator cranked?"

Elvis isn't certain its a good idea, but he's beginning to fight his own impatient demons. He finally tells the agents, *Yeah*, he'll go and do that.

Torres is surprised, in the sudden barrage of light, to discover the bloody carcass still twitching. Still alive. The guy moans a couple times, on the verge of coming around. She wants to take a closer look but something moves behind her and she turns to discover Deputy Russell and his wife standing amid the shattered remains of the hallway arch. The woman appears to be in shock, cradled snuggly beneath her husband's arm. She has mascara stains down one cheek, her eyes wide and disbelieving. The deputy surveys the surrounding carnage with a rigid expression, gripping his pistol with a white-knuckled intensity.

Russell's gaze catches Torres' and she blinks at the

severity of his unspoken accusation. Not at all the look of a man prone to cold feet, the guy Ben Roman told her had split for Jamul this morning.

"Deputy Russell," she says, braving a smile that feels empty against her face. "You came back?"

"Never left."

She nods silently, frowning at nothing, trying to make sense of it. "Seems we have a communications problem, deputy."

"You think?"

"*Angie?*" Jeannie says suddenly. "Where's Angie?"

The words immobilize each of them with a heartbeat of dread. Torres and Cutter touch gazes.

"Mr. Manetti?" she says.

"Angie?" Jeanne says again, louder, her gaze darting frantically. "*Angie?*"

Trip Cutter finds Manetti's body, calling out to the others with a resigned voice. He bends down and closes the young man's eyes. Just a street punk—not a word spoken between them—but Cutter feels an anxious knot of remorse. The last twenty minutes have done that, have bonded them somehow. Lying there, Manetti looks barely old enough to drive, his smooth skin porcelain white, a smudge of blood against his cheek.

Cutter sees Renee and Zapata in the doorway, the big Mexican staring at Manetti with a strange and muted expression. Deputy Russell and his wife appear in the hall behind them and Cutter shakes his head.

"You maybe don't want to see this," he says to Jeanne,

but she's already pushing her way between Torres and Elvis. "Where's Angie? Is she here?"

"I don't see her."

"*Angie?*" Jeanne screams the word and Torres reaches out, puts a reassuring hand on her shoulder. Cutter stands, scrutinizing a bloody print on the washing machine. Another crimson dribble leading to the doorway.

"Hey, take a look at this," Jeff says from the hall.

A second handprint. Midway through the hall Cutter discovers a faint smudge, already dry. A door leading to the garage is ajar.

"Angie's blood?" Jeff wonders.

"Likely Manetti's. It's not from an open wound."

"If they took her," Jeff says, then silences his thoughts, realizing what nobody wants to hear.

A man's scream echoes through the hallway. They turn, aware that Elvis is no longer present.

Jesus, now what? Torres thinks.

They find Elvis in the dining room. The bloody pile he's dragged from the patio is more or less human again, sitting in one of Micky Logan's expensive hardwood chairs. Elvis is binding the man's legs to the chair with duct tape, his arms already wrapped behind his back. And because he'd been bleeding profusely from a gash over one eye, Elvis has circled duct tape around his head, a gray band that mushrooms the man's hair into a crazy pompadour.

"What's going on, Mr. Zapata?" Torres asks.

Elvis glances up, pushing the words toward his mouth. "Gonna find Angie is wha's goin' on." He plucks a coiled extension cord from the arm of the chair and Torres' gaze follows its length to the dining room table. She spies the attached steam iron and gets the gist.

"Mr. Zapata, you do realize we're federal agents?"

Elvis gives her another look—a *different* sort of look— slowly uncoiling the cord in his hands. He jabs the plug into a wall socket.

Vinnie's eyes dart back and forth. "What's he doin'? Shit, what's he *doin?*" He emits a muted nasal whine, his nose tilting toward one cheek, Vinnie's objections made through a mouthful of blood.

"We get answers quick," Elvis says, "else Angie dies."

Cutter's been silent, staring at the guy in the chair, trying to place the face. He steps toward Vinnie, extends a finger and straightens out the broken nose.

"Oww. Shit! That hurts!"

"I'll be damned," Cutter says. "You know who we *got* here, Agent Torres?"

Her expression tells him she doesn't.

"It's Vincent Sparanzano."

Torres squints, trying to make the face through the duct tape and blood, the pompadour and tilted nose.

"'Scuse me," Elvis says, stepping between them and wedging the still-cold iron tightly against Vinnie's crotch.

"Shit! Hey, shit!"

"Mr. Zapata?" Torres' voice hitches cautiously. Elvis remains oblivious, staring down at Vinnie.

"Mr. Zapata, if you think for a mo—"

"Yo, Renee?" Cutter says, stepping toward the bullet-gouged liquor cabinet, picking through splinters and glass shards. Pools of sticky fluid have oozed a wide oval stain on the carpet. Torres stares after him with a frown.

"They killed the Smirnoff's, the Johnnie Walker," he says. "Damn shame about the Glenfiddich. Looks like what we got left here is some peach schnapps." He reaches for a single bottle, still intact, takes a sniff, then a tentative swallow. He winces, then glances back and motions to Torres.

"Let's you and me have a coupla hits, alright? Chat a little bit over yonder."

"Hey, *noooo*," Vinnie whines. "You can't let him do this! Shit. What's he gonna do, huh? What's he *doooin'*!" Vinnie stares at his crotch and glances wild-eyed around the room, finding no friends at all.

"Trip? He's right. We can't allow this." She watches Cutter take another swallow.

Cutter smiles, enjoying the burn. "This ain't bad. Here, take a jolt."

"Trip?"

"Seems you and I have a little problem to resolve. Ben was wrong about Deputy Russell hightailing it back to Jamul. Seems to me—" He glances around the shattered room. "—that Deputy Russell and his pretty wife were supposed to die here this evening."

Cutter's still holding the bottle of schnapps toward her, waiting.

"Something else Ben forgot to tell us," he says. "So happens, Micky Logan's dead. But you knew that, didn't you?"

She blinks back her surprise. "I swear I didn't, Trip. I heard cheap talk, but I didn't believe it. You *know* I wouldn't hold back intel like that."

"Uh huh. Well, Deputy Russell told Ben yesterday. At the coffee shop." He gives her a moment to think it through. "Ben's turned on us. That's what you wouldn't tell me in the car."

Torres finally takes the schnapps, uncertain, raising the bottle to her lips. She feels the alcohol sting the roof of her mouth, then burn its way down her throat. "God's truth, Trip, I didn't believe that either." She shakes her head, on the verge of tears. "That's what coming here tonight was all about. I needed to prove it to myself."

"He's gone and slimed us."

Torres holds his gaze. "I don't know what to do."

Behind them, Vinnie starts to scream. The two agents turn to watch.

"You got maybe ten seconds," Elvis says, "man, before your *cojones* begin to hiss an' pop. Maybe just enough time to tell us where's Angie at, huh?"

Vinnie feels the first waves of heat radiating from the metal plate; he tries without success to suck in his crotch. "Hey, I don't *know* no fucking Angie. It's gettin' hot! It's motherfuckin' hot!"

Torres says, "Who brought you here, Vinnie?"

Vinnie tries to pull his hands free. He doesn't have much time to consider his options, to make things up. "Shit! Turn it *off*! Turn it off, man!"

Elvis says nothing. The heat begins to sear through Vinnie's pants. "Al!" he screams. "It was Al Liola, okay! An' Moya. Richie Moya! Swear to God! It was them."

"You're sure about that?" Torres asks.

"Yessss!" Vinnie jerks backward, arching his body, the

chair jumping a couple inches. The iron dislodges and falls to the floor. A puff of smoke drifts from Vinnie's scorched pants.

"Moya's part of Fortuna's crew," Torres whispers.

"That's not Moya in the back hall neither. Must have been Moya who killed Manetti."

"Then it's Moya who has Ms. Breusser. You know his file?"

"I know he's a sociopathic freak," Cutter says.

"We tell the Russells?"

"They're going to find out, one way or another."

"You know we've got Vincent Sparanzano sitting here," Torres says, her voice still low. "He's never stuck his neck in the mud before. We connect some dots, link Vincent to Fortuna, then Fortuna to Teddy Sparks. We can finally put Sparanzano on the map, Trip."

"Getting a freak like Vinnie to turn over on his uncle won't be too difficult," Cutter agrees.

"Thirty minutes and we can have can special ops tearing this place apart. Bring in the FBI and—"

"What about Ben?"

Torres hesitates.

"Besides, you're forgetting one small detail." Cutter glances at Jeff. "If Moya took the deputy's sister-in-law, he's not going to drop her off at the nearest church."

"Maybe that's the price we pay?"

She looks for confirmation in Cutter's eyes, wading through the passing seconds—but he smiles gently, aware of the uncertainty clouding her gaze—and shakes head.

"It's too damn high, Renee. The tag's too damn high."

Elvis has been holding the iron the last few seconds, looking at Vinnie with menacing intent. He spits on the metal plate and the iron sizzles. "So where'd he take Angie?"

"How the fuck should I know?"

Elvis shrugs and moves the iron back toward Vinnie's crotch.

"Wait a minute, *wait* a minute! Maybe over on Gil-more. I dunno. Swear to God, man. Maybe there."

"Gilmore?"

"Yeah, yeah. A fuckin' warehouse, man."

"One of the Duke's safe houses," Cutter says, this time loud enough for Jeff and Jeanne to hear. "Off of Century, near the airport. Odds are Vinnie and his boys rendezvoused there, picked up a hot ride before coming here. We know the place. Been watching off and on the last year or so. Always came up empty."

He glances at Torres. "I guess now we know why."

Jeff moves between Vinnie and the agents. "How do I get there?"

"A good chance she's not there," Torres remarks.

"Maybe a chance she is."

"This isn't your town, deputy."

"Look, I'm done playing your rules. Wherever this warehouse is, they're probably halfway there by now. Whoever took her—"

"We think a mob guy named Moya," Cutter says.

"—Yeah, well once he gets there, then what? No way I'm going to sit here and wait for you to figure things out."

"You're out of your jurisdiction," Torres reminds him.

"You know what? Fuck you. I'm getting Angie."

Torres frowns. "I don't appre—"

But Cutter raises a hand and, surprised, she closes her mouth.

"Maybe a forty-five minute drive from here," he says, "this time of night and if we hustle. We can call in a tac-op team, but they won't put anything together quicker than that. LAPD might fuck it up, not knowing the all kinds of crazy Richie Moya can be. I know some roads. Maybe we can shave a few minutes off."

"Trip?"

"Deputy's right, Renee. Game's changed somewhere along the way. We stand here yapping any longer, Miss Breusser's gonna be toast."

"This is wrong."

"Doing it right, all these years, I don't see where that's got us." Cutter motions toward Jeff. "I got car keys, deputy. I think we need to hurry."

Jeff nods, turns to see Jeanne coming toward him, eyes terrified. "We don't have time," he says gently, aware of the conflicting emotions etched against her face. She opens her mouth and he puts his finger against her lips.

"No, you're not. You're staying here."

Jeanne's unable to find the words and feels the tears coming, tumbling unabated down her cheeks.

"I can't worry about her and you too. I'll bring her back. I promise. Look, babe, we gotta run."

"I'll take good care of your deputy, ma'am." This from Cutter, regarding her with an uncertain smile.

"I love you," Jeff says. He kisses her and tastes the salty wetness of her tears. He looks at Torres, grateful to see that she's ditched the 'tude, the agent glancing toward Jeanne and giving him a silent nod. Giving him a silent promise.

10:00ᴘᴍ SUNDAY

Renee Torres realizes that she's lost control of the situation. She doesn't like her world unraveling and here she is, swimming in chaos. Drowning in it. She knows maybe half a dozen people she can call, ways to circumvent Ben Roman, but she still can't bring herself to believe he's gone dirty. Part of her still needs to hear it from Roman himself. She watches Elvis begin to unwrap Vinnie Sparanzano, feels her insides twisting in a myriad of conflicting emotions. Elvis moves quickly, with purpose and, suddenly suspicious of his intent, Torres' mind snaps back.

"Can I ask what you're doing, Mr. Zapata?"

"You lettin' me go?" Vinnie's voice rises with childlike innocence. Unbound, he scrambles to stand and Elvis shoves him back into the chair.

"Me an' Vinnie, we're goin' for a ride."

"Absolutely not," Torres tells him.

Elvis gives her a glance with—*damn that man*—casual disregard.

"I'm not permitting this," she says tersely. "Vincent Sparanzano is not going anywhere. He's under arrest."

"Maybe you can arrest him tomorrow, huh? 'Cause right now, Vinnie's goin' with me." He begins to retape Vinnie's wrists together.

Torres feels the weight of the Ladysmith in her hand, lifts her gun and points it at Elvis. "Vincent Sparanzano is *not* leaving this room."

"Then shoot if you're gonna. Thing is, see, I'm dead anyway. Teddy Sparks ain't gonna cancel a contract just 'cuz his crew screws up. But he might if we trade him Vinnie. The punk here for our lives."

Teddy Sparks. There—the name out in the open. And yet everything's happening too damn fast, the name a passing whisper beneath a roar of indecipherable static in her ears. Torres swallows, fighting back a shiver of frustration. "I'm afraid that's not good enough, Mr. Zapata."

Vinnie glances back and forth between the two of them, this angry looking lady with her pointed gun and the big spic who scares the hell out of him. A rock and a fuckin' hard place. He's not certain of his best option and, for once in his life, Vinnie keeps his mouth shut.

"*Can't* you arrest him tomorrow?" Jeanne says. Torres and Elvis look at her, as if aware of her presence for the first time. Jeanne stands demurely in her pink sweatshirt and natty-kneed jeans, a polite expectation on her face. For an instant Elvis swears it's Angie standing there—then blinks and sees Jeanne again.

"I can't do that, Mrs. Russell."

Elvis pulls Vinnie up out of the chair, holding him by the collar. "Then you might as well shoot the lady here while you're at it, 'cause she's dead, too. She and her husband."

"What?" Jeanne says.

"Yeah. Way I figure, you're part of the contract. Supposed

to be dead now like me. Like the Kid. We trade Vinnie for
our lives, else we got nothin' to deal."

"They want to kill *us*? Jeff and me? Why?"

"On account of wha' you seen here," Elvis says. "Or wha'
they think you seen. What you maybe heard."

"You mean that Micky Logan's dead?"

Jesucristo, the whole fuckin' world knows? Elvis shakes his
head. "Yeah, tha's what I mean."

Torres' gun doesn't move. "Mrs. Russell, the DEA can
offer you protection."

"Nothing personal, agent Torres, but I don't think my
husband is going to give a rat's ass about your kind of protection." Jeanne turns to Elvis. "You're serious about this?
About Jeff and me being killed?"

His look tells her that he is.

"Because there's something you should know," Jeanne
says. "Something that can maybe help."

Elvis hitches an eyebrow, not sure what she's talking about. Vinnie's getting antsy, wiggling around in
his grip, his weight shifting from one foot to the other.
Elvis squeezes the back of Vinnie's neck and he stops
moving.

"You're taking him to see this man Sparanzano?" Jeanne
asks. "He's with the Mafia, right?"

"Yeah."

"Then I'm going with you."

"Uh, tha's maybe none too smart."

Jeanne pauses. "Wait a second. I'll be right back."

"Mrs. Russell — ?" But she's already gone. Torres presses
her lips. "Mr. Zapata, I'm warning you." They watch each

other for a long moment, saying nothing, until Vinnie gets antsy again, finally fills the silence.

"Lady, shoot this fuckin' beaner here an' I'll give you ten large. You let me go an—"

"Shut up, Vinnie."

"My uncle, Teddy? He'll buy you a new car. You want a Cadillac? A new Lincoln? I swear to Christ. If that's what you want, you take me back an—"

Jeanne returns, out of breath and carrying Micky Logan's three ledgers. Carrying her jacket, ready to go.

"Mrs. Russell?" Torres says sternly. "You're not leaving this house."

"But we have *more* to trade than Vincent," Jeanne tells her, looking at Elvis.

He stares at Micky's books in her arms. He doubts that whatever she has is enough to square them with Teddy Sparks, but he also knows that help is one thing he could use more of. Elvis gives her a slight nod and shoves Vinnie toward the door.

"Mr. Zapata?"

Jeanne follows.

"Mrs. Russell?" Torres swings the revolver from Elvis to Jeanne, back to Elvis and then to Jeanne, thinking, *what the hell am I doing?* The two of them waiting, watching her with curious uncertainty.

"Are you going to shoot us, Agent Torres?" Jeanne asks.

"Goddamn it." Torres exhales with a sigh and drops the gun to her side. "Get out. Go. Kill yourselves, I don't care." She grabs the bottle of schnapps off the table and picks her way to the couch, knowing the closest bit of evidence she has to finally nailing Teddy Sparks is walking out the door. Without turning, she calls out; "First thing tomorrow morning, Vinnie, you're under fucking arrest."

She's lost track of time, the moments melding together, passing in a blur. She's done everything this man has asked of her without complaint, without a sound, walking along the dusty edge of Barranca Vista under the sliver of moonlight, aware of their two shadows mingling on the asphalt. Walking the way lovers might walk, she thinks. Ahead of them, parked against the side of the road, a white pick-up truck.

She can still see Dwight's image — his torn body soaked in blood and the death in his eyes. It seems surreal, like a dream, her mind caught in the relentless depths of a nightmare she can't shake. She knows enough to be afraid, although her fear remains tucked away in that place deep inside her brain.

The man reaches for something up under the rear wheel well — it's not until she sees the flicker of a key that a surge of reality startles her into awareness. Angie begins to cry.

"Shu'p," he says angrily. He pushes her toward the cab and she sobs again, feels his fingers grab a tangle of hair. Angie's forehead slams against the roof of the cab. She feels more than hears herself moan, expelling air and tasting blood before a rush of descending blackness envelopes her. She wonders, a final wisp of awareness, if it's really this easy to die.

10:15 PM SUNDAY

Ben Roman pulls his BMW into Logan's driveway. The front gate is wrenched from its track, lying twisted on the ground—somebody impatient, in a hurry. Roman slips his gun from its hip holster and places it on the seat beside his leg. He switches off his headlights, maneuvering up the long drive by the wedge of moonlight.

He's surprised to see Logan's place lit up, more surprised at the light flooding from the front doorway, both big doors yawning open. He brakes a good distance from the house and leaves his car, gun in hand. He climbs the front steps and glances inside, tasting the residue of cordite in the air. Roman crouches low and goes in, follows his gun through the entry, into the foyer, into the shattered living room and—

"Renee?"

She's sitting on the couch, head down, the house in shambles around her. Bullet holes pock the walls, marble chips gouged out of the fireplace, furniture splintered. Torres has her little revolver in one hand, a bottle of schnapps in the other. "Renee?" he says again. "My God—"

"Oh, hello, Ben. You've come for a body count?" She doesn't bother looking up. Her voice is a little slurred, not enough to conceal the acrid tone of her words. "There's a DB in the hallway. Another in the laundry room. One MIA. I suspect we'll have more before morning, but that's just one girl's opinion."

Her attitude puzzles him, at the same time scares him in a way he can't decipher. Roman holsters his sidearm, moving around the scattered pieces of debris. Inspecting the gaping wall of nothingness between the living room and patio.

"What the hell happened, Renee?"

"Shit hitting the fan, Ben. Just shit hitting the fan."

"Where's Trip?"

"On what I'd call a hostage rescue mission."

"A what?"

"With Deputy Russell." Her gaze finally meets his and Roman realizes that he's arrived too late for games.

"If you're curious," she says, "Mr. Zapata took Mrs. Russell over to visit Teddy Sparks."

When he doesn't reply, she adds, "I mean, sure, why not? Tonight's been one big Loony Tune anyway. They went to return Vincent to his rightful owner."

He's confused now and assumes she might be drunk. He turns slowly, a full circle, taking in the magnitude of the destruction. When he returns his gaze he finds hers scathing.

"You son of a bitch," she tells him.

Their gazes lock, mutually probing. For the first time in a long while, maybe his entire life, Roman blinks first. "Renee, listen — I need to tell you a few things."

So much to explain and not enough time. He searches

for a place to begin and takes a deep breath. "You're not going to understand what I have to say."

Torres stands up. "There's nothing to understand, Ben. I'm sure it's a wonderful excuse. But, here's the thing—I don't care. You sold us out. All this fucking time you were sleeping with Sparanzano. In my book, nothing else matters."

"Yeah, I broke a goddamn rule. I had my reasons."

"I don't want to hear about your fucking reasons."

"Maybe you'll realize I did this for all of—"

"Stop!" She puts both fists to her ears, still with the gun in her hand and the bottle of schnapps too, splashing some across the floor. Standing there with goofy rabbit ears, trying to block out whatever he wants to tell her. "I don't care, Ben. Whatever it is, I don't goddamn care."

He's silent and she watches the twisted agony of his expression. "It smells in here. I'm going outside." She turns her back on him, stepping over splinters and shards of glass. Getting halfway to the shattered wall of French doors before she hears the distinctive metallic click.

It stops her, mid-step. She doesn't look back. Her breath escapes in a jagged rush.

"Renee?" His voice is both apologetic and desperate. "I need you to hear this. I need you to know why."

She ignores him and takes another step.

"Renee, please. Don't."

Another step, then another. "Renee—?"

An eternity wedges into a fragmented instant of uncertainty. Another step and she'll be to the French doors. She feels her mind tilt and whirl. Feels Roman's gun pointing at the back of her head. She wonders if she'll feel pain, if her head will shatter, wonders what—

The gunshot forces a small rush of urine from between her legs. She stumbles forward, trembling, both the bottle and her gun flung from her grasp, her fingers outstretched. She catches herself on the broken doorjamb and stands for maybe a minute before she realizes she's crying. She can't remember the last time she's cried, the tears a hot memory down her cheeks.

She doesn't have to look back, but she does.

Ben Roman could have eaten the gun, but Roman knew the kind of embarrassing problems that would cause—problems without easy answers. And Ben Roman was nothing if not a methodical man. So he tilted the barrel against his chest and pulled the trigger.

Somewhere along the chain of command, questions will undoubtedly be asked, but Torres knows those voices, those questions, will ultimately be dismissed. She understands human nature well enough; whatever the enormity of his transgression, Roman's apology will be accepted, received with accolades and posthumous commendations. The lines he crossed were lines without distinct borders and, tonight, Ben Roman died a hero. The *Times* will likely espouse his life and spout sanctimonious bullshit about an elusive war against a non-existent enemy.

He'd told her once; "Drugs don't kill people. Despair kills people." Walk that line long enough, maybe you begin to realize that more often than not, those borders don't even exist.

What Torres also understands, even if nothing else

makes sense at the moment—Roman's death leaves
Sparanzano deaf and blind. Her one undeniable truth is
that Teddy Sparks' invisible grip on L.A. has already begun
to dissipate, had begun to crumble the moment of Ben
Roman's final breath. Reason enough, she knows, to keep
his secret.

Elvis thinks it better that Jeanne drives. He sits in back of
the big Mercedes, keeping his Glock pressed against Vinnie's kidney. Every now and then Vinnie whines or com-
plains and asks for a fuckin' aspirin. Elvis jams the gun
harder under his ribs and shuts him up. He keeps an eye
on the dark roads ahead, now and then telling Jeanne to
turn, or go straight at the light. Other than that, they don't
speak.

Elvis decides against calling Teddy Sparks too quickly;
if this isn't going to work, he doesn't want Sparanzano
getting his people ready before he has a chance to speak
his peace. He hopes Teddy Sparks won't be in crazy mode
tonight, all that incense and mystic shit, naked on the floor
and surrounded by candles.

They drive south for several minutes and then turn
inland, toward the brightly lit heart of the city.

"Up here, take a left," he tells Jeanne.

In ten minutes Elvis can see the Bonaventure. He picks
up his cell and touches the speed dial, Sparanzano all the

way at #1, the number Sparanzano had given him on Saturday. He hears the click. An answering machine beeps and a pleasant female voice tells him, *You have reached the offices of Gavinetti Exports. Please leave a...*

And Elvis without a damn thing he wants say to a machine. What? *We got Vinnie, let's make a deal?* Probably not.

"Here?" Jeanne asks, the Bonaventure rising majestically on her left.

"No, go straight," Elvis says, trying to think.

"What's the matter?"

"Ain't nobody home."

10:30 PM SUNDAY

Richie Moya isn't certain what to do. He pulls into the warehouse complex off Gilmore, fingers a key code into a little metal box and cruises past a security guard who's not paying attention, the guy huddled inside his little hut and probably half drunk, this time of night. Moya steers the truck down a few blocks of deserted warehouses. He gets out of the cab and unlocks the flimsy metal delivery door, slides it open, making all kinds of racket this time of night. Listens to echoes fade back toward silence. He climbs back behind the wheel and pulls forward, crawling past wooden crates stacked against the walls, throwing shadows in spooky angles. Moya coasts toward the little plywood office and brakes, sitting through a tangled moment of rage and paranoia before he glances down at Angie, doubled in half on the floor, her head and one arm draped across the passenger seat.

"Fucking bitch," Moya says under his breath. He plucks the gun from his lap and taps its long snout against the back of her head, ready to pull the trigger—but once again a thought pops into his head and stops him cold.

The thought wears the face of Danny Fortuna.

Moya has a suspicion that Al Liola's dead. With any luck, Vinnie is too. Danny's not going to be happy about that. With his luck he kills the blonde and Danny will want her alive. Keep her breathing and Danny will want her dead. *Sheesh.* But even to Moya, the latter seems the more easily remedied dilemma.

He walks around the Ford and drags her out of the passenger door, leaves her unconscious on the concrete floor and returns with a length of yellow nylon rope. Goes off again to call Danny Fortuna from the phone inside the office—an assortment of unregistered guns and clips and boxes of ammunition strewn everywhere. Danny will tell him to pop the woman or not and, the way Moya feels, killing her quick will be the best thing to calm his nerves.

Killing her slow might even be better.

The three men sip espressos, Danny Fortuna's with a jolt of Courvoisier. A small electronic chirp interrupts their silence. Sparanzano watches the others reach for their cells—Fortuna this time—although Sparanzano's already turned off his phone and disabled his voicemail for the evening. The last thing he wants is Ben Roman calling twenty-fives times, leaving frantic messages. Dead agents at the Logan estate and how's he going to explain a bunch of phone traces between him and the DEA? Tonight, he stays incommunicado.

"Hey, I'm *eatin'* here," Fortuna says tersely. His listens, then suddenly forgets his food.

"—No fuckin' way."

"—He *what?*

"—Shit.

"—What? There *with* you? I don't care. Cap the bitch."

But Sparanzano, as if somehow aware, shakes his head.

"—No, wait a sec. Not yet. I'll get back at you."

Danny Fortuna ends the call and looks miserably at Sparanzano. He whispers, "*Vinnie.*"

Elvis gets endless rings, glances at his watch and swears to himself. Micky probably has a half-dozen numbers knowing how to reach Teddy Sparks, but Micky isn't talking.

"We gonna drive all fuckin' night?" Vinnie says, watching Elvis hits the auto redial, then shake his head.

"What are we going to do?" Jeanne wonders.

"Keep drivin'. Take a left up here at the corner. Then another left."

"In circles?"

"Nowhere else to go," Elvis supposes. He hits the redial, waits a long moment and hangs up. A few more times

before he catches Jeanne's worried expression in the rearview.

"I don't know what to do," she says, "but there's a police
car behind us."

Vinnie twists around, starts to call out, to raise his duck-
taped hands. Elvis jams the Glock between his legs, tight
against his crotch. Says, "Turn around an' shut up," and
Vinnie, wearing a new jag of pain, complies with a whimper.

"Take a right up here," he tells Jeanne. "Loop around but
don' get on the highway. We wanna stay close, in case I
get through, I don' wan' Teddy Sparks having a lot of time
thinkin' about this."

Jeanne looks in the rearview a few times and eventually
relaxes. "It's okay. He turned the other direction."

"Fuckin' spic," Vinnie mutters.

Elvis looks at him—and suddenly has an idea. He'd
patted Vinnie down tonight in Micky's living room—back
when Vinnie was a bloody lump. No wallet, no blade, but
Elvis found an iPhone in Vinnie's pants. Slipped it into his
own jacket pocket and forgot about it. Until now.

Vinnie sees the cell in Elvis' hand and says, "Hey, fucker,
gimme that."

The window displays a photo of some naked redhead
and it takes Elvis a moment to figure out the menu. Vinnie's got nothing but initials: A.F., C.C., D.F. J.T., J.Z.,
N.P... *what the fuck?*

There, finally, a single name displayed in the menu.
Teddy. Elvis raises an eyebrow. Vinnie's ego getting the better of him.

"Man, that's fuckin' mine," Vinnie whines, staring out the window.

But Elvis gets nowhere fast. Uncle Teddy's not answering for anybody. Not even for blood.

"Take a left," he says to Jeanne. He has another idea and searches the iPhone's menu again.

Sparanzano suggests they have a nightcap at the Bonaventure before retiring—it's rare that he turns in before midnight, and another room filled with impartial eyes might prove a worthy precaution this evening. Danny Fortuna drives, the three of them buzzed on Chianti, all three men with rooms on the thirty-first floor tonight. Fortuna tosses the valet the keys and they're midway through the lobby when his phone buzzes again.

"We're becoming a regular switchboard," Sparanzano remarks to Joey Segal.

"Fuckin' shit," Fortuna mutters, expecting Moya with another problem. He says, "Yeah?" Then stops in his tracks.

Sparanzano raises an eyebrow.

"It's for *you*."

Teddy Sparks is suspicious, but also curious. He takes the phone. "Yes? Who is this, please?"

Elvis spends a moment trying to find his voice.

"...Hello?"

"Mr. Sparanzano, it's Elvio Zapata."

Silence.

"I know it's you who hit us at Micky's place tonight. I know 'cause I got Vinnie here—"

"I'm all fucked up!" Vinnie calls, craning his neck. Elvis pushes him away with the Glock.

"—An' I wanna settle this thing with nobody else gettin' hurt. Can we talk about this, Mr. Sparanzano?"

"Where are you?"

"Here. Downtown."

"Oh?" Sparanzano turns in a circle, observing the lobby, the parking lot, his gaze alert. "You and Vinnie are alone?"

"I got Mrs. Russell with me."

"May I ask why you brought her along?"

"She sorta brought herself," Elvis admits.

Sparanzano inhales deeply and lets the breath out in a soft sigh. "All right. Drive to the service entrance, the alley off of Flower to the freight elevators. Five minutes. The security gates will be open. Speak to no one. I'll have someone meet you there."

"And you won't try nothin' on me or Mrs. Russell?"

"No, I will not."

"I got your word on that?"

"If you're telling me the truth, Mr. Zapata. So long as Vinnie's alive, then you have my word."

Elvis breaks the connection. "Turn right up here," he says to Jeanne.

10:45 PM SUNDAY

Two men in wrinkled sport jackets await them on the concrete lip of the service entrance. A few dim lights provide an anemic glow amid dark, sprawling shadows. Jeanne feels a tinge of fear.

"Those are Teddy Sparks' guys," Elvis tells her.

She pulls the Mercedes to a stop. Neither man at the service entrance moves. Elvis looks at Jeanne. "You sure you wanna do this?"

"I'm sure."

They climb out of the car, Elvis pulling Vinnie out by the scruff of the neck.

"Hey, Eddie! Tony! It's me, Vinnie!"

The two men exchange glances but neither says a word. Elvis watches their hands. Jeanne, arms filled with ledgers, waits by the driver's door. She stares straight up at the night-shrouded oval towers, then back at the men watching them. The moment seems utterly surreal.

"Shoot these fuckers, will ya!" Vinnie's voice echoes between the walls. When neither man moves, Elvis nods toward Jeanne.

"Hey, an' get me some fuckin' aspirin!" Vinnie calls.

They ride the service elevator in silence. It smells of raw meat and wet cardboard. Elvis is still gripping Vinnie by the collar. "Hey, lemme go. Cocksucker. Guys, c'mon— shoot this motherfucker. Cut me loose, huh?"

The two men stare at Vinnie in his bloody clothes, his broken nose and ruined face; stare at Jeanne, a small blonde hugging a bunch of ledgers. Elvis opens his jacket and, without a word, one of the men removes the Glock from his holster. They're big and burly guys, but they top off at Elvis' chin. They stare at Jeanne again.

"She packin'?" one asks.

"She's an accountant," Elvis tells them.

They pat her down anyway, taking their time.

Danny Fortuna meets them inside the marbled foyer and dismisses the two guys with a grunt. Fortuna frowns at Vinnie, then motions with a finger for Elvis and the woman to proceed. Vinnie pushes ahead, holding his taped wrists in front of his face. "Who put those two schmucks on fuckin' autopilot? Will somebody fuckin' unwrap me here or what?"

Sparanzano has changed into a navy blue bathrobe, over silk pajamas. He gives a nod toward Fortuna, who reaches in a pocket and produces a penknife. Vinnie extends his hands and Fortuna deftly slices the tape.

"Mr. Zapata," Sparanzano says politely. His eyes shift to Jeanne. "And this must be Mrs. Russell?"

She nods.

"How do you do?" Sparanzano notes the three leather books in her arms. "I'm sure this has been a horrible ordeal for you. My apologies."

"Thank you." Speaking softly, holding her own.

"Won't you sit down? Would you like some Chianti, Mrs. Russell?"

"No. Thank you." She turns in a slow pirouette, looking for the closest chair. The room is huge, magnificently opulent, a sea of white shag. A crystal chandelier winks pinpricks of light. Sparanzano guides her toward a long, leather couch with a motion of his hand.

"What you must understand, Mrs. Russell, is that what happened tonight was not personal." Jeanne listens to this man with his soft voice, in his elegant bathrobe, seating himself in a padded armchair across a squat glass-topped table. A vase between them blossoms with fresh flowers. He looks more like a priest than a Mafia hood—although the short guy standing behind him is right out of the late show. Well dressed and a little too Italian. A little too squinty-eyed. The short guy scares her. Vinnie's already charged to the bar. He pours himself a tumbler of vodka, muttering and swearing to himself.

"If it had been up to me—" Sparanzano puts a sympathetic hand to his chest, glancing at Elvis, then back to Jeanne. "—I would have paid."

Elvis raises an eyebrow.

"Unfortunately, the decision wasn't mine to make."

He's wearing slippers, Jeanne realizes. For some reason she doesn't think a man wearing slippers would do them harm. "Excuse me," she says. "But one of your—your *people* is holding my sister."

"I can promise that she's quite safe at the moment."

Jeanne closes her eyes, clutching the ledgers even more tightly to her chest. "Thank you," she whispers.

"As I told Mr. Zapata, that you've returned Vinnie is very important to me."

"Yeah, well, here I am—so gimme a fuckin' piece," Vinnie says, coming around the bar. He's gulped most of his drink, smirking now, ridiculous in his duct tape bandana and stuck-up hair, his face crusted in drying blood. He moves to within a few feet of the couch and says, "Lemme pop 'em right here. Swear to Christ, I'll blow 'em both to hell."

"Vinnie, be quiet."

"Fuckin' spic nearly roasted my balls off."

"That you're here now is all that matters." Sparanzano cocks his head and says; "By the way, Danny spoke with Richie a little while ago."

"Yeah?"

"Most troubling."

Vinnie takes another gulp of vodka and regards his uncle with a sudden smirk. "Tol' you stuff got all fucked out of whack, huh?"

"Told us the situation got out of hand, yes. Told Danny that you spooked, Vinnie. In all probability got Al Liola killed."

"Al got wiped? No shit. Richie tol' you—what? That *I* spooked? No way. Richie's fulla shit."

Jeanne's watching Sparanzano, aware of his disappointment, Sparanzano with his eyes closed, and she has a fleeting impression that he might be praying. From the corner of her eye she senses a quick motion, the little Italian guy behind Vinnie with a black garbage bag out of nowhere, the guy on his tiptoes—suddenly dropping the bag over Vinnie's head. He tugs sharply backward with one hand, reaching inside his jacket with the other.

"Hey!" Vinnie drops his glass and jerks forward. The little guy withdraws a long-barreled pistol and places the tip against the back of Vinnie's head. Jeanne can see the impression of Vinnie's face pressing against the taut, smooth surface, his mouth open, nose tilting to one side. The gun makes a small cough and the bag abruptly bulges in front.

Sparanzano opens his eyes again.

Like in a movie, Jeanne thinks. The little guy yanks

sharply backwards on the bag, catching Vinnie before he
can stumble forward, easing the limp body to the floor with
an almost gentle concern. She watches with a slack-jawed
fascination, forgetting to breathe and somehow not even
believing it might be real. She tears her gaze from Vinnie—his left leg spasms a bit—and refocuses dizzily on
Sparanzano, the same man in the same slippers, same soft
brown eyes. She's aware of the little man's gun, pointing
at her now.

Sparanzano spreads his hands, an apologetic gesture.

"You tol' me your word, Mr. Sparanzano," Elvis says.

"So long as Vinnie was alive," Sparanzano reminds him.

Elvis thinks about it, unable to refute the logic of Vinnie lying there with his brains blown out.

"But *why?*" Jeanne asks, finding her voice.

"A matter of honor, Mrs. Russell. It may seem harsh to
you, but I abide by a strict sense of principle. As perhaps is
now obvious from my nephew's regrettable death, and now
Mr. Zapata's. Disturbingly, I'm afraid your own as well. Mr.
Zapata killed an associate of ours and, in return, I'm bound
by honor to avenge that killing."

"Are you talking about Micky Logan?"

"That's right."

"Then I think you should look at these." With shaking
hands, Jeanne places the ledgers on the little glass table.

"And why might I do that?"

"Because Mr. Logan was doctoring his books. The money
he owed you every month. If this is the type of principled
man you intend to avenge, you may want to take a peek
before you shoot us."

A crescent of a frown forms against Sparanzano's lips. "There's so much you don't understand, Mrs. Russell. Let me try—" He holds up a finger. "Very briefly."

As if she might be *bored*? Jeanne can't believe it.

"I exist in a world that exudes a certain amount of greed. While Micky Logan was a man of financial wiles, Micky's accountant was a man of decidedly split loyalties. I'm well aware of Micky's finagling. I simply adjusted my percentages accordingly. While Micky assumed he was outfoxing us, we'd actually achieved a state of what you might call harmonic symbiosis. The yin and yang of the universe, after all. So you see, I have no quarrel with Mr. Logan."

Sparanzano spreads his hands again, a resigned sadness in his gaze.

Jeanne gives the man a stern-looking frown. "What you don't understand is that Micky Logan was cooking the books on his own accountant. The amount you're talking about is roughly one hundred thousand a quarter. Those are the numbers reflected in his accountant's books. But what Mr. Sussman didn't know is that Micky Logan was keeping a *third* set."

Finally, a glint of surprise touches Sparanzano's expression.

"Micky Logan was taking you to the cleaners. Roughly three million dollars over the last two and a half years. It's all there, in the third ledger."

Sparanzano leans forward, his eyes flitting between Jeanne and the ledgers. Almost as an afterthought, he gestures for the gunman standing behind him to lower his pistol.

"I *really* wish you'd look," Jeanne says.

For the longest moment Sparanzano studies her gaze. He motions again to the gunman. "Get Joey over here. Wake him with my apologies, Danny, but get him up *now*."

Despite his apparent nonchalance, Elvis finally begins breathing again. He turns toward Jeanne with a half-raised eyebrow and, for the first time since she's met him, Elvis smiles.

Cutter drives in silence, occasionally glancing over, telling Jeff, "Hold on, only a little further," but otherwise neither man with any compulsion to speak. Maybe because words at this point won't help. Maybe because neither man expects to find Angie alive tonight.

A plastic yellow duck on the dashboard snags Jeff's attention. The toy stares at Jeff with a painted, loony smile. He notices the loose crayons on the floor, Disney hair clips, the incongruent, silenced machine gun against Cutter's leg, young life and life's aftermath swirling together in a crazy, surreal sort of way.

Something bumps against Jeff's heel. He reaches down, picks up a blonde-maned Barbie, the naked doll with a plastic bicycle streamer wound several times around her neck.

"Hold on, deputy," Cutter tells him. "Not much further."

Pacific Coast Highway merges with Route 10 and Cutter

quickly turns off at Lincoln—the street a neon-tinged mirror of working class L.A. The area's seen better times but
it's doing the best it can, settling in for the night, shadows flitting around the edges of light. The shadows *watching* him, Jeff feels. Cutter cruises through a series of red
lights, the traffic thin at this hour. He makes a few turns,
storefronts gradually giving way to industrial buildings, the
darkness at first penetrating, then permeating. Desolation
encroaches on the side streets around them, an occasional
liquor store or bar flashing its intent like a Siren's song.

"We almost there?" Jeff asks.

"Almost."

It's a ritual they repeat several times.

11:00 PM SUNDAY

Moya's been obsessing the last half-hour, alternately pacing and watching Angie lying on the concrete, all tousled
blonde hair and torn denim. He looks at the clock and
thinks, *fuck Danny Fortuna.* He walks over and stares at
her for a long, twitchy moment. Moya has a sudden urge
to unzip his pants and piss on the bitch. Instead he nudges
her a couple times with his boot, then leaning into it, gets
a steel toe under her shoulder and flips her onto her back.
Gets a moan out of her. Unaware, he begins to snap his
fingers.

One side of her blouse is drenched in the dead punk's
blood but Moya barely notices. He's staring at her breasts.

A good, long look. One hand absently brushing back and forth against his crotch. Moya walks over to the plywood office, picks up a cutting blade from a cabinet and comes back, feeling the weight of the tool in his hand, then reaches down and squeezes her left breast. Soft. Bitch isn't even wearing a bra. Moya moves the cutting blade to where her nipple puckers her shirt—but he pauses, not sure if she would bleed out before he's through with her.

He reminds himself to take her nipples when he's through with her. Later say, *Hey, look what I got?* and maybe get a chuckle out of Danny. Fortuna told him she was a whore, but she doesn't look like one. All that gold hair. White skin. He can smell her perfume. She looks more like the type of girl who thinks she's too good for him, sneering at him in bars, on sidewalks, crossing to the other side of the street sometimes, to avoid any chance of eye contact.

Moya cocks his foot and kicks her, hard, then boots her again for good measure. No response. Moya needs—*more.* His gaze roams the warehouse and he spies a series of heavy chains drooping against a wall, pulleys suspended from a ceiling winch.

Yeah, there we go.

A throb of pain pushes Angie back toward consciousness. She wakes with the stench of motor oil in her nostrils and a vague, dizzying uncertainty as to where she might be. She stares into the cold grayness of a cement floor and hears scraping metallic sounds behind her. She realizes that her hands are bound and tries to move, feels a jackhammer stab of pain in her side and gasps, starts to moan—then pulls it together and thinks, *shut the fuck up, Angelina.*

Listening again to the metallic clink-clink-clink-clink-clink.

She remembers now, waking up once or twice on the floor in the cab, smelling of turpentine and old cigarettes, hearing traffic sounds before drifting off, the taste of blood in her mouth. Now she's—*where?* Here. The metallic noise grows closer. An echo of footsteps on cement. She shuts her eyes, coaxing herself to stay limp as long as she's able.

Moya grabs a ribbon of chain, gives himself some slack and slips the attached J-hook through Angie's nylon bindings. He yanks sharply. Like a marionette flirting with life, her forearms give a fluttery jerk upwards. Moya pulls again and Angie's jolted to her knees, arms extending over her head. A savage new pain sears through her shoulders and she forces herself not to scream. She lets her head loll back and prays the forced grunts from her lungs won't give her away. Another jerk and she feels her feet leave the concrete. She sways slightly, only the tips of her bare toes brushing the floor. Her head rolls forward and she tries to catch a glimpse through barely-opened eyes. She sees the man in front of her as a silhouette, aware only of his smile.

That same terrible smile she remembers coming at her through the darkness, the moment Dwight died in her arms.

"There is, of course, another problem," Sparanzano says and Jeanne glances intuitively again at Vinnie's faceless body. The moment is too bizarre and, even in her terrified state, she can't help but wonder, *How will they get him through the lobby like that?* Reality floods back and she realizes that Micky Logan's ledgers aren't going to help her out of this.

"I don't think your nephew was a very good person," she tells him.

"You have moxie, Mrs. Russell." Speaking in a chagrined tone that makes her shiver.

"You speak of honor, Mr. Sparanzano. Is *this* what you call honor?"

"This is what I call business. What happened to Vinnie is a family matter. Between him and me and his maker. That you've witnessed this particular family matter—yes, I'm afraid it becomes a matter of business."

"So you're going to shoot us?"

Sparanzano stares at her in silent pain.

"Hey, she's an accountant," Elvis says. "She don't know none of this."

"Whatever she knows, it's unfortunate."

Jeanne feels a new surge of gnawing dread. She watches the little guy watching Sparanzano, the little guy excited, almost anxious. Thinking, just like that, it will be all over. She wonders about Jeff, about never seeing him again. Never having babies. She's so afraid the fear feels like a physical weight, an unbearable pressure against her chest.

"It don't seem right," Elvis tells Teddy Sparks, "whacking us over a piece of *basura* like Vinnie. Bad karma," Elvis says, the words pulled out of nowhere and Jeanne only half listening, still thinking about Jeff. About the first time they'd met. The first time they'd kissed.

But Sparanzano is very much aware. Surprised, in fact. Sparanzano studies Elvis closely. "You know about such things, Mr. Zapata?"

Elvis tries to remember. Forces the words toward his tongue and finally says, "I know you do this thing, it really fucks up your *destino*—you know, man, your future. Maybe haunts you the rest of your life." He looks expectantly at Sparanzano, not sure if he's made any sense or not.

Sparanzano sits in a thoughtful muse, silent for a long moment, then waggles a finger absently at Fortuna.

"Get my cards, Danny. On the bed stand."

"You shittin' me, Teddy?"

When Sparanzano says nothing, Fortuna shrugs and goes to do what he's told.

"You're willing to let the fates decide?" Sparanzano asks.

Elvis nods. It's more than he had two seconds ago.

"You and the lady both?"

"We came in together," Elvis says. Jeanne's attention has returned, cognizant that something's happening but not certain of what. They're still alive, at least. The little guy's gone and Elvis is talking. Something about playing *cards*?

"Then I suppose you'll understand that whatev—"

Sparanzano closes his mouth because Fortuna returns,

carrying an intricately carved wooden box that he places on the glass-topped table. Sparanzano removes the lid and exposes a deck of heavy, oversized cards.

"What?" Jeanne asks.

"Tarot," Sparanzano says. He gives the cards a loose shuffle, watching Elvis with unflinching interest.

"What are we doing?"

"Maybe dyin'," Elvis tells Jeanne with a shrug. "Maybe not. I dunno yet."

"Mr. Zapata and I are about to reveal the future, Mrs. Russell." Sparanzano places the cards carefully on the table between them. He spreads the deck with the palm of his hand and gestures.

Elvis hesitates and looks at Jeanne, then reaches forward and selects a card. Flips it over on the table in front of Sparanzano. They stare at a solitary figure in a flowing black robe, carrying a sythe. Ominous black letters at the bottom.

DEATH.

Jeanne thinks, *two out of three?*

For a long moment silence permeates the room. The little guy with the gun seems confused. Sparanzano remains transfixed by the card. Jeanne blinks between Sparanzano and the card several times—the grim, skull-like face grimacing but hard to perceive because the figure's upside down, facing Sparanzano. When he finally looks up, his gaze is thoughtful, probing.

"I spoke of honor, Mrs. Russell. Our way of life. I have, in my own life, only one greater loyalty."

Jeanne finds herself unable to speak, to react.

"You have a husband. A pretty sister. Children?"

Reading her silence, he says, "No? Someday, perhaps. Happy young children, so full of life, playing their innocent children's games in your yard."

Without a sound, Jeanne begins to cry.

"During the remainder of your life, Mrs. Russell, should you mention Vincent's demise to anyone"—he pauses, a stern finger raised—"to *anyone*, and one day a man will appear at your door. You will not know this person, but he will do great harm to your family. To your husband and to your pretty children. Do I make myself understood?"

"Yes," she whispers, forcing the word through her tears.

"Put Vincent and Micky Logan and whatever happened this evening out of your mind forever and you'll have nothing to fear from me. *Capisci?*"

"Yes."

"What about Joey?" Fortuna says, the little guy's voice tinged with regret. A bullet in his gun with nowhere to go.

Sparanzano regards the ledgers on the table. "I believe Joey will find matters precisely as the lady has informed us. I don't say this very often, Mrs. Russell, but I believe I can trust you."

Jeanne finally manages a smile.

"It was a pleasure to make your acquaintance. You remind me of my wife many years ago. A compliment to you both." Sparanzano sits back in his chair and Jeanne is aware of his paleness. His gaze flits quickly to Elvis.

"Mr. Zapata? Tomorrow you'll come work for me, hmm?

Maybe perform more admirably than poor Vincent. There's a great deal about Micky Logan I'd like to—"

"Mr. Sparanzano, no disrespect," Elvis says, "but I don' wanna do this no more."

"Oh?"

Elvis shakes his head. "Drugs an' shit."

"May I ask?"

"He wants to be a bartender," Jeanne says, putting a hand gently on Elvis' sleeve.

Sparanzano opens his mouth, but closes it again—not understanding, but accepting whatever the fates have decided this night. He nods dismissively toward the doorway. "And so the world goes on, hmm?"

Elvis stands and pulls Jeanne up beside him. She wants to say something, anything, but Elvis guides her hurriedly toward the door. She looks back—aware of the little guy regarding them with a lingering doubt. Also aware of Sparanzano studying the card again.

"What?" she says.

Elvis keeps her moving.

"What?" she asks again in the doorway.

"The card," Elvis says.

"It was a *death* card."

"Upside down," Elvis whispers. "Upside down to us. Not to him."

"Upside down?" Jeanne says, still not comprehending.

"Wasn't *our* death card," Elvis tells her, closing the door behind them, and Jeanne finally understands.

11:15ᴘᴍ SUNDAY

Angie's known predators like this. She's spent the last eighteen months avoiding these men on the streets or in motel rooms and bars. She knows the look, the warped thrill of intent that simmers behind their eyes. Men like this, they prey on their victim's fear. This isn't about lust, or even about sex. It's about domination and submission and humiliation—and when they've drunk their fill, it's about snuffing out life because life means nothing to them. Angie realizes that she is going to die tonight.

The smiling man spends several minutes watching her sway from the chain, then moves closer. He becomes suddenly impatient and grabs her hair—she can feel blood trickling against her scalp—then jerks her head backwards until she thinks her neck might snap. She feels his lips, his tongue thickly on her throat, leaving a hot ooze of saliva. Angie moans, fighting an urge to scream and pull away. He moves behind her, rubbing his hands roughly along her thighs, up her waist and to her breasts, his fingers clamping hard. Squeezing her nipples, pinching, exploring weakness. Angie chokes off another scream, desperate to deny him her acknowledgment of any pain. He presses himself against her back and she can feel his throbbing bulge poking her jeans. He is arousing himself with her helplessness.

She feels him moving again, his stiffness at her side. He brushes against her belly. She can smell his breath, a cloying staleness that makes her want to vomit. A man as decayed inside as out. An instant later his lips mash against hers, his tongue penetrating deeply into her mouth. His movements, his hands, are becoming rougher, more anxious, more painful.

Angie feels herself succumb to another realm. Feels herself transformed to that tranquil place inside her head, snatching her away from the reality of the smiling man's violent world.

At the front gate, the old guard reeks of whisky fumes. The guy's nearly eighty, watching soft porn on a little TV set, telling them with a shrug that a coupla cars maybe came and went tonight. The gate's automated if you've got a magnetic card, or if you press the right key code. The guy shrugs again, basically letting them know that he doesn't have a clue. Cutter holds up his badge but the old guard doesn't really give a damn—he waves them through with a grumble.

Cutter drives past a few warehouses bathed in utter darkness. "This is the place," Cutter says. "Up ahead."

"You're sure?" Jeff's aware of the desolation surrounding them, shuddering to think that Angie might actually *be* here.

Shuddering again to think she might not.

Angie's dream-reality settles around her mind like a warm blanket. But it's ultimately a helpless place and for the first time she can remember, bits of reality drift in with her. Compelling voices inside her head insist that *helpless* is one thing she cannot afford to be. Not this time. She stirs and fights against the familiar cloak of paralysis. She feels reality flood back—all the fear and loathing—then twitches and opens her eyes.

The smiling man's gaze burns in front of her like a hot ember. "*Bitch*," he seethes.

No fear, she thinks. No fear no fear no fear no fear no fear—

"What?" she hears herself say. "Did I miss the party?"

For an instant, confusion dances across the feral face. Then the smile returns, the aura of dominance. "Hon, you ain't missed nothin' yet."

"You have a reservation, sailor?"

The smiling man doesn't like her contempt. *Too much, Angelina.* He slaps her. "Whore."

She feels the far-away place begin to seep again around the edge of consciousness. Angie fights to push it away. "Look, I'm only saying it doesn't have to be this way." She wonders if she can play coy, wearing all this blood, all this pain.

"Shut up."

"It can be nice… between you and me."

"I'll show you how it's gonna be." His fingers claw at her thighs, find her belt loops and he yanks her jeans down around her knees. Her panties are dislodged over one hip. The smiling man fumbles, pulling off one denim leg, bending there a brief instant and—*Yes!* she realizes—vulnerable. With an adrenalin rush of strength, Angie drives both knees sharply upward toward his throat.

He senses her sudden movement and jerks his head sideways. Her right knee catches his cheek and unbalances him. Her momentum carries her knees toward her chest and she jackhammers her legs outward. An instant of bewilderment flashes across the smiling man's face as her heels connect with that fucking animal smile.

Cutter coasts another moment, then brakes in front of 118, the minivan's headlamps splashing an oval of light. Jeff scans the complex—a long concrete building, large and pitched-roofed, with corrugated tin doors situated every thirty or so feet. Small windows set high and dark. They've already passed several rows of identical buildings, tiny numbers stenciled on each metal door. Only asphalt and pitted concrete around them. He feels a frantic clawing of dread.

"This one here, we occasionally keep an eye out," Cutter says. "Surveillance cameras when we can get a court order—but every time we've show up, the place is empty. I guess now I know why."

Jeff peers at the surrounding darkness. If Angie's not here, he doubts they'll have time to find her—or even know where to look next. He peers the length of the looming structure, black against black. "Wait a sec," he says, "turn out your lights."

Cutter does so, and then dims the van's console. Jeff searches the facade, giving his vision time to adjust. The moon's lost behind the warehouse. The night is absolute.

"Damn," Cutter mutters.

"Look, *there*. Window on the left," Jeff says, nodding to a unit a few doors away. A glass window is blacked out, the barest outline of light seeping into the darkness.

"Uh huh, I see it."

"You think?"

"I think."

Jeff draws his Smith .38.

"We can do this one of two ways," Cutter says, shifting the minivan into first gear. "The sensible way or the *other* way."

The smiling man wobbles back several steps, a gash in his lip dripping blood. He nearly falls, eyes glazed, but Angie sees awareness snap back, the man regaining his balance. He's come away with her jeans in one fist and holds them up, like a trophy, oblivious to the flow of blood that dribbles from his chin. He gives her another smile, his teeth coated in a crimson sheen.

"Fuckin' whore," he says, his voice a whisper that chills her. He spits blood and drops her jeans to the floor, then steps away, a few paces, staring back and forth at the cutting blade and the silenced pistol he's left atop a wooden crate. He makes his decision and returns holding the gun next to his face, curling his other hand around its long black snout, pumping up and down, up and down.

"You wanna fuck, whore? Fuck *this*."

Angie moans and tries to kick him again, lashing out, but he sidesteps her effort, grabs for her panties and misses. She manages a glancing blow against his arm. Her momentum swings her sideways, her legs flailing. He makes another attempt to snatch her panties, misses again but catches her above the knee, his fingers digging into her flesh. He thrusts his gun upward toward her crotch. She squeals, suddenly very afraid.

"When it comes, baby, it comes *hard.*"

Another thrust, but the angry black barrel misses its mark. Angie twists and struggles to free herself from his grip. She tries to kick him again but he leans sideways, standing wide of her reach, still holding her leg. She tries again, exhausted by this final attempt, her foot finding only air.

Angie feels herself running out of chances.

"Yvonne's gonna be pissed," Cutter says. He grinds his foot on the brake pedal and guns the engine. "Hold on, deputy." The minivan's engine screams in an angry crescendo of noise and unfamiliar vibration—then launches toward the tin door. Jeff puts one hand on the dash, the other extending his .38. Thinking, *Oh, shit*—

Angie watches the gun weave toward her crotch. She gathers the last remnants of her strength and wonders, *Maybe one last time?* Yet the thought shrivels behind an apocalyptic screech of metal as the far wall implodes. A sudden blur of motion displaces shadows across the cavernous room, the smiling man instinctively spinning toward the sound, his gun raised. Angie glimpses a battered minivan, a whirling cascade of corrugated metal shards and, with a final surge of adrenalin, she kicks out. Her foot connects with the smiling man's shoulder blade and propels him toward the van, unbalanced, stumbling, firing wildly. He snarls a final obscenity.

The van nails him, dead on, the smiling man so much like a bug splattering against the windshield. His arms fling wide, his gun gone, fingers groping at nothing. She hears a squeal of brakes and glimpses her brother-in-law, grim-faced, pistol extended — Jeff, who doesn't like taking need-less risks — firing his revolver twice through the windshield. The smiling man's face dissolves in a crimson smear, and she thinks *Good, good, good*—knowing that terrible grin is gone forever.

She spasms, trembling, and consciousness begins to recede into some dark crevice. Angie wonders if Jeff is really here at all. Wonders if seeing his face, feeling his arms around her, might simply be a figment of her dying brain, a surreal dreamscape that lingers in that final moment between life and death...

12:30 AM MONDAY

"You have two minutes," Torres tells Jeff, sober now and hating it. "Before I call in an ops team." She glances toward Trip Cutter, who isn't saying much, seated on a couch a few paces away. Every few seconds he glances at Roman's crum-pled body, shaking his head, trying to make sense of it all.

Torres looks at Jeanne and Angie—the two sisters who've yet to release each other, their last few minutes spent in a barrage of tears and murmurs. No help there either. Torres wonders if anyone's even remotely here.

"Meaning what?" Jeff asks.

"Meaning that I need you—I'd *like* you—to leave. That's not a threat, deputy. Not an order. I'm asking for a favor, cop to cop."

Jeff's aware of a single tear crawling from the corner of her eye and she brusquely palms it away. "I'm asking that you allow us handle this," Torres says. "The fewer stories about tonight, the better."

"What about us?" he asks.

"You're not here. You left this afternoon. You took your family home because that's what Ben Roman told you to do."

Jeff's gaze wanders around the shambles of Logan's living room. It takes him a long moment, but he realizes something is missing. No, not something—some*one*.

"Zapata?" he asks. "What's going to happen to him?"

"There's a body buried somewhere in the backyard. Mr. Zapata and I thought it prudent that he not be in the vicinity when it's found."

Jeff nods, not pressing the issue.

Torres holds his gaze. "Look, deputy, we fucked up. Go home," she says. "Give Trip your gun; ballistics will need a trace. We'll log it as being in Agent Cutter's possession this evening. You'll get it back, sooner or later, with some bullshit story. We're going to clean this up. We're going to start over. We're going to make it right, I promise you."

Jeff nods without expression—he moves past Jeanne and Angie, pausing long enough to lightly kiss the top of Angie's head. He goes to the bedroom and collects their bags, returns to find Jeanne and Angie still in their silent embrace. He dumps the luggage in the Volvo and returns, pulls his Smith .38 and places it on the couch next to Cutter.

"You okay?"

Cutter looks up from the couch. "Tell you the truth, man, I don't know *what* I am."

"Well, you're good in a crunch. Thanks," Jeff says. He reaches out and shakes the agent's hand.

"Jeannie?"

"I'm ready," she whispers.

"Me, too," Angie says. She's washed her face. Her forehead and cheek are bruised, her lip split, but already she knows she's somehow on the mend. She feels almost radiant standing there, wearing her teal summer print dress. The one with the white flowers. The one Manetti likes.

"We better get going," Jeff tells them.

They step carefully over the glass and debris, toward Micky Logan's elaborate front entrance. Angie hesitates a moment, looking back from the doorway. "*Dwight,*" she says, barely aloud, a gentle farewell to whatever ghosts that might still linger. Jeanne doesn't hear and ushers her forward with soothing words toward the Volvo.

They make Orange County forty minutes later, Jeff alert and silent. The radio's on, *Desperado*—an old Eagles' tune—playing low. Jeanne's spent much of the trip looking back at Angie with brimming eyes, occasionally reaching out and the two of them clutching hands. But Jeanne's sleeping now, her head resting on Jeff's shoulder.

Angie watches the darkened world pass from the back

seat and feels her eyelids grow heavy. She stretches out, trying to find a comfortable spot, resting her legs on those few items piled on the seat and finally deciding to dump everything on the floor. A couple of jackets and, underneath, a brown satchel that reminds her of—Angie frowns. *Dwight's* satchel. She brushes her fingers against the smooth leather, content with the sensation for a long moment. Curious then, she unzips the bag and peers inside.

The satchel contains crisp stacks of blue-banded hundred dollar bills. A good many stacks of packaged hundreds, the bag nearly full, piles and piles of money. "Elvis," she whispers with a tired smile. She re-zips the bag and glances at Jeff, his gaze unwavering from the road ahead.

Angie lays back, eyes closed, and wonders how she's going to explain *this* time.

TUESDAY

Trip Cutter finds a moment, takes his Styrofoam cup of tepid coffee down the hall and makes his way to Renee Torres' shared office—six metal desks, shiny black under an array of fluorescent lights. Only a couple of the desks are occupied. It's late in the day, the afternoon already a memory. Cutter raps a knuckle on a corner of Torres' desk, startling her out of a stupor. Her gaze darts up from a glowing monitor.

"Jesus, Trip. I thought you were another friggin' AI snoop. What's up?"

They've been ping-ponged through a hectic schedule of affidavits and interrogations and debriefings since Monday morning. More of the same tomorrow, most likely. Torres appears gaunt and drained, stacked manila files neatly on her desktop, caseload files that can't wait. Another agent will be assigned during the time she'll be out of the field. Reassigned to banality, the way she figures. *Routine*, they tell her. Until the investigation is complete.

He manages a smile. "You hanging tough?"

"Yeah, doin' okay. Hobart came by a while ago. Suggested a little getaway might be in order. Administrative leave while they sort things out. What do you think?"

"Hawai'i has a nice ring to it," he tells her.

"Yeah, it does. Maybe I should think about—" But she pauses, aware of the mood behind his lingering gaze. "Trip? What's wrong?"

"Thought you'd want to know. A drive by, about half an hour ago. Bunch of pissed-off brothers in a purple Mercedes took out Danny Fortuna. Waiting for him and Teddy Sparks, coming out of a restaurant over on West Sunset."

"You're serious?"

"Most likely making a move on Duke Capriccio's territory," Cutter says with a nod.

"What about Sparanzano?"

"Amazing thing is, not a scratch. Fifty, sixty rounds fired, and they didn't touch the guy. The dude's luckier than a long horse on a short track. Too bad it didn't rub off any on Fortuna."

"Dead?"

"Life support at USC. Three in the chest. Took a couple

in the face, one in the throat. ICU doesn't expect him to pull through the night."

"Anybody find the car?"

"Abandoned. Smoldering in Watts. All we know is three men of color ran from the vehicle," Cutter says. "One of them a little gimpy. A bunch of LAPD's *white* boys out there, ringing doorbells in the 'hood. That's as good as it's going to get."

"It's beginning," Torres says with weary amazement. "It's already starting."

"Feeding frenzy," Cutter admits, "for Logan's successor. Lotta people gonna die before they find one."

"Do you ever ask yourself why we bother? Why we even try? Because it's never going to end, you know. This shit's never going to end."

Cutter says nothing, but thinks to himself, *ended for Roman.* He brushes away the funk and says, "Hey, you wanna grab some coffee in a bit. After hours?"

"Sounds a little tame, under the circumstances." Renee Torres forces her own smile. "How about I buy you a few shots of peach schnapps. We'll talk."

"You're on, girl." Cutter winks at her, and moves back through the corridor in no great hurry. He feels empty inside, ambivalent, wondering where the silver linings have gone. Wonders if they've ever really existed at all.

WEDNESDAY

She's walked this dirt path nearly every day for seventy years, a stooped woman with fragile bones and stark white hair, wearing a faded woven shawl. She's walked this way and prayed and wondered about life and sung songs and smiled at whomever she's chanced to meet. This afternoon, her old eyes become aware of a figure looming at the dusty crossroads ahead. Standing there for a long time now. *Waiting*, she thinks.

She presses on slowly, wary of loose stones. The big man seems out of place in his dark suit, under the azure sky and yellow sun. And yet—is there something familiar about the broad shoulders? Her heart beats faster and she quickens her pace. The old woman narrows her eyes, another few moments before her mouth expands in a wide, toothless grin.

"*¡Elvio? Eres tu!*"

"It's me, Gran'mama." Telling her in Spanish.

"You've come—"

"Home," Elvis says.

"To stay?"

"To help Simone."

"And your sisters?"

"They are coming also. On an airplane."

She takes his arm, feeling his strength and energy and she sings again, in her heart.

"Walk with me, Elvis."

"*Si, Gran'mama.*"

"I like your haircut."

"*Si, Gran'mama.*"

Elvis smiles at the old woman and guides her along the path, all the time in the world to be patient.

EL FIN

Author's Bio

DAVE WORKMAN has served as a Los Angeles-based film critic, newspaper columnist and magazine writer for many years. *On The Rocks* (2012) is his second novel.

An excerpt of *On The Edge* (2017) follows this page.

Dave's books can be found on Amazon.com and at Muse Harbor Publishing (www.museharbor.com). Also a book designer and editor, Dave's blog, *Rules of Engagement*—notes of encouragement for new writers—can also be found on museharbor.com. He currently lives in Northern California with his wife, Eileen (also a writer) and a perpetually hungry Golden Retriever.

Dave Workman's *Like A California Dream* (A novel about surviving Hollywood) will be available in 2018.

On The Edge

Dave Workman

(an excerpt)

1

Bobby Leland felt himself drifting toward a peaceful sleep, his thoughts fading when the woman beside him said, "Here's what I want, Bobby. Are you listening to me?" Her finger tickled a path across his chest, her breath a hot whisper against his ear. "I want you to kill my husband."

They lay naked upon chamomile-scented satin sheets, in a room with a marble fireplace, French doors opening to a balcony that overlooked the distant Pacific. Because he and Erica had made a kind of full-throttled reckless love for the last forty-five minutes, Bobby felt mellow to his toes.

"Did you hear me?" she asked. "Bobby?"

"I heard you," he said, safely cocooned in the darkness behind his eyelids. "You want me to kill Elliot."

"I want *us* to kill Elliot. You and I together."

"Both of us," he said, wondering if he might be already dreaming.

"Yes."

He gave it a few seconds, remembering Erica's previous evening's attempt to microwave Cordon Bleu. "You could always make him dinner."

Her tongue tutted. "Bobby, I'm *serious*."

For some reason, he wasn't surprised.

At forty-two, seven years older than Bobby, few people could have guessed her age. Long and sleek and perfect, happenstance and heredity had gifted Erica Garmond a graceful neck, high cheekbones and hypnotic cobalt eyes; platinum blonde hair that fell straight, curling slightly inward where it brushed against her throat, and lips poised on the verge of a chronic pout. Erica appeared to be one of those women who'd simply stopped aging.

Not that she didn't work hard to maintain herself: up for aerobics at 6:15 every morning, her afternoons occupied with tennis or jogging. Almost too rich and certainly too thin, the way Stan Muca described her. Stan was an artful observer and carouser himself, head pro and Bobby's boss back at Rancho Madera Tennis Club.

Bobby had been Erica's teaching pro for the last eight months. Her occasional lover for the past four. Occasional because he'd learned early on that Erica enjoyed calling the shots, Bobby responding whenever the warm La Jolla breezes blew favorably in his direction. The few times he'd phoned to suggest dinner or maybe cocktails near the beach she would turn cold, spurning him in one natty way or another—sometimes canceling her twice-weekly lesson at the club. So he would wait patiently for the winds to change again.

The thing about Bobby Leland, he was good at adapting.

"*Bobby?*" she said.

He'd begun to zone out again, caught himself and dragged his mind back. He floated in that twilight area between sleep and consciousness, still not certain this conversation was happening.

The sheets rustled beside him. "Are you paying attention to me?"

He absently sucked a crescent of saliva from the corner of his mouth. "You, what? Want it like an accident or something?"

"It doesn't matter. Yes. I don't care. No. I don't want him found. I want this a complete mystery. It doesn't matter *how* we do it. I simply need him dead."

"And you want me to help you."

"I don't think I'm capable of doing this alone." Bobby felt her lean close, her breasts pressing against his rib cage. "Please?"

He felt detached, fuzzy somehow. He assumed she'd be over this particular compulsion tomorrow or the day after. And the last thing he wanted to do was piss her off, give Erica a reason to toss him out when every muscle in his body screamed for sleep.

"Sure," he told her. "Whatever."

THINKING BACK, Bobby decided that Erica must have wanted Elliot dead since the club's Fourth of July doubles tournament. She and Carl Faulkner had lost the semi's in the third set, an occurrence that would have typically sent her off sulking, then later blame Bobby for not working her strokes hard enough. But losing seemed less on Erica's mind than getting him alone that evening, Rancho Madero's traditional aprés-tournament *Beer n' Lobster Bash* in full swing on the clubhouse patio. Fireworks splashed the distant horizon above the shimmering San Diego skyline. When Bobby wandered through the bar and into a service closet to fetch another keg, Erica followed. He heard a noise in the dark behind him and turned.

She laced her arms around his neck, suddenly all over him. "*Fuck* me, Bobby," she breathed, nuzzling his ear and biting hard, thrusting herself against him, her weight slamming them both against stacked boxes of Chinette plates and paper towels.

"Christ," he said. "What—?"

"Here," she breathed. "*Now.*" She groped for his crotch, squeezing in a way that brought him to his tiptoes. Bobby could hear wisps of conversation and laughter carrying from the patio. She unzipped his tennis whites, feeling for him, not giving him an easy out.

"Jesus, your husband..."

"Is a prick," she told him.

"...is out*side.*"

"We won't have to worry about Elliot much longer, Dearheart. I promise you that."

He hadn't understood at the time. But, replaying the

moment in his mind, he realized that probably should have been his first clue.

BESIDE HIM in bed, Erica said, "Do you know why I want Elliot dead?"

"Because he's a prick?" Bobby asked, remembering.

"Because—" He heard her feathered sigh. "—because I suspect he's going to murder me, if I don't kill him first."

Which finally prompted Bobby to open his eyes.

Erica lay waiting, her gaze probing, her delicate chin cupped in one hand. "So what I'm asking, it's simply a matter of survival. You understand that, don't you?"

He might have believed her fear—*might* have, except for intensity of her gaze, her eyes crystalline, mesmerizing, the color of a still mountain lake on a frigid winter's day. Despite the way her lip trembled, Erica couldn't pull off playing the helpless female.

"It would be self-defense," she told him, "you and I killing Elliot."

"You're imagining things."

"Believe me," Erica said. "I know the way his mind works."

She had thrown subtle tantrums in the past, although Bobby had never felt himself jerked around quite like this before. He'd met Elliot numerous times at the club, of course; Erica's husband a patent attorney, a full partner in a downtown law firm and probably a good lawyer, but a mediocre tennis player. A little demanding and self-centered, but he paid for that right on the first of every month. Erica occasionally alluded to a darker side of Elliot's profession, although she'd never been specific. Bobby had never considered the man particularly dangerous.

"He's planning something," Erica said. "I've seen... *nuances.* The way he's been acting, treating me lately. Looking right through me. As if I no longer exist."

"Sounds like half the couples at Rancho Madera."

"No," she said, "there's more."

He waited.

"The telephone conversations. Elliot with his morning coffee by the pool. Making calls on his Android, always suddenly finished when I come outside to swim laps. Last week I overheard him. I was upstairs, listening from the sun deck. Somebody asked if he had an alibi. Elliot repeated the word like a question, then said 'I'll be at the office, hard at work.' As if he had it all planned out."

"Maybe he's having an affair?" Bobby offered.

"He's had his share, trust me. The thing is, he doesn't give a damn if I know or not."

Bobby shrugged. "He's goofing on you. Isn't that Elliot, always the life of the party? I mean, no offense, but the guy's got a few, y'know, idiosyncrasies." More than his share, in Bobby's mind. Erica's husband always calling him *Bobster* at the club, for instance. Or the way he carried crumpled Post-it Notes in his pockets, sometimes a dozen or more, constantly jotting reminders to himself. And his obsession with gadgets—Elliot's life filled with expensive doodads. He'd bought a drone a few months ago, something called a *QuadCoptor*—a football-sized hovercraft equipped with a micro-camera that he could control from his cell phone. Elliot asked if Bobby could video him on the court one day, whacking at the ball in all his glory. But Bobby was pretty sure a buzzing drone would freak out the other guests.

"Cost me six hundred bucks," Elliot told him, because the man loved to drop price tags. Bobby assumed he'd end up ogling all his neighbors lying topless by their swimming pools. A while back, he brought in a radar gun so Bobby could clock his serve. It had cost Elliot close to a grand, and Bobby had never seen the damn thing again.

Erica told Bobby that her husband wasn't any different at home. Elliot's frivolities included a BMW M6 Coupe equipped with a windshield-equipped HUD and a night-vision infrared display, not to mention his Lagoon 400, a 40–foot catamaran that he could barely handle on breezy days in the bay. He often buzzed through eighteen holes at Rancho Santa Fe Golf Club on a balloon-tired Segway PT, maneuvering the vehicle like some deranged adolescent, his leather bag of titanium Honma Beres braced beneath the handlebars. "Boy toys," she'd once said in a huff.

Erica often inferred that Elliot's sound system cost more than her diamond—oh, yes, and the man absolutely *mad* about surveillance equipment. Nighttime laser trips at the windows and doors, motion-sensitive cameras monitoring the grounds. Erica would venture into her husband's study and pause the HD video feed whenever she expected Bobby. She knew a blind spot around the far side of the garage where he parked his Jeep before she reactivated the cameras.

She couldn't be certain if Elliot schecked the surveillance data stream after his occasional weekends away, although she did consider her husband paranoid enough to peek now and then, curious about what he might have missed. But she took a perverse delight in knowing Elliot hadn't a clue that she'd so easily bypassed the system.

"Our little secret," she'd informed Bobby with a smile.

Their entire marriage, it seemed to him, resonating with capricious little secrets.

Erica drummed her fingers against his chest, watching him with a mixture of annoyance and quiet expectation. Bobby threw the covers aside, suddenly very warm, and draped a leg over the side of the bed. "Couldn't Elliot be involved in something—I don't know, *illicit?*"

"Dearheart, Elliot's always involved in something illicit. He flaunts what he can get away with. This is different, something far more devious. Secretive. Something that involves me."

"But *killing* you?"

"Believe me, he's quite capable."

Bobby slipped out of bed and stood naked, smiling at her with a goofy grin, expecting to crack her façade. But she stoically held his gaze.

"This is a little weird," he admitted.

"Not in Elliot's world."

He shook his head, walked to the window and pulled aside a drape. The sun had descended, the clouds reminding Bobby of a lipstick stain against the horizon.

"I realize this is difficult for you to comprehend," she said.

He peered down into the palm-dotted yard, at the pool and private tennis court where they'd played a couple of hours before. Elliot had left that morning for San Francisco,

Erica fairly certain he wouldn't return until tomorrow evening or maybe Thursday. She had phoned the club, Elliot's BMW barely out of the driveway, asking Bobby for a private lesson.

Daring, but that was Erica.

Behind him she said, "Promise me, Bobby — if I turn up dead, you won't just let it drop. Won't assume I slipped on the soap or something."

He turned from the sunset. "Jesus, you're serious."

She blinked. "Yes, of course. Haven't you been listening?"

"This is crazy."

"Will you at least think about it?"

When he didn't respond, she said, "Don't take this wrong. I don't want it to sound whorish or anything — but I'll pay you. I'm not offending you, am I? If I offered you, say, fifty thousand dollars for your help?"

He stared at her, his thoughts swirling like paper streamers on a Marti Gras breeze. Erica's smile trembled. "Fifty thousand doesn't sound so terribly offensive, does it, Bobby?"

"I think you're trying to get me drunk," Nikki Song told Stan. She swiveled on the bar stool and wrinkled her nose, peering suspiciously at the two cards confronting her — a red five and a black eight.

Stan Muca stood behind the polished oak counter in his peach Polo shirt and white tennis shorts. He held a deck of playing cards in one hand, the other splayed in mock chagrin against his chest. Between them stood a bottle of Cuervo 1800 and a partially-filled shot glass.

"Darlin'," Stan said, "the thought never crossed my mind." He grinned at Bobby, sitting nearby, content to observe Stan's little ritual from a safe distance.

A dozen or so club members meandered about Rancho Madera's darkly wooded lounge, sipping cocktails, chatting at distant tables. Nobody paid much attention to the head pro trying his luck with the new masseuse, most of them having already witnessed Stan deal off the bottom.

He nudged the glass toward Nikki's elbow. "Bummer of a draw, huh?"

She warily eyed the shot glass. "I've already *done* three."

"Lucky in love," he countered.

"If only," she said with a laugh and turned her head to glance at Bobby.

Bobby sipped his beer, thinking, *yeah, right.*

She tapped a finger on the bar and said, "hit me."

Stan flipped up the king of spades. "Busted."

Nikki tossed her hair and arched her back as she tilted the glass against her lips. Bobby liked watching her from this angle, liked the profile of her bare legs and slim hips and flat tummy. Liked the way she always smelled of eucalyptus oil or sandalwood. She was small and well-toned, an extraordinarily pretty girl with almond-shaped eyes and golden skin, shining ebony hair that flowed past her shoulders.

Stan dribbled another finger of amber liquid from the bottle. Nikki glanced at Bobby again and said, "How come *you* don't play him?"

"Because Stan doesn't particularly want me between the sheets."

"So *that's* how this game works?"

"See? You can't lose," Stan told her with a smile.

STAN WAS TWELVE years older than Bobby and already prematurely sun-pruned, his salt-and-pepper hair thinning in front. Not bad looking, but past his prime and fretting about it. He and Bobby worked the pro shop, earning a commission from sales, giving lessons and restringing an occasional racquet. Rancho Madera had been Stan's home for a decade and he was content, aspiring to nothing more than playing tennis and teaching housewives, drinking away his evenings in the lounge. He'd been married twice and divorced twice, with a rum-soaked pledge to Bobby there'd never be a third Mrs. Muca. Although the way he'd been puppy-dogging Nikki Jade Song these last few weeks, Bobby wondered if Stan might be considering an exception.

She'd been working at Rancho Madera for barely a month. The club's previous masseuse had taken off for parts unknown, probably sick to death of Stan's flirtation—although nobody knew for certain. Nikki had wandered in a few days later and Stan hired her on the spot. Hadn't much mattered that her credentials were sterling, certified in Swedish deep-muscle therapy and Japanese *shiatsu*, and with a list of health club references from the Santa Cruz area. Bobby wasn't sure if Stan had even noticed her résumé that morning, more engrossed in Nikki's Spandex attire—emerald green running shorts over a black body suit that nicely accentuated just about everything.

She called herself a *mutt*—because Stan had asked— a little Chinese, a little Hawaiian and a big slice of Seattle thrown in as well. Whatever the mix, it looked good on her. That first day at the club, Nikki didn't seem to mind Stan's overt preoccupation with her breasts, her smile playful and attentive. Bobby realized he'd have to be careful around that smile; keep his hormones at a safe distance. The last thing he needed was Erica catching her using that smile on *him*.

Nikki watched stan shuffle the deck and said, "A girl could get into some serious trouble, playing with you guys."

"More'n you realize," Bobby said.

"Nah, hey, we're harmless," Stan replied, throwing her a glance both roguish and pathetically childlike.

Bobby downed another swig of beer, heard laughter, and glanced toward the doorway. He watched three men coming off a doubles match he'd set up on Court 5 earlier that afternoon. They carried Italian leather racquet bags and wore expensive threads, Ellise and Taccini and Versace; maybe two or three grand apiece. Bobby recognized them as attorneys from one of the downtown law firms that perked its elite with full club memberships—not an inexpensive carrot, Bobby knew.

A fourth man followed, older than the others by a decade; a tall, sharply angled man named Peter Dumas. Dumas paused in the doorway and gazed toward the bar with sullen intensity. Bobby was fairly certain of Dumas' irritation, Stan not the only hormonal junkie since Nikki Song's arrival. Bobby held Dumas' gaze until the man turned and followed his companions to a table across the lounge.

"…and we could drive to Vegas next weekend," Stan was telling Nikki. "I'll show you a few things. How to count cards—you know, beat the system. Totally fuck with the casinos."

Bobby recalled Stan's previous two-thousand dollar fiasco at the Monte Carlo and tried to remember if his friend had *ever* come home ahead.

"We could walk away with a lot of cha-*ching*," Stan said.

Nikki gave Stan a distracted nod; she'd been likewise aware of the attorneys' arrival across the room. Bobby had the distinct impression that Stan's fifteen minutes were up.

"Might be fun," she said absently. She slipped off her stool and feigned a sigh. "Well, guys, time to go earn my keep."

"Just one more," Stan prompted.

Nikki hesitated a heartbeat, then obligingly waved for two cards. He dealt her the queen of hearts and an ace.

"Hey, blackjack! You *lose*, amigo."

Stan snatched up the shot glass and offered an affable toast. "Story of my life, darlin'."

Nikki's hand brushed Bobby's shoulder as she passed. He watched her stroll across the lounge, her touch still a warm tingle beneath his shirt. As she approached the attorneys, their voices rose in a chorus of fond greeting. Peter Dumas had remained standing beside their table— as if he'd been expecting her, Bobby realized. He watched Dumas' arm slide easily around her waist. Nikki tilted her head to accept the man's kiss against her cheek.

Stan leaned across the bar and whispered, "Maybe she only fucks money."

"She's being friendly," Bobby said stoically.

"They had dinner a couple of weeks ago."

"Who did?"

When Stan didn't answer, Bobby swiveled on his stool, saw Stan ruefully pouring himself another splash of tequila.

"Who do you think?" Stan prompted.

"Nikki and *Dumas?* Where'd you hear that?"

Stan lifted the glass and downed its contents in a quick gulp. "You know Vincent Ciano?"

"Your ten o'clock Tuesdays," Bobby said. "Left hander. Plays with a Yonex?"

"Uh huh. Vince bartends at George's. Y'know, over on Prospect?"

"And...?"

"Told me he saw her and Dumas gettin' it on."

"Getting it *on?*"

"Having dinner together."

"Oh."

"Last week," Stan said.

One of the young attorneys stood and crossed the lounge, slipping behind the self-serve bar to hustle his buddies a round of drinks. Bobby sipped his beer, listening to the clink of bottles. Stan fell silent, playing with the empty shot glass until the man departed, hands laden with cocktails.

"...fucker's old enough to be her father."

"Stan, *you're* old enough to be her father."

"Yeah, but I'm dope."

"She's relatively new in town," Bobby said, giving her the benefit of his doubt. "She's still getting acquainted."

"Getting laid is what she's doing. Hey, what's that joke about inscrutable Asian chicks?"

But Bobby didn't know and shook his head. Truth was, if Nikki Song's intent *was* to screw money, he figured she'd come to the right place. A good number of the club's members were attorneys or brokers or surgeons from Scripps. Rancho Madera was private and exclusive; a small club with four TruHard and four clay courts, a high-ticket pro shop and an expensive-label cocktail lounge. Outside, a cantilevered sun deck overlooked center court and, in the distance, a wide swatch of the Pacific. Downstairs, next to the richly wooded, white-carpeted locker rooms, the club sported a Nautilus weight room and twin saunas. All the amenities.

Watching her casually chatting up Dumas, he wondered if Nikki Song might be one of them.

Bobby didn't know much about Peter Dumas. He would have known even less if Erica hadn't told him that Dumas and Elliot Garmond were law partners. Bobby had been surprised at the time, neither man having made any noise about it at the club. Dumas was a few years younger than Elliot, maybe forty-five; thin and agile, with sun-toughened skin and a full head of graying-to-white hair. He wore it parted in the center, curling past his eyebrows and long in the back, occasionally tied in a ponytail. He drove a black Porsche Carrera and didn't invite idle conversation, so Bobby seldom hit him up with small talk. He'd watched Dumas play a few times, a pretty good tennis player, although he never seemed to be having *fun*. Bobby knew guys like that, fueled by a consuming intensity, either taking the win or going home angry.

As if aware of the scrutiny, Dumas' attention shifted toward the bar. Bobby held his stare for a long moment before Dumas leaned close to Nikki and whispered. She nodded and took the vacant chair as Dumas started across the lounge. Bobby felt an uncertain knot tighten inside his chest.

"Circle the wagons," Stan said quietly.

Neither Bobby's gaze nor Dumas' wavered.

"Howya doin', Mr. Dumas," Stan said.

Dumas stopped in front of Bobby's stool, one hand casually tucked into the pocket of his tennis shorts, his gaze flitting between Bobby and Stan long enough to strain the silence. Bobby finally raised an eyebrow and Dumas said, "She's a little out of your league, boys, don't you think?"

Bobby opened his mouth, closed it again and allowed himself a sip of beer, rinsing away the words that had gathered on his tongue. Stan's one and pretty much only rule at Rancho Madera was not to piss off the clientele. Bobby had never found a reason to break Stan's rule, although he realized the next couple of seconds could go either way.

"Hey, we're just having a little fun," Stan said.

"From now on, why don't you have your fun without Miss Song, hmm?" Dumas waited long enough to weigh their silence, long enough for Bobby to make up his mind. When he said nothing, Dumas broke his gaze and turned back toward the table.

"What a turd," Stan whispered.

"At least she's not sleeping with him."

"Yeah? How you figure?"

"A guy with that much testosterone backwash," Bobby said, "sure as hell ain't getting laid."

Stan slowly nodded his agreement and Bobby went back to contemplating the silence, staring vacantly across the room, aware of the wake that Dumas had left gently rocking his psyche.

※

WHEN ERICA'S HUSBAND strolled into the pro shop on Thursday evening, Bobby felt a twinge of unease. Part of him already saw the man as a walking ghost.

Elliot Garmond stood an inch or two shorter than his wife, grown thick and slightly bowl-shouldered with the approach of middle age. A rug of dark curls matted his forearms and chest, his hair graying at the temples. Bobby suspected that Elliot might be wearing a toupee, not quite certain, meaning it was an expensive toupee. The one time he'd asked Erica, she told him *of course not*, sounding indignant, as if her husband's baldness might somehow reflect poorly on her.

Elliot sipped a Jim Beam over ice, raising his glass toward Bobby in a casual toast.

"Mr. Garmond," Bobby said neutrally. He stood restringing a racquet on an old Ektelon, half-listening to the day's Wall Street recap. The TV usually remained tuned to CNBC or CNN, unless Stan was watching a Lakers game. Bobby silently followed Elliot's progress toward one of the striped Captain's chairs in front of the pro shop's flat screened TV.

Elliot snorted a laugh, motioning toward the screen with his glass. "Shit, Apple's up, Cisco's up, Alibaba's up—hey, Intek's up another eight bucks today. Man, to have gotten a piece of that action, huh?"

Bobby nodded absently.

"Always somebody wanting to blow up the fuckin' world," Elliot said and Bobby knew what he meant. Intek USA manufactured high-tech weaponry, smart bombs and laser guided missiles—an arsenal of highly-secretive lethal gadgets.

Elliot had a streak in him, loved to talk about golf or sailing or the market. Bobby wasn't much of a golfer or into sailing, but he wasn't half bad when it came to picking stocks. His focus was generally long-term, although he occasionally dabbled in puts and calls or played hot trends on the upswing—usually bailing out early, before he could get hurt. Not that he'd gotten rich, buying in small lots he could afford. But Bobby drove a year old Jeep Grand Cherokee, a top-end model with a moon roof, GPS and heated seats. Not the kind of vehicle a local pro usually acquired teaching bored housewives to hit an overhead lob.

Elliot took another sip of whisky. "Been out of town a few days, Bobster. Haven't been keeping up with the Street. Anything to die for?"

Bobby remained silent, wondering how to answer *that* one—fretting until he realized Elliot had turned in his chair, watching him.

"Bought some Amgen the other day. Up three."

"Amgen, huh? Elliot pulled a crumpled Post-it from

his jacket pocket, found a pen in another pocket and jot-ted down the name. He glanced at Bobby again, waiting for more.

"Heard it might beat street talk by maybe half a buck. Morgan Stanley's upped it to an aggressive buy."

"No shit. Hey, I get a chance an' I'll check it out." Elliot shrugged and turned back to the TV. Bobby suspected the man would be on the phone to his broker the first thing in the morning. Not that he cared, although he would have been surprised to learn how much Elliot *had* made from their occasional chats. Then again, it wasn't as if Bobby hadn't received anything in return. He'd gotten Erica, along with an uneasy feeling that Elliot knew he was sleep-ing with his wife. Not really minding, but perhaps only so long as the numbers held up.

"Got a question for you," Elliot piped, waggling a fin-ger at the screen. "All this new technology shit, I can't keep up. Still kicking myself for missing out on Google way back when. Or when fuckin' Facebook made their LBO? I kept asking myself, *What's to fuckin' buy there?* Now Spo-tify, Quara, Snapchat, man — I don't get it. Everybody's got some voodoo magic smart phone app and I'm gettin' too old to understand all'a that shit. Got any ideas? Know any-thing I can tuck away for the long haul?"

Maybe you should stick to day trading, Bobby thought and visualized Erica with a pick and shovel, planting Elliot's corpse by the swimming pool. Getting shivers because, for a second, the image seemed too real.

"Gotta plan for old age," Elliot said. He stood and

rattled the ice cubes in his empty glass, letting Bobby know his intent. "Keep the little woman in a 24-carat rocker, you know what I mean?"

"Lemme think about it."

"Nothing on the tip of your tongue, huh?"

"Not at the moment."

"Too bad. 'Cause you know what they say. Money's the ultimate aphrodisiac." Elliot wandered toward the lounge, then paused in the pro shop doorway. "Can't keep 'em happy, and pretty soon they'll be humping the mailman."

"Is that what they say, Mr. Garmond?"

Elliot gave him a wink. "That's what they say, pal."

Bobby watched Elliot walk away and wondered how his life had become so complicated. Everyone playing games that didn't need playing. You share a few drinks with a woman and maybe there's a spark, even a gentle hint of romance — and the next thing you know she wants her husband dead. Wants you along for the ride. Simplicity always a distant, fading song in Bobby's ears.

www.ingramcontent.com/pod-product-compliance
Lightning Source LLC
Chambersburg PA
CBHW030418180626
46812CB00005B/2065